TUSKEGEE TALES
MAKING DO:
Growing Up Colored In The Jim Crow South During The Great Depression

info@matjointl.com

For more information about bulk purchases, please
contact Matjo International at info@matjointl.com

Cover design by Frank Espinoza
ISBN 978-0-9996107-7-0

*To Mama and Daddy, the two "love birds,"
who taught me, my sisters and brother how to live
a life of love, hope, and faith in God, and to all of my
elder relatives and friends who have contributed their
stories to make this novel a true period piece.*

*And to Doug, my husband, who patiently
loved me through the birth of this series.*

Acknowledgments

Now faith is the substance of things hoped for, the evidence of things not seen. Hebrews 11:1 (KJV)

This Bible verse best describes my journey in writing *Making Do: Growing Up Colored in the Jim Crow South During the Great Depression.* It honors my parents, Mattie and Joseph Wright. They inspired this book and its theme: having faith in God.

My own trust in the Lord was established and nurtured by their daily example. This faith, guided by Father God, His Son, my Lord and Savior Christ Jesus and the Holy Spirit that enabled me to find and assemble this remarkable team:

I'd like to thank the award-winning novelist John Rechy and the exceptional biographer Anne Edwards. I have had the pleasure of attending workshops by both, and have benefited from my numerous conversations with them about writing.

Frank Espinoza - we met twenty years ago through a fellow author. Frank has a great business that includes design, typesetting, and printing. Frank also designed the awesome cover of Vol. 1: Faith and Dreams!

Amanda Pisani - I met Amanda through her husband, Ken, a fellow WGA West member. She is a phenomenal copy editor. Knowing it was my first novel, Amanda gave me critical information and assistance in creating and polishing this beautiful story.

Emily Ransom Miller - my very talented niece is the graphic artist who created the masthead of my series, Tuskegee Tales, and the chapter icons. Her incredible talent always wows me!

Brae and Jill Wycoff, the founders of the Kingdom Writers' Association (KWA) - have inspired others, like myself, to become God's scribes. Their monthly meetings have honed my writing skills through their scripture-based teachings.

My KWA writer's cadre - Steve Bonenberger and Lo Mehnert have inspired me to make this idea into a series of novels. My friends kept my feet to the fire of inspiration and dedication to what they knew I wanted *Making Do* to become - a legacy and homage to my parents.

My early manuscript readers - primarily Kim Allen, Gail Morris, Phyllis Larrymore Kelly, William Grooms, and Joanne Smith gave me great feedback and encouragement along the way.

Sherry Ward - who I met through Brae and Jill Wycoff, is an incredibly brilliant marketer and publisher (Square Tree Publishing). With Sherry's exceptional insight and talented team, *Making Do* was prepared to reach its many readers.

I'd like to thank my family - William Porter King (Uncle Bill), Robert Hamilton Zander (Cousin Johnny), his son, Robert Mackenzie Zander, and my cousins Joseph Caver, and Joshua Wright, Jr., and my dear sisters and brother: Gloria, Sharon, Lydia and Joseph Jr.

Finally, I cherish my husband, Doug. His love and steadfast belief in me kept me going through many challenging days!

TABLE OF CONTENTS

MAKING DO:
Growing Up Colored In The Jim Crow
South During The Great Depression

Preface

I am a fourth-generation storyteller. But I'd like to think that this family craft extends even further back to our ancient traditions, the "griots" of Africa.

According to my mother, who was an exceptionally creative storyteller and poet in her own right, our great grandfather was one of those griots. Mama shared many stories with us that her grandfather, "Papa," told them.

As children, she and her brothers and sisters would eat roasted peanuts and baked yams around the fireplace in Birmhill Alabama, the "home house," listening to Papa spin yarns based on the oral tradition.

These stories included tales from Africa, family history as well as his and my great-grandmother's exploits in traveling from Virginia to Alabama.

TUSKEGEE TALES
MAKING DO:
Growing Up Colored In The Jim Crow South During The Great Depression

Preface

I am a fourth-generation storyteller. But I'd like to think that this family craft extends even further back: to our ancient traditions, the "griots" of Africa.

According to my mother, who was an exceptionally creative storyteller and poet in her own right, our great grandfather was one of those griots. Mama shared many stories with us that her grandfather, "Papa," told them.

As children, she and her brothers and sisters would eat roasted peanuts and baked yams around the fireplace in Burstall, Alabama, the "home-house," listening to Papa spin yarns based on the oral tradition.

These stories included tales from Africa, family history as well as his and my great-grandmother's exploits in traveling from Virginia to Alabama.

Following this tradition, our family lore includes a story that Papa's daughter, my grandmother, wrote a movie script. Her love for romances and writing evolved into a screenplay that she supposedly sent to Cecil B. DeMille.

I hadn't heard this story until only a few years ago, long after I had become a member of the Writers Guild of America. While the story hadn't been corroborated, the thought of her pursuing this path in the early thirties filled me with pride.

My mother carried on this tradition, telling stories to her sisters and brothers - and later, our family. She would tell us fairy tales and bedtime stories that were filled with action, love and mystery.

They were so vivid that I went to our neighborhood bookmobile and asked for one of these books, by title.

But the librarian was unable to help me find it. "I've never heard of that one," she said.

When I asked Mama where she had seen the book, she laughed and told me, "I made it up!"

The stories I remember with clarity were those she and my father told us about growing up in the South. They would reminisce about their own experiences of a time when people made their own soap, used mules to plow the land, and even in the city, kept cows and hens.

It was also a very frightening time. This was the age of Jim Crow, an era that occurred after slavery and the Reconstruction period, just before the Civil Rights Movement.

This was a period of worldwide economic and political upheaval - the Great Depression and World War II. It baffled me how they survived and navigated through these difficult events in our nation's history.

It was from listening to their stories (abridged for young minds) that the seed of interest grew into a greater desire to share with others this rich period. This was for two very specific reasons.

First, I wanted to capture the events of this time in a novel. When I began writing in the early eighties, my mother's recollections of the events of her childhood were the centerpiece of the story.

As time progressed, I found that many outside sources were giving texture to this piece. Through research and talking with relatives and contemporaries that actually walked the streets of Bessemer and Billingsley at that time, my understanding of the landscape and timeline began to shape the construction of the novel.

As in many fictional works that are inspired by actual events, the events and characters of *Making Do* are invented, although some characters and incidents are based on real people and places. In those cases, names were changed to protect the identities of individuals.

While *Making Do: Growing Up Colored in the Jim Crow South During the Great Depression* is not a literal story of my parents' lives: it is an homage.

Secondly, as a teacher and educator, it was my hope to create a thoughtful, engrossing young adult novel (that also could be enjoyed by adult readers) would encompass some of the events that happened in the early forties leading up to World War II.

I also hoped to delve into the spirit of this age that motivated and shaped my family's lives. It is a spirit that I hope to convey in each volume of this series.

This spirit is one of faith in God. It is the spiritual force that kept families afloat during these challenging times when personal safety, finances and emotional confidence could have easily been shaken by the forces at play.

This is a story of winning a triple victory over fear: through family friends and faith in God.

Prologue

I was born in a slop jar. Mother was giving birth to me and had to go.

As Mother tells it, "Miss Minnie gave me the pot and there you were!"

Minnie Bliss, Mother's midwife, caught me just in time. She saved me from falling headfirst into that bedside commode.

Miss Minnie and Big Mama Dee, my grandmother, were taken by surprise by my sudden arrival. It was a strange way to enter the world. They had a good laugh about it.

My older brothers and sister, who always teased me, loved bringing up this tale when they wanted to get my goat. A story like that swiftly got passed around Burstall, our small, colored community. It added a lot of laughter to everyone's day.

A good laugh is a priceless thing, especially in the South during the 1920s. While Miss Minnie rescued me from landing in a pretty nasty spot, my life began in a troubling predicament.

The South, since slavery times, was a dangerous place to grow up bein' colored. After our being freed, Alabama became one of the main Jim Crow states.

The Jim Crow laws were set up by folks who wanted to keep us colored folk down as far as our schoolin' and working were concerned. It did allow colored folk to be mistreated or given some terrible physical punishment if we didn't follow their rules.

These cruel rules made life hard. We feared for our lives. Worst of all, some of us accepted them as a part of life.

It was a scary time made worse when the Great Depression hit our country. This was a financial calamity that closed banks and caused people to lose the money they had scrimped and saved.

People lost their jobs. Even worse, since the Great Depression was affecting people all over the world, it made finding jobs near impossible. It seemed like no one had any money.

But our family, like so many colored folk, were used to shouldering hardships. My parents continued doing the one thing that always helped in hard times—making do.

By the grace of God, Daddy was able to keep his job at the steel mill, but his hours were cut in half. Mother took up the slack doing laundry with Big Mama Dee. Papa Bell's food from the farms gave him extra cash to tide us over.

With hard work and perseverance, my folks kept food on the table and love in our home during those desperate times.

Throughout all of it, God sheltered us. We were blessed and found ourselves better off than most.

God held onto us, just like Big Mama Dee did, upon my birth. She took me from Miss Bliss and, after making a fuss over my small size, wrapped me in her clean, sweet, sun-dried flour sacks and held me, singing a lullaby, "honey, lil' baby mine!"

If I'd been crying, which I'm sure happened, the comfort I received from those strong, loving arms chased all of my fears away.

Over the years, my family taught me to fight my fears with faith because God was always there. That to have faith in Him would keep me safe.

Big Mama Dee was sure to remind me, "The Lawd will see you through, baby girl!"

But in the spring of 1937, I needed to draw on that faith like never before. It was the spring that would change our family and my life forever.

****

CHAPTER 1

An Uncertain Future

I stood at the doorway of my bedroom, unable to speak or move. Fear welled up in my throat as I stared through the cracked door. Sherrie Lee, my oldest sister, was writhing in pain on our bed. Sherrie Lee was dying.

She moaned as she tossed and turned, her pale brown forehead wet with fever. Her copper-colored ringlets covered the pillow like a flame.

I wanted to go in to hold Sherrie Lee's hand. I thought maybe I could reassure her that she had found true love. Although I reminded myself there was nothing to fear, my eyes told me a different story.

Staring at her lying helplessly atop that big, homemade cotton-filled mattress, my faith faltered. Nothing I could do or say that would change a thing.

Just ten years earlier, Mother had sewn our mattress using blue and white ticking. It quickly came together on her treadle machine. She told me that she had stitched double rows with her Singer to keep it strong.

Papa Bell stuffed the mattress thick and fluffy with cotton he picked and cleaned. He grew them on one of his "gentleman's" farms. These were plots of land he rented after retiring from the tarpaper factory. My grandpapa loved farming!

Our sheets were made from cotton flour sacks that Mother washed, ironed flat, and sewed together into a patchwork pattern. They were extra soft. It was a cloud of a bed that felt like heaven.

We laughed and teased each other when we got to lie in it. The five of us slept like brown sardines—two up and three down.

Was it just a few years ago that Sherrie Lee and I whispered so many secrets, hopes, and dreams about finding true love on that bed? This was the type of love we'd seen so many times on Bessemer Theater House's big silver screen.

We watched the romance movies in the upper balcony. The peanut gallery was the section where other colored children like us had to sit, away from the white theatergoers.

But even though it had old chairs with their springs busting through the leather and was littered with empty popcorn and peanut bags, the gallery was the place where our dreams began.

Watching the movies filled our minds with hope about love and happy endings. Those fantasy-filled images made love seem so reachable and simple.

It also gave us one important piece of the puzzle that we clung to. We knew that the key to true love would be simple. The perfect man, our prince, would give us a single, magical kiss.

Sherrie Lee had met her prince. Fred was her true love.

But now, she lay dying on that same bed!

I was only fourteen, but I can still recall every detail of that sultry Alabama afternoon. It was as if my mind were an album of Kodak pictures!

I even remembered how the air, fragranced with the cloyingly sweet smell of honeysuckle, wafted inside the kitchen from our screened back door. It was a stark contrast to the stern and worried expressions worn by the men around the kitchen table.

The strong, acrid aroma of Daddy's freshly brewed coffee, forgotten on Mother's water heater stove, mingled with the honeysuckle whenever a gasp of air happened to find its way into our kitchen.

The house felt almost empty without my other six brothers and sisters around. Early that morning, my older brothers had taken the younger ones out for a scavenger hunt.

They regularly made finding the coal nuggets that dropped along the railroad tracks near our house into a game. This morning, it served two purposes: getting the little ones away from being underfoot for those tending Sherrie Lee and replenishing our coal supply.

Daddy sat at the white enameled kitchen table with Fred, Sherrie Lee's husband. He consoled Fred while Papa paced the floor, twirling his handlebar mustache.

This was something Papa did when he was worried. It was an odd sight, as there was nothing our big, fearless Papa couldn't tackle.

But now, my grandfather, along with everyone else, was worried about Sherrie Lee.

When Daddy got up to pour a cup of coffee for Fred, I took in his sadness. His brow was furrowed, and his slight frame was bowed by the weight of the heaviness in the room.

Not wanting to disturb his thoughts, I tried to quietly collect water from the stove. Daddy must've caught my movement out of the corner of his eye. He must've figured out that I was carrying a load heavier than that bucket of hot water.

"Baby girl, just hold on to God's unchanging hand. He's got yo' sistah an' he's got the lot of us, honey."

He gave me a pat on the back to encourage me. But I knew there was nothing any of us could do. God was certainly in control.

Earlier that morning, I was sent to fetch Miss Minnie. When I told her what Big Mama Dee said, she didn't even take down her rag rollers or shed her housecoat.

The midwife's concern was immediate. Her eyes flew wide open, made larger against the dark chestnut brown of her ageless face.

She threw the last of her coffee on her barren lawn and sprinted to our house, faster than her age should have allowed.

"Oh, Lord!" she exclaimed and took off running. Miss Minnie ran all the way up the front porch steps, straight into the bedroom where Big Mama Dee and Mother had Sherrie Lee.

As I stood outside that cracked doorway of our bedroom, mixed feelings filled my heart. While fearful, I was also hopeful that they could turn around Sherrie Lee's condition.

It was then that I glanced up at the hallway mirror. For the first time that afternoon, I saw myself. What a specter I had become!

I stared at my image, the thin legs, large head, and huge, expressive eyes. I hadn't slept or eaten well since Sherrie Lee's turn for the worse.

It reminded me of when I was sick with typhoid fever some years before. While I laid in bed, I tried to cheer myself up with a little song:

"Skinny legs, kindle thighs;

A bullfrog belly and terrapin eyes;

and a watermelon head!"

I was near death, but Big Mama Dee was able to rescue me. Would she be able to save Sherrie Lee, too?

At that moment, Sherrie Lee uttered a moan that reached down into my soul.

"Please, dear God," I whispered before I entered the room.

Mother held my big sister's hand in a vise-like grip as Big Mama Dee tenderly dabbed the festering wound.

Sherrie Lee flinched each time the cloth touched her. It was though a hot coal instead of a soft, cool washrag was touching her skin.

"That old white doctor coulda had her admitted into Birmingham General! They takes colored folk there!"

"Ya know as well as me, Miss Dee, they ain't takin' no po' colored folk over in that there hospital!"

Miss Minnie fretted as she wrung out another towel for Big Mama Dee.

"An' if they do take 'er, I hear tell they puts colored folk in they basements! Tha's what they do at them white hospitals! Yo little baby don't belong there!"

My grandmother didn't reply. She was focused on what she could do for the angry red incision.

Big Mama Dee had practiced the healing arts for many years. They had been passed down to her from her mother. She was known throughout the community as a medicine woman.

We didn't know if her knowledge came from Africa or from some Indian tribe of Virginia where her parents had lived as slaves. All we knew was her great knowledge brought people outside of Jefferson County to our house seeking her help.

She gave Sherrie Lee's swollen incision a thorough inspection and shook her head.

"Press down on it while I go and find where that chil' . . ."

It was then that Big Mama Dee, my namesake, spotted me cowering near the doorframe.

"Girl! You'd best to be gettin' over here! Bring me that hot water 'afo it get cold! An' tear these clean sacks!"

I remembered entering as quickly as I dared. The blue-speckled, enameled bucket was filled to the brim with boiling water.

Gingerly setting the bucket down on the oak floor that I had helped Mother wax a week earlier, I attempted to take the stack of colorful flour sacks from the nightstand. But Big Mama Dee put the flat of her hand down on them with a "thump!" She held onto them until my eyes locked with hers.

"Now I want you to tear up these old sacks like you did the last bunch, chil'! But this time, I ain't got time for you standin' 'round wool gatherin'!"

Big Mama Dee, who usually looked spry and energetic, had a fine network of wrinkles around her eyes. She stared at me but seemed to be looking through me.

Her expression reminded me of one of the boys I had once seen at Deacon Jone's boxing club. He had taught my brothers and the other boys in our neighborhood how to fight.

Out of curiosity, I once peeked into the old blacksmith's shop to see what they were learning.

One time, I saw a boy on the ropes under my brother Luke's fighting skills. His face looked like Big Mama Dee's did now.

They were not winning this fight. Not by a long shot.

Just then, Sherrie Lee let out a loud moan. It scared me so badly I jumped in my skin.

It didn't seem possible that this was my brave big sister! She was the one who could face pain without a whimper.

When Sherrie Lee was ten, she'd had a bad tooth. Mother pulled it out with the pliers. My big sister sat still and didn't flinch throughout the ordeal.

Finally, when Mother yanked the tooth out, Sherrie Lee just got up, spat some blood into the commode, stuffed the socket with a piece of cotton and went back to her studies. Never once did she complain!

In desperation, I grabbed her hand. She had to be strong! It was more than I could bear seeing her in so much pain!

"It's gonna be all right, Sherrie Lee!"

"I . . . I . . . know, baby . . . girl!" Sherrie Lee was able to gasp. She looked up at me, then shot a worried glance at her daughter, Mae.

Someone had pulled in the old bassinet Papa had found and repaired for the baby. Mae had been placed near the bed.

Mae's little legs kicked the air. Her caramel-colored face was scrunched in a smile.

Watching the baby was Sherrie Lee's only desire. Mae contentedly sucked her fists as she smiled at no one in particular.

At that moment, Miss Minnie let out a gasp of shock. I turned to see that she had lifted the cloth and had exposed Sherrie Lee's incision.

The cut had turned into an angry, purplish-red gash. The edges of the wound had become swollen and filled with dark-yellow fluid.

I almost cried out, but quickly covered my own dismay with the flour sacks. Sherrie Lee's once smooth, creamy stomach was now ravaged by this awful incision.

"Girl, go! Tear up them clean rags and make it snappy!"

I rushed out of the room, gasping to hold back my tears. It shouldn't be this way!

Was it just last summer when we'd compared bras and girdles? Posing in the mirror, Sherrie Lee's perfect figure filled out her undergarments like a movie siren.

"You know, Lena Horne ain't got nothin' on me!"

That same flat, perfect stomach was now marred by the infection—the infection that sought to claim her life.

That night, I woke up to muffled sounds of crying. I felt a wave of guilt.

Sherrie Lee's cry caused every bit of sleep to flow right out of me. I ran to the sickroom, feeling horrible.

Pausing at the door, I felt a pang of guilt. I should have been praying for my sister instead of sleeping!

I touched the cold, brass knob but was unable to turn it. I didn't know what I might find on the other side.

Mustering all my courage, I pushed the door open. My feet were like lead as I shuffled into the room.

Fred sat on the edge of the bed, holding Sherrie Lee's hand. Mother had little Mae propped up on her shoulder so Sherrie Lee could see her baby.

Fred glanced up, realizing my presence. Mother motioned me to come closer. Fred changed places with

Mother and took the baby so that I could hold Sherrie Lee's hand while she slept. Quietly, Mother stepped out.

As soon as I took Sherrie Lee's hand, her lashes fluttered open. Startled, I flinched. I felt so unsure of myself. I wasn't prepared for any of this. I didn't know what to say!

"Dee Dee!" Her expression was that of relief. It melted away my anxiety.

"Yes, Sherrie Lee, I'm here."

Sherrie Lee's voice was barely audible. I leaned closer.

"I have to tell you . . ."

It was a struggle for me to keep the tears back. I turned away, not wanting her to see me with my face all torn up.

"Dee Dee, no matter what happens . . ."

She broke off. My tears were coming so fast, I could barely see her lovely face. It had an angelic quality without so much as a wrinkle in her usually furrowed brow.

I wiped both her and my tears away. We held each other, knowing that we had but a short time together.

". . . just know that I love you. Hold onto your faith, Dee Dee. Jes' like Big Mama Dee says. You got the strength, and God's gonna bless you even more so, baby girl..."

Lifting off the pillow, Sherrie Lee fixed her eyes on mine. They held a great intensity.

I tried to encourage her to lie back down. Instead, she shook her head and smiled at me.

"Jes' don't let anything quench that spunk of your'n!"

With that comment, she sank back into the pillow. I was stunned. I had hoped to comfort her, and she had comforted me!

"Oh, Sherrie Lee, thank you! I'm sorry . . ." I hugged her not wanting to let her go.

"Don't be sorry, Dee Dee. God gave me everything I ever wanted . . . a beautiful wedding, a wonderful husband, and a lovely little baby girl. He's been so good to me, now I get to be with Him in heaven…"

I gulped and quickly glanced at Fred. His expression was filled with anguish, too.

I had to escape before I started crying. I didn't want to make her feel any worse, seeing me crumble.

I mumbled something about wanting them to have some time together. Then, giving Sherrie a last squeeze, all I could say was, "Bye."

I felt so ashamed. I wanted to tell her that she was the best big sister I ever could have wanted, but fear choked the words off in my throat!

Later that night, I heard Mother's wailing cry but didn't return to the room. I stifled my own tears in a pillow until I fell asleep.

I knew I would awaken to a very different world. I just prayed, with every fiber of my being, that the Lord would be with me. I knew He would give me faith to make it through my tomorrows. But this tomorrow would be one without Sherrie Lee.

****

For an uplifting poem that Mattie Wright, my mom, wrote please contact me at josanwrightcallender.com

CHAPTER 2

Pods Of Genius

Charles mopped his brow, gazing at the rows of green plants in amazement. The peanut crops were remarkably resilient. They stood invincible in the withering heat of summer.

The early morning sun crept high in the bright blue Billingsley, Alabama sky, promising another blisteringly hot day. Its heat seemed to glare down on Charles as he worked his way down the rows of peanuts.

White cumulous clouds were too high to promise rain. There was just enough moisture in the air to ensure another sultry autumn day.

In many ways, it was a carbon copy of all of the harvests Charles could remember while working on the farm.

However, this day was different. Something had shifted.

Charles tossed another big, tan-colored burlap bag of freshly picked legumes into the wagon. The sun warmed the pods, filling the air with the aroma of roasted peanuts.

A smile tugged on Charles's lips. A chuckle escaped. Then, he laughed outright, revealing a straight row of white teeth against copper skin.

"Daddy's going to slap his leg and let out a holler when he sees all of these peanuts, Ol' Bess," he chuckled.

Bess tossed her head with indifference. Her only concern was the large green flies. They swarmed the mule's big ears and attempted to torment her no matter how many times she swatted her tail.

Charles absently brushed Bess's dark brown flank. She chomped on her bit and tossed her head again, giving Charles a quick, wide-eyed glance.

Bess was ready to proceed down the evenly tilled rows filled with peanut bushes. Stamping her heavily shod hoofs, she indicated that it was time to move on in order to hasten their trip back to the cool interior of the barn.

"Hang on, ol' girl, we gotta pace ourselves 'til Henrietta and Martha come out to help. We've got thirty-nine and a half acres of these peanuts to pull!"

Charles inhaled deeply. The sweet-sour smells of the damp earth, the peanut pods, and the mule's sweaty flanks were comforting and familiar.

The Stevenses had been farmers since his earliest memory. His daddy made sure of that with the purchase of this plot of land.

Benjamin Stevens was only sixteen years old when a neighbor, an Italian man, offered him the forty acres for five hundred dollars. It was a section of Mr. Romano's own land, but later, he explained his reasoning to Daddy Ben.

"I came to this country with nothing. Somebody gave me a chance," Mr. Romano had said.

His heavy Italian accent was very odd for this part of the country. But the kindness was universal.

He told Daddy Ben he wouldn't have to pay him anything the first year. The men shook.

Ben was under the legal age, so his mother, Mama Edna, signed the papers. The deal was done.

Charles understood the lure of fighting the elements to make this land into something productive. However, over the past few years, there was a subtle shift in Charles's focus.

He had gotten up early, like so many other mornings, to beat the heat. But, that morning, his mind became firmly locked on a new train of thought.

He was sharing a cup of coffee in silence with his father, as was their routine. They knew the full house would not remain quiet for long.

Sister Martha was out collecting eggs and Mama Edna was milking the cow. Any minute, both would be returning to the house to fix breakfast.

Soon, his brother Adam and his new wife, Henrietta, would be stirring. Adam had had an accident at Bishop's sawmill in which his finger had been severed. It was a horrific event that reminded them all of a previous family tragedy.

However, Adam's setback had a silver lining. He and his wife were able to return to the family farm to save money while he recuperated.

Finally, Daddy broke the silence.

"Might as well work the field today, son. You ain't gonna be worth a plugged nickel to me and the foreman if yo mind's on them peanuts."

By being allowed to miss a heavy workday like Friday, Charles knew his father had spent some time reflecting on the importance of this harvest. It had taken Charles years of working odd jobs to earn enough money to buy his peanut seeds.

"Thank you, sir. I'll have something to show for it once you get back."

Daddy Ben just grunted. For a season, he had watched the little seeds grow. Their yellow flowers had germinated, growing more plentiful every day until the entire field had blossomed.

Their bobbing flowers indicated that the pegs had burrowed into the ground and were sprouting legumes. Shortly thereafter, it was time to harvest.

Methodically, Charles moved along the field collecting the pods. His plan was to have at least a wagonload completed before his father returned from the lumber mill.

Obviously, Charles thought, his father had made note of his preoccupation with the fields for several months.

Daddy Ben must have connected Charles's enthusiasm for this project with the trip he had taken years ago to the

Tuskegee Institute with the Future Farmers of America. It was a life-changing experience.

Charles's excitement for farming this particular crop came from his belief that Dr. George Washington Carver was right. His lecture on the profitability of peanuts made Charles see that they were the farm's best chance.

Later, Charles had shared with his father that Dr. Carver said that peanuts would help to enrich the soil and make future crops more bountiful.

At the time, Adam felt it was a passing novelty. He expressed his disbelief one day over lunch at the sawmill.

"Y'know, it'll all go to dust, Daddy. Remember all the other years? Charlie's no farmer. He waits until you almost come home, most days, to even start clearing the field!"

Charles would feel the familiar anger rise up in his throat at his older brother's admonition. While Adam spoke the truth, it didn't make it any easier to swallow.

"I get the work done, don't I?"

Although he held his peace after that comment, Charles knew it would be difficult to try to vindicate himself. This crop would show how much he believed in its promise.

In a way, Adam was right. He hadn't a passion for farming. To Charles, it was a means to an end.

Seeing his family and others struggle over the past ten years brought this fact to light. Charles had to admit that working so hard, year after year, for failed crops had taken the taste for farming out of his mouth.

The crops would either be eaten up by boll weevils or parch quickly from fallow ground. There didn't seem to be any way to correct it.

The Depression only added to the misery. The combination of bad soil, boll weevils, and poor finances had taken its toll on many farmers.

However, two things kept Charles going in the midst of this: the books he borrowed from neighbors to continue his education and that one visit to Dr. Carver's lab at the Tuskegee Institute.

Dr. George Washington Carver had told his class that peanuts would grow faster than cotton and were a lot easier to harvest.

Looking at his current yield, Charles knew Dr. Carver was right!

In the next year or two, the Stevenses should have a field that would be fertile and rich for planting whatever they wanted. This would more than make up for the poor cotton yield of the past ten years.

However, beyond the success of the farm, something else had burrowed into his mind. It stuck in his memory like burrs to his socks.

Charles remembered how he felt standing amidst the other young men that had crowded in Dr. Carver's small, dusty lab at Tuskegee.

While Dr. Carver talked at length about a new method he and other colleagues had discovered regarding crop rotation, Charles felt a new excitement rising in his spirit. He knew that this feeling went beyond Dr. Carver's lectures on legumes.

The man's generous spirit struck Charles as much as his brilliance. Dr. Carver wanted colored farmers to know how peanuts could make a difference in their futures.

Charles felt deeply blessed and honored to be in the laboratory that day. It opened up a new world of exciting possibilities.

Since he had joined the Future Farmers of America, Charles had learned about farming and planting. But the trip to Tuskegee and his meeting with Dr. Carver opened his eyes to ideas that went beyond the scope of farming.

As Dr. Carver, a man of strong faith, spoke, Charles knew that God had given him this particular field trip. It was an opportunity for the young men to learn at the feet of a genius, a true master in the science of agriculture.

Dr. Carver had been sought after by world leaders like Joseph Stalin and had even worked with Thomas Edison and Henry Ford. He had worked with these American scientists and both wanted him to come to work with them fulltime on their projects. Many others revered his knowledge and insight.

But his heart and soul remained in botany, art, and farming or agricultural science as fields of interest. He wanted to give back to his people and had made Tuskegee Institute, the University founded in 1881 by Lewis Adams, a former slave, the birthplace of his home laboratory.

Booker T. Washington, the school's first teacher, and Dr. George Washington Carver were two men of stature who had a similar goal—to find ways to help people like themselves, people who were former slaves, succeed.

His teacher told them that Tuskegee Institute was one of the beacons of the New South. The men involved ranged from the former slave, Lewis Adams to W.F. Foster, a state senator who was a former Confederate Colonel, and George Campbell, a former slave owner.

According to the teacher, the three men all took an active role in building the University which included the recruitment of Booker T. Washington from Virginia.

"You are part of a very select group of young people to visit this University. Dr. Carver is making a difference not only in the lives of people in this area, but in the world, too!"

When Charles's class arrived at the lab, the older gentleman greeted them, dressed in a shabby lab coat that was once white. He took off his gold, wire-rimmed spectacles to wipe their much-fingered surfaces with a small, flannel towel.

Particles of lint from the cloth ascended in the bright light that flooded the lab from its many windows. The scientist eyed his eager audience with a steely gaze.

"You boys got land? You got to hold onto it. Some say, 'Why peanuts?' Well, I've sat in the peanut gallery at the motion picture theater and noticed how many people were eating peanuts: colored and white alike!"

"Everyone likes peanuts. So I say, 'Why not peanuts?'"

He strolled down the tables of samples of experiments he had underway, gesturing at them to emphasize his point.

"That's why y'all here. To see that there's more to the peanut than it just being a goober!"

Dr. Carver explained to the young men that peanuts were thought to have come from the African continent, perhaps from the area of Angola. The word nguba was Bantu for "peanuts." He deducted that, most likely, slaves brought them to the Americas.

"You see, boys, I've a heritage and responsibility from God to unlock the secrets of this little pod. It's part of our history. I've been privileged to discover thousands of ways this hardy little legume can be used to benefit mankind, and I'm discovering more uses every day!"

Charles looked at the different displays Dr. Carver had spread across his lab. Everywhere he looked, there were tables and charts proclaiming products made from the peanut: shoe polish, tires, medicines, household products, and food products.

The air in the lab held a combination of aromas, a mixture of shellac, turpentine, oils, paint, and peanuts. It seemed to bubble up into an alchemy of excitement that touched each young mind.

Dr. Carver gathered everyone around and spread something he called "peanut butter" on pieces of fresh bread. Charles had never tasted anything like it before.

He'd never forget its dense, oily, yet nutty taste. He chewed it appreciatively, but thought it would be better served with something sweet. Mama Edna's sweet-sour crab apple jam came to mind.

Charles could hardly wait to get back to the farm. He wanted to be one of the first to plant and gather his crop to see what the yield might be. Dr. Carver predicted most would yield close to 90 percent or more.

All forty acres needed to be fertile for the farm to be self-sustaining. Crops with corn and peanuts would produce a cycle that would fetch them more money each and every year. It would give the farm a new lease on life.

His mind awash with the possibilities, Charles absently picked up the shoe polish can. It promised an "un-scuffable shine" due to its main ingredient, peanut oil. He took a sniff but couldn't immediately detect the aroma of peanuts.

"Look with your eyes, son, not with your hands."

Dr. Carver had walked up beside him. He spoke in his low, soft voice that held both a warning and a touch of humor. Charles hastily returned the can to its display.

"Peanuts are going to be everywhere, mark my words!" He glanced around at the boys' transfixed faces.

"It's time that colored farmers get on the wagon and not get left in the dust of change and industry!"

Then, he did something remarkable. He tapped Charles on his shoulder and looked him in the eye.

It was as though he saw in Charles the same thing he saw in himself. Was it his natural curiosity, or could he have seen the barely contained excitement Charles held?

"You boys represent the future, not only of Southern farming, but of other intelligent endeavors. Learn as much as you can. Try to go as far as you can in your education. Men like Mr. Edison, Mr. Ford, and others are working together with me in getting this country to move ahead of the world on many fronts.

"We're going to put this Depression behind us! To realize its potential, we need young, educated minds."

Dr. Carver's unwavering gaze was directed to each of the young men. Charles thought that every one of the boys felt that Dr. Carver was talking to him, personally—as though no one else were in the lab but himself and the famous scientist.

"You see, education is the way to unlock the golden door to freedom for our people. I know it'll take hard work, but guess what? Opportunity shows up in overalls looking like work!"

Charles flicked the reins. Old Bess shook her flanks and allowed Charles to guide her to the next row. It had taken him five years to earn enough money to put in this peanut crop.

The excitement of collecting this harvest was tremendous for many reasons. Somehow, he felt in his soul that it held the key to his future.

Charles knew that furthering his education in whatever way possible was something he had to do. That was locked firmly in his mind. He knew that with a solid education, he, too, could make a difference in his future. But how?

He had to drop out of school when he turned fourteen to help out with the farm. High school was in Clanton, too far away unless they paid room and board.

Daddy couldn't spare the finances, or Charles, as he was needed on the farm. While he knew the finances couldn't be helped because of the Depression and the poor crop yield, it hurt Charles to the quick. He decided to turn all of his attention to reading and learning as much as he could on his own.

But as he studied, he would often pause, perplexed. How in the world was he going to provide for his future family as a farmer?

His father had started early. Daddy Ben had already saved up a great deal of money toward buying the farm before he was sixteen.

Mama Edna had taught him how to save a penny here and a penny there. Ben had saved a bit more from his stint in the Army during the Great War.

Daddy Ben always knew that he wanted to own land, get married, and raise children. But he had to work several jobs and leave the family for long stretches of time to make ends meet. He had paid a great price for this land.

Gazing over the fields, Charles wondered how different his life would be from his father's if he were to take another path.

He wanted to get married and have a family too. But the Depression hit everybody hard, especially farmers. It seemed as though the city held more promise for financial success.

Some felt that the war going on in Europe might have an impact on their lives. Charles had seen it in the headlines every time he went to the feed store in Billingsley.

While he had hoped that it would remain just idle talk, a lot of folks believed it would be the war for world freedom.

There was no way to know for sure what the future held. But Dr. Carver's words continued to resonate with him and give him new energy and hope. He did have a future, a positive calling. But where?

Movement in the Romanos' field across the way caught Charles's eye. A wagon filled with white canvas and tent poles was struggling to cross the deeply rutted field where the corn had just been harvested.

The wagon pulled up and stopped in the middle of the field. Several men exerted themselves in an attempt to pitch a large, white tent. The boss, a man smoking his cigar down to the nub, motioned and gestured vigorously.

"Looks like a tent meetin', Bess. And it's close enough I won't have to think two times about visiting. Sure hope it's gonna be a good one—full of fire and brimstone!"

He frowned and tugged his hat lower on his forehead. His mind raced back to his mother, who'd taken them to church with her every Sunday.

Mother Cora.

Even though he was only three at the time, he remembered how she had scurried around the house, "like a chicken with its head cut off," Mama Edna would say, to get everyone ready. They'd walk down the dusty road to her parents' church for Sunday school outside the little town of Billingsley, while Daddy slept off his workweek. He would join them later for the church services.

Charles watched the men put up the large tent and fought the temptation to go over to help. Helping out was second nature to him.

But he had already promised that a couple of acres would be cleared that day. Standing there musing over the past and other possibilities wasn't going to get any of the work done.

Charles whistled between his teeth, causing Ol' Bess's head to jerk up. As she lurched forward, Charles felt a strange sense of buoyancy.

He felt that his life was about to shift. He knew for sure that, while there were no guarantees, he was heading to a brighter future.

CHAPTER 3

MY FIRST DAY AS A SENIOR

"Lil' Sister! Come on outta there! You gonna run us late!"

Matthew pounded on the bathroom door. His booming voice made my hand jump, and I had to touch up my lipstick.

I determined, right then and there, as it was my senior year, I was going to start a new direction in my life. I would not let my brothers push me around!

Not that morning. I pursed my lips, dabbed them, and resolutely squared my shoulders before opening the door.

Matthew stood right outside with his arms folded. He wore a scowl, but when he saw me, there was a hitch in his performance.

Immediately, his overall demeanor changed. That positive appraisal was worth all the extra time it had taken to put my look together.

Luke whistled. He pushed his way past Matthew, because our hallway was too narrow for both of their well-built frames. Luke shook his head as he gave me a brotherly once over.

"Now, you know Mother and Daddy had some pretty babies!"

"That includes you fellows!" I smiled demurely and gave his arm a little squeeze, whisking by the bathroom sentries.

"Y'all best to be movin'! It's almost seven!"

Mother had her hand on her hip, in her "I mean business" stance. We knew better than to dawdle. Mother wasn't foolin'.

I kissed her good-bye before picking up my lunch pail, book bag, and jacket.

"Thank you, Mother."

Mother, usually stern of visage, also confirmed my hopes. I could almost swear that she gave me the same approving smile she'd saved for Sherrie Lee!

She said nothing but nudged my brothers and me out the door. When I asked Big Mama Dee why Mother never said anything about how good I looked, she laughed.

"She don't want ta give any of ya a big head, chil'!"

None of that mattered, today. No one could pull my head out of the clouds.

It was 1940. My senior year!

Matthew and Luke escorted me to school my first day. They started this tradition when I first entered Paul Lawrence Dunbar High School, three years ago.

Matthew was attending the Methodist Seminary and Luke was at Tuskegee studying engineering.

"You're lucky Dunbar starts a week earlier than our classes, Lil' Sister," Matthew said. He led the way to our regular shortcut, the railroad tracks.

Following the tracks made it a straight, three-plus mile walk. But most importantly, it took us away from Bessemer Senior High, the white high school.

We didn't want to have a rough start. Avoiding the mean white students was our primary focus. It was easier to avoid that area of Bessemer, which we always did like the plague.

I was worried that I had run us late, but I had to pick out the perfect outfit for this special day. I chose my newly-made brown corduroy skirt and the white blouse that Mother had sewn for me last spring.

This outfit made me look like a serious student, but was attractive, too. I even stayed up late polishing my loafers until they had a high shine.

Sunday afternoon, Mother had helped me with my hair. I wore my headscarf all through dinner 'til I went to bed, afraid that the look would not be my best if one hair was out of place.

I woke up with my right eye twitching. While I don't lay truck to superstitions, I knew that old folks had their reasons for them.

Was some good luck really awaiting me on this beautiful day? I silently thanked the Lord that we had that shortcut, because now, we needed it!

Along the railroad tracks, sweet gum trees towered above us on either side, a hundred feet tall. Their branches filled with red, orange, yellow, and purple leaves created a carnival canopy to celebrate this wonderful day.

The prickly little gumballs attracted a menagerie of finches that flew high overhead. Not to be left out of the festive fall gathering, I saw several black squirrels scamper along the branches.

The brush was alive with crickets and grasshoppers. The smell of fall was in the air. How beautiful fall was in Bessemer!

As we walked to school, each of us were lost in our own thoughts. We nodded and waved to men and women along the way. Many were day laborers and domestics.

They reminded me of the many times Mother and Daddy told us that they wanted us to have a better future. Our parents insisted that we all go to college. It was exciting to think of what my work would be once I graduated.

My magical senior year! It would be my last shot at high school. Soon I'd become the person I always dreamt of becoming. After high school, I would be ready to face the real world as an adult.

Bessemer Colored High School was built the year I was born, in 1923. It was the only school that colored boys and girls could go to because Jim Crow laws didn't allow us to attend Bessemer High.

Later, our school was renamed Paul Lawrence Dunbar High School after the famous, colored poet. People always said when you finished Dunbar, you could get a job. A good job!

The school offered a large number of academic classes as well as vocational classes such as sewing, auto mechanics, and typing. But picking out one field as my vocation was very hard.

I wanted to be the secretary of our senior class because I liked writing, especially poetry. I entertained the idea of going to a business college. Rosalind Russell made smart women working in offices look beautiful and industrious.

Taking care of people, like Big Mama Dee, was another one of my interests. I thought about it often since she'd saved my life when I had typhoid fever from falling into a bad part of the Branch where a dead cow lie upstream. I became deathly ill. So much so, the old family doctor gave up on me.

"There's nothing that could be done, folks. Sorry."

"The Lord is gonna help me save my baby girl!" Big Mama Dee had declared.

People had come from all over to set up a watch meeting for me, thinking that I wouldn't make it through the night. However, Big Mama Dee had other plans.

She began to cook her concoction on the kitchen stove. We still don't know what it was she cooked, because she never shared the mysteries of her healing arts with anyone.

Boy, did it stink!

It made such an awful smelling brew that it must have scared all of those watch folk clear off the porch! But whatever that medicine was, it worked.

After Sherrie Lee's illness and death, I knew medicine was not for me. I still cringe at the sight of blood.

Thinking about Sherrie Lee made my eyes well up with tears. It had been three years since her death, yet she was constantly on my mind.

Our dreams and plans for the future changed forever that day. Now, it was just my future.

To avoid getting blue on this special day, I forced myself to think of the fun things; the good times we'd had together.

I owed Sherrie Lee so much. I promised myself, that senior year, I'd follow her lead to be glamorous. I'd make all of her effort count. That thought buoyed my spirits as I got myself ready.

That morning, for instance, my thoughts immediately went to Sherrie Lee as I put on my face. They were joyful memories. I always admired how beautiful she looked with her reddish, copper hair and her bright red lipstick! She had it down!

I spent two years begging her to show me how. Sherrie Lee always refused each of my pleas.

"You're too young, Lil' Sister! You only twelve!"

"Mother got married when she was thirteen! So, whatcha got to say about that?"

"Hush!"

Sherrie Lee made pretend she was going to swat me, but I dodged and ran off. I loved running. I was very fast and knew she could never catch me.

After Sherrie Lee and Fred were married, we all looked forward to the birth of their child. All of these things changed Sherrie Lee.

She shifted from the gruff, sour-tempered sister I had grown up with to someone patient and loving. Maybe it was because of the changes her body was going through. Whatever the case, she began treating me with respect—as an equal.

One day, she sidled up to me while I was reading Black Beauty, my favorite book. That she had something on her mind was obvious, but I knew better than to look interested.

"Girl, y'know you worry the horns offa billy goat? C'mon back in our room, and I'll give ya the first makeup lesson."

I started to hug her, but she pushed me away.

"You just better not let Mother know! You gots to wipe it all off before you leave the room!"

Maybe it was because she was pregnant and bored, but whatever the case, I was in seventh heaven! She gave me a little bit of her old makeup and put me to work.

It made me smile thinking about how excited I was. It was the first step in having my dream come true!

Not a few times did she remind me I needed to get ready for my senior year. As I began practicing for my new role five years ahead of my seventeenth birthday, we figured we had plenty of time.

Every day she'd come over and show me how to pinch my fluffy eyebrows together to make them thinner, more defined. Then she helped me apply eyebrow pencil, lipstick, and rouge. We did it in secret, so Mother wouldn't pooh-pooh our plans.

"You gots to practice doing this every day, Lil' Sister. When your senior year comes, you'll be the belle of the ball!"

I remember scrunching up my face at her calling me "Lil' Sister." I hated that nickname.

"Aw, Sherrie Lee, c'mon!"

Lil' Sister was a name that my family had the hardest time letting go of. It didn't make any sense for me to have this nickname with five sisters and brothers in the family that were younger than myself!

I never liked nicknames. It kept people from ever getting to know a person's real name!

While Mother wanted us to remain grounded, it was Big Mama Dee who'd tell us, "Aim for the stars, even if you hit the stump!" We knew we could become anything we set our minds on. Even movie stars!

"So, who should I fix you up like? Nina Mae McKinney, Marlene Dietrich, or Dorothy Dandridge?"

"I'd rather be made up like Maureen O'Hara or Lena Horne."

Sherrie Lee was quick to interject, "Hey, I'm the Lena Horne of this family! You can be Bette Davis . . ."

When I gave her the look Mother gave us when we said something outrageous, we both cracked up.

During the last few years, I hadn't had much time to do anything special for myself. Taking care of the little ones became my job after Sherrie Lee got married. Whenever I could squeeze some time out for myself, I kept practicing my makeup and dreaming about my senior year!

The first part of that dream was, when senior year came, I would start the first day of school looking glamorous. The second part was that I'd find my prince!

Thinking back on that day, Sherrie Lee and I had never felt closer. That thought saddened me with her being gone.

"Time to focus, Lil' Sister!"

Matthew was quick to see that I wasn't paying attention. We were almost at the First Street trestle bridge. As always, my heart started racing.

If the bridge had been made for pedestrians, complete with railings and walkways, it would have been different. I tried not to think of the fact that twenty feet below me were cars, horses, and wagons going about their morning business.

When I was fourteen, stepping out on these trestle tracks for the first time, I was so scared. I felt like crawling over them on my hands and knees. But I couldn't have done that.

My hesitation was already enough to get Matthew and Luke on my case. It was as if their jeering would suddenly fill me with courage!

But it didn't take crossing over some trestle bridge to get my brothers going. I often felt that if I had ever gotten some encouragement from them, it would mean that I woke up in the wrong house.

Teasing was their way of showing love, if that's what you call it. I guess, in their minds, they were hoping to make me tougher. At least, that's what Mother always said when she scolded us.

But to me, I'd rather call it as it was. It felt like I was constantly being raked over the coals with a big, heaping shovel of back-biting!

Looking down the four-foot wide trestle, it suddenly came to me how much I'd grown over the past three years. Now I could walk across this wood and steel bridge one tie at a time in my brown corduroy skirt and nice loafers.

I learned the secret was to distract myself as I walked across. Down below, I could see people making their early morning deliveries in Ford Model BBs and Studebakers.

As I took steps along the trestle's wooden beam, I wiped my slightly moist hands as if smoothing my skirt. Feeling its little ridges took my mind back to how the corduroy fabric had become my pleats under Mother's deft hands.

With a serene expression, made soft and golden by the glow of the china lamp on our side-boy, she would sew up the sides of the fabric, humming a gospel song. It was one of the few times when we could see Mother relaxed.

She had taken down the brown, nondescript dress that was given to my Aunt Thelma, who worked for a well-to-do family. My beautiful new skirt seemed to leap out of the mounds of fabric. There was nothing mammy-made about Mother's sewing.

In reality, every single thing we wore came from the Banker Lewis's. They seemed to take a liking to Aunt Thelma. Their children called her Auntie Thelma.

The family never gave anything away without first letting Aunt Thelma take a look at it. It seemed that Banker's sons would wear their clothes for one season, then send the practically new items home with my aunt.

"Almost there, DeLois Ann."

It surprised me to hear Brother Luke's encouraging, gentle voice behind me. I had taken my mind off of the trestle for most of my journey.

I thought, with a chuckle, that maybe he was being kind because this was the last year they'd have to walk me to school.

My two brothers towered over my five-foot frame, fore and aft. Luke kept an eye out for trains. His football and boxing training had given him the power of an athlete.

I watched the back of Matthew's head to keep the proper pace. While Matthew looked chubby, he was built like a tank; he was the family's champion wrestler.

His job was to spot the wrong sort and to make sure we made good time.

Matthew's concern was sincere. He'd seen a lot of friends beaten up by the students of Bessemer High.

Although he was a full two years older than Luke, he looked shorter because of his girth. He shrugged it off and said that he never lost his baby fat.

His chunky size and chubby cheeks caused people to think he was the younger of the two boys.

Even though Luke was the youngest, he had been double promoted back in elementary school.

Luke was so smart! He started reading before he started school.

I was so proud of my brothers; they were both very handsome, but I couldn't let them know. They might've gotten big-headed.

Luke's handsome face glistened in the morning light. I knew the shine wasn't from sweat, 'cause we'd barely walked two of the five miles.

Luke always swathed his face with a light coat of bacon fat when mother wasn't looking. He did it every morning after he'd washed up.

He said it was to cut down on the ashiness. But I knew it was because he was particular about his looks. The grease made his face look amazing.

People said we looked like twins, even though he was two years older than me. We both had a wide, perfect smile, the same high forehead, small nose, and wide-set eyes, but they looked a lot more becoming on him than me.

Again, Matthew noticed that I had slowed down. His expression grew rancorous.

"Hurry up, Lil' Sister! You don't want to run into none of those poor whites on our way, do you?"

I couldn't get mad at him. He was just trying to protect us. I saw that we were getting closer to Dunbar. We were also getting closer to Bessemer High.

Picking up my pace, one thought circled my brain: I wish I were prettier.

I flipped my bob and smiled, now thinking, maybe with this makeover, I am!

I'd always loved movies where the heroine would suddenly appear as a beautiful swan transformed from an ugly duckling.

All of my life, I saw myself as that ugly duckling. I'd worn pigtails and was very shy. I didn't want to call any attention to myself.

I had an age-old problem. It was a secret that I tried to keep to myself. I was filled with dread that others would find out.

That secret held hostage my best intentions. I knew in my heart that if I were to overcome that horrible secret, someday, I'd be able to blossom into a swan and meet the man of my dreams!

I was a bed wetter. On top of that, during that period of my life, Mother thought that making me wear my pee-stained clothes would embarrass me into stopping. It just made me very sad and lonely.

Burdened with the secret and low self-esteem, I went through all of those years of agony. It was impossible for me to stop something I had no idea of how to fix!

For the longest time, I couldn't bear to stand near anyone, thinking that they may smell me and find me repulsive. It was just easier to keep to myself.

After the doctor told Mother that I was a sound sleeper and couldn't have anything to drink after six o'clock, nobody could pay me to take a drink.

Even if it were ice-cold buttermilk! From then on, I had a new lease on life!

The year before Sherrie Lee died, she said something that always stuck with me. She and I had walked home from a movie we'd just seen, Dark Victory, with Bette Davis.

"Now, DeLois Ann, when you start high school, especially on your senior year, it's your last shot to be the person you've always wanted to be!

"I know that your condition really frightened you and made you feel bad. But you can't always live your life 'fraid of your own shadow, Lil' Sister."

Remembering her last comment about how I had to have courage and to keep my spunk, I knew Sherrie Lee was trying to help me to conquer my fears.

Going into my senior year meant that I was almost an adult. I wouldn't always have folks around that cared about my well-being. It was time to grow up.

CHAPTER 4

A FUTURE AND A HOPE

The moon peeked from behind billowing clouds. Its light allowed Charles to make his way across the freshly harvested cornfields. His eyes were trained on the brightly lit tent.

The sound of music could be heard faintly, in the distance. As he drew closer, it seemed to rise like a wave, swelling up to heaven.

Sacred songs served many purposes for his people. During slavery times, they gave his people solace from the barbaric work conditions of slavery as well as the hope of future deliverance.

His grandparents had told him that many of the songs were used to guide folks to the Underground Railroad, to freedom in the north. The lyrics gave its listeners secret instructions.

Charles could now make out a few words of the old gospel song the tent meeting group was singing. He blended his baritone with the chorus. The old songs flooded his soul with many memories. Old songs with lyrics about the glory of God and Zion and reaping harvests made his pulse quicken. And, along the excitement, he felt a tinge of remorse.

He had not followed his mother's example about regularly attending church. The services had been a great part of his early childhood.

Daddy Ben had helped to build the church that sat a stone's throw from the tracks in a small clearing. But with the workload he had been juggling, Charles felt lucky when he was able to make it there more than once a month.

How vividly he remembered his mother standing in that little church with a straight back and eyes focused on her songbook. When Charles, the youngest, squirmed or tried to sit down, she squeezed his hand so tightly it hurt.

"You's in the Lawd's house! Stand up and honor Him!"

He flinched, but he dared not pull away. Somehow, even at that young age, Charles sensed that his mother needed to hold his hand just as much as she needed to be filled with the Lord's Spirit.

When they finally sat down, Daddy Ben sat ramrod straight. He was a stern figure.

Charles' oldest brother, Samuel, was almost a carbon copy of his father. He emulated Ben's posture for all of his twenty years of practice. Charles sat on the other side of Mother with Adam and Martha. Mama Edna anchored the family at the end of the pew.

Ben's focus on the minister's message was something to behold. His eyes flashed with excitement.

It told Charles that something marvelous was going to happen at any minute. It made him want to watch, too.

That night, as Charles approached the tent opening, he wasn't sure if he'd ever found what his father and mother were expectantly searching for those Sundays. He only knew that it all changed after Samuel died.

While he could barely remember his older brother, it was the first tragedy that struck the Stevenses' household. Soon after, Cora was admitted to a home.

His father had become more preoccupied with the business of keeping the farm going and making ends meet. He worked twice as hard to pay for Mama's keep at Mt. Vernon, which was clear across the state.

Earlier, he had worked with Samuel at the sawmill. Two salaries helped to pay down the mortgage faster. Ben knew that he could rely on Mama Edna and Cora to take charge of the day-to-day chores.

Later, after Samuel's death at the mill, the farming fell on Adam and Martha. Ben took on more hours at the mill and Cora became more distant, nervous. The death of her oldest son began to take its toll on her health.

The family periodically attended church, but life wasn't the same. Something had been lost.

It was tangible to Charles in many ways. Especially after his mother was placed in a home for mental illness. It was as though the Lord's Spirit had left him.

He had wandered away from the teachings of his youth and found his own way. In doing so, he had made mistakes. Many mistakes.

But for some reason that he couldn't explain, that evening felt different. Maybe the fervor of the song rekindled some smoldering ember of hope within his heart.

Charles found himself smiling as he entered the tent. A small, elderly man stood at the doorway. He was dressed in a shiny, well-worn suit, his dark face a stark contrast to the bright white, well-starched shirt he wore, with fraying cuffs and collar.

The man handed Charles a book. It was a scruffy, well-used brown hymnal.

The older man's smile was so engaging that Charles felt its warmth.

"Have a seat, brother. I thank the Lord for your presence."

It was an odd greeting, but it did help make Charles feel at home. He sat next to a middle-aged gentleman who kept his head bowed the entire time.

Charles gazed around at the small gathering. He saw people he knew from the nearby farms, white and colored alike.

In attendance were mothers with children, young girls and boys he had gone to school with, and older men who frequented the little feed store that stocked everything in Billingsley from flour to harnesses.

In the front, behind the pulpit, were four chairs. A group of graying men of different hues sat in these seats. Their faces were lined and worn by hard work in the hot Alabama sun.

But they didn't look weary from their toiling. Somehow, they appeared to be refreshed and happy. Perhaps inspired by the songs?

He listened closely to the words to see if he could gain any insight.

He closed his eyes and thought about Heaven. The Book of Revelation said it had streets paved with gold. Perhaps that thought and rest for the weary was what his mother had held onto, so long ago.

The singing stopped. Charles glanced up. He found that the older gentleman who had greeted him at the door was on the small stage. The elderly man held up his well-worn Bible and leaned over the pulpit.

The sweet night air blew into the tent. The breeze, fragrant with freshly tilled soil, gave its members a cool respite.

"Brothers and sisters! This evening, I want you to turn your hearts to the Lord. Put the picking of cotton, making the mortgage and bills, or what tomorrow's meal is gonna be out of your heads. Tonight, we're going to feast from the Lord's table!"

The room was awash with "Amens!"

A smile tugged at Charles's lips. This minister wasn't wasting any time.

He sat back in his seat, preparing himself for a message that would help him sort out his own strange mixture of fears, feelings, and thoughts. Maybe he'd get some direction this very night!

A young boy handed him a Bible. Charles thanked him.

He had left his father's Bible on the mantelpiece, not wanting to disturb Ben's nightly reading. Ben's routine was to have dinner, discuss the current events in the paper, and finish with his Bible before going to bed.

Charles wished his father could have come to the meeting with him. However, he knew that the work at the sawmill made it nearly impossible. Between the peanut fieldwork and his own work at the sawmill, sometimes-church services seemed the only thing that he could barter off.

But at what price? Charles shook his head.

If giving up a good nights' rest was hard for him, he knew it would be harder for his father. Yet, he still chose to ask his father to come with him.

"Right now, yo' mind is like wax. Maybe there's somethin' that minister can give you from God's word that'll stick."

Charles could see that Ben had that faraway look that seemed to come more frequently as the years passed.

Was it remorse? Charles wondered.

There would be little rest for him after attending that tent meeting. It made him almost reconsider his plans. But somehow, that meeting was important.

"Open your Bibles now to Jeremiah 29:11. That's chapter 29, verse 11."

The old preacher leaned forward, his nose barely inches from the book and his glasses perched, forgotten, on his forehead.

"And it reads on this wise, 'When seventy years are completed for Babylon, I will come to you and fulfill my good promise to bring you back to this place.'

"Now listen, church! This next part is what tonight's sermon is built around."

"'For I know the plans I have for you,' declares the Lord, 'plans to prosper you and not harm you.'"

Charles sat up straight, eyes wide with excitement. Quickly thumbing through the Bible, he found the verse and read along with the minister.

"'... plans to give you a future and a hope.'"

Charles stared at the minister, dumbfounded.

"'Then you will call on me and come and pray to me, and I will listen to you.'"

He had not heard these verses before!

They unlocked something in Charles's heart that had been pounding at its door for a long time. Was there forgiveness, as well as a release from his fears? More importantly, was there a future outside of Daddy Ben's farm?

He knew the importance of having land. Land was what colored folk and lots of white folk could only dream about owning.

Charles knew how God had intervened in Daddy Ben's life with Mr. Romano. That had clearly been God's plan for his father. But what was God's plan for him?

"Brothers and sisters, the Lord won't let you go wandering around in the wasteland of Babylon without a road map! He has a plan and a way for you to make it to the future He has for you!"

The minister held his Bible in the air, shaking it for emphasis.

"Listen, church! He never intended His children to stay in Babylon. It was just a way station! Use His map and He'll guide you!"

"Amen!" The words peppered the air. A few men slapped their knees.

"C'mon, now!"

The minister mopped his head and raised the white handkerchief to the heavens.

"The Lord, my Lord, never meant to keep his people down! He always has a plan for them!"

"Preach on, brother!"

"No, my friends," the minister shook his gray head, "my Lord says, 'I' . . ."

He paused to gaze around the tent at the expectant faces of the crowd.

"Now, wait a minute. Would you want your plans to come from the Creator or the created? I want the plans of the Creator, brethren! Not man!"

"But it is the Lord that says here, 'I . . . I have plans to prosper you and not harm you!'"

The congregation rose to its feet, clapping in agreement. Charles stood, too. He felt the spirit of joy returning to him, engulfing him.

"He has plans to give you a hope and a future! Can I get an 'amen'?"

A thunder of "Amens" met the minister's challenge. A heavyset woman in front of Charles got up and pranced around. Bouncing on the balls of her feet, she held her Bible high, weeping.

"Your future ain't here, church! It ain't workin' for pennies in the field or at the hands of the master of this Great Depression world here on Earth! Your future is a rich one with the Lord! In His hands, you can go as far and as high as He gives you strength, ability, and courage to go! You are just beginning to receive His promises, His blessings!"

The minister looked around the assemblage, finding and staring into each set of eyes. When he found Charles's, Charles felt the familiar charge. It was the same type of charge he had felt long ago when Dr. Carver had singled him out.

But that time, it was stronger. Charles caught his breath and bowed his head in prayer.

The minister closed his Bible and, once more, held up his handkerchief.

"That's part of the promise, my friends. You have to call on the Father for him to answer you. You have to pray to Him before He can listen to you and give you what He promised you!

"The gift is already there, church. Will you come and offer your heart to the Lord so he can take you into His kingdom? Let Him take you the rest of the way and enter into His promise!

"His true gift is a heavenly home—we're just on the road of life. But all of His gifts are here for the asking, church.

"He wants to give you the biggest gift of all—an eternal home with Him and His Son, our Lord Jesus Christ.

"Won't you come? Give your hearts to Him? He knows all of the burdens and trials you've gone through. He knows the sins."

Charles's head shot up. He stared at the minister.

"Give your heart to Jesus, believing He came and died for you to take away those sins, nailing them to the cross. He arose on the third day in the newness of life, God, and man. He had breakfast on the beach with his disciples and was seen by many others, finally, taken up to live eternally in glory with his Father, the Lord of hosts!

"Someday, folks, He will return to gather up His people. Are you ready? Won't you come, today?"

The congregation began singing, renewed and revitalized. Charles's voice rose, yet cracked with emotions he hadn't felt in years.

Involuntarily, he found himself walking toward the front of the church. He fell to his knees, tears flowing.

It was the path he had been searching for. He wanted God to lead him. He wanted God's future.

The minister and one of the older men on the pulpit came to him. They prayed and cried with him.

The older man raised his head and stared at Charles.

"Son, do you accept that Jesus is the Son of God, that He died for your sins?"

Charles nodded his head. "Yes, I do, sir."

"That confession brought death to Jesus Christ but will bring life to you, son."

The men led Charles to an area on the stage where there was a small baptismal tub. Taking off his shoes, Charles stepped into the water.

"I baptize you in the name of the Father, Son, and Holy Ghost!"

As he was lifted up out of the water, Charles felt his burdens lifted too. Climbing out of the tub, he was ecstatic; his face, radiant.

The churches' "amens!" and claps on his back encouraged him. He knew for the first time that he was on the right path for his future.

As Charles strode back over the dry stalks of the threshed cornfields, he was soaking wet, but lighter in step. He knew what his life had been like before, but now, felt what was yet to come—this next part of his life—would be full of God's promises.

He now had a future and a hope! He also knew, as clear and as bright as the moon that shone down on him, his future was not going to be on his father's farm.

CHAPTER 5

TROUBLING TIMES

"Lost ten minutes! We coulda been there but for waitin' around for you, Lil' Sister!"

Matthew snapped the silver case of Papa's old pocket watch shut for an extra, dramatic flair. His comment was something I didn't need to hear. I knew I'd lost track of time getting ready for my first day.

Turning toward Luke, he shouted, "And I figured she'd walk a lot faster without those pee-wet clothes weighing her down!"

I quickly looked around, hoping no one was near enough to hear. I went from having all of those great feelings of faith growing in my spirit a moment before to being crushed. I was a balloon that had suddenly lost its air.

Matthew had dared to utter my dreaded secret in public! Just as quickly that old feeling of shame washed over me. I grew hot. My temper flared.

"Go ahead, Matthew! Tell everybody in Bessemer!"

My face burned with anger.

"Nobody needs a radio with you broadcasting all of my business!"

He hadn't exactly shouted, but his loud voice was nearly as bad as a yell. Matthew was almost "deef," as he would say, from the time he was a baby.

Mother believed that Matthew's hearing loss was caused when he was in her womb. She said it came from her taking quinine water for leg cramps when she was pregnant with him.

I guess he used a loud voice so that he could hear himself. But it was unsettling, even though we were in the woods by ourselves.

What made it hurt so badly was it made me aware of the truth: I was still the old me inside.

I turned my fiercest glare on Matthew.

"Who needs enemies with brothers like you?"

Not surprisingly, Matthew smiled at my comment. He loved getting my goat.

Suddenly, his smirk evaporated.

Three very rough-looking white boys stood in our path. Their expressions told us that they wanted to teach us something in the worst way. Something unpleasant.

Mother told us that the meanest people were the ones who had nothin' and didn't want you to have anything, either. She also told us that some people used money or its lack as an excuse for doing bad things.

"And don't be surprised, chil'. Bad people come in every color. But, no matter the person, God don't like ugly."

All the same, it just seemed that in Bessemer, with Jim Crow, most of the meanness directed toward us came from poor white folks.

Jim Crow was something that had been around the South for many years. Daddy said the evil rules were set up to keep colored people in their place after slavery ended.

He figured that since there were so many of us, now freed, the white people were afraid. Maybe they thought we'd rise up and get even for the cruelty done to colored folk during the slavery days.

Whatever the case, these laws had a set of horrible, and sometimes deadly, consequences. We had to protect ourselves and be very careful at all times.

I felt very sad when I ran into people who didn't like us. It was frightening to have people call me terrible names. Worse yet, they treated us unfairly, like we weren't human.

I noticed this when we went outside of our little community of Burstall. We couldn't go into certain stores, or when we could, we had to use the "colored" entrance.

Even though some of our family friends worked in downtown Deli, they couldn't buy a soda there on a hot summer's day.

Over the years, I became more aware of the unfairness of what I saw. As I grew up, I had more than a few questions. Jim Crow just didn't make sense to me. Slavery had ended more than sixty years earlier!

At the age of ten, I decided to ask Mother about it. While Mother was often very stern, she was very loving and kind. I knew I had to catch her when she wasn't hard at work. That took some waiting!

I found the perfect opportunity while she was hanging up the Monday wash. Mother was singing one of her gospel hymns about heaven. Mother's singing told me that she was in a good mood.

"Mother, why is it that whites treat us like we don't count? Why don't they act decent like Banker Lewis and Papa Gallo?"

Papa Gallo was an Italian man who made the best pistachio ice cream, which he called gelato, in the whole of Bessemer. He owned a store near our house.

Both whites and coloreds would come to his store to buy cones and pints of it. He treated everyone as equals.

"One line! First come, first served!" he would bark when someone tried to cut the line or became rowdy about being next.

Mother stared at me and thought for what seemed a long time before answering. Finally, her expression softened.

"Chil'! Only th' Lord knows about that one!"

Mother paused, thinking as she held up one corner of a sheet. Absently, she realized that she had used the last wooden clothespin Papa whittled from her apron. I handed her another one from the clothespin bag tied to the wicker basket.

"Decent is as decent does. Some folk knows how to act decent to other folk, like the Banker and Papa Gallo.

One thing I do know, baby. A lots o' folk are gonna hafta answer to the Good Lawd some day. He'll do the sortin' out on that account, that's fo' sho'!"

Mother returned her attention to her work as if to say, "that was enough of that!"

She had no time for such foolishness. I knew I was lucky to get as much out of her as I did. Quickly, her expression grew pensive.

Maybe she was reflecting on the story Papa often told us. The incident happened when he lived in Coaling near Tuscaloosa. The traumatic event caused him to flee the area.

Papa was a big, imposing man who didn't take any guff off of nobody. It was hard to imagine him taking flight unless he was in real danger.

He told us that he had spent an entire hot summer's day tilling a plot of land of a farm he had rented. On the way back to the barn, a white man stopped him.

"I need to use yo' mule, Campbell. I'm fixin' ta move a load of hay this afternoon."

"Cain't do that, Mista Larry. Yo' can see my mule's lathered up from workin' in the field all day. Workin' him any mo'll kill him, sho!"

Papa said that any fool could look at the mule and see that its back was lathered up with sweat and dirt. This man knew that, too.

"Bible sho' talks poorly 'bout a man who don't take care o' his animals!"

Mr. Larry was surprised when Papa said no to him. Papa told us that with Jim Crow just taking hold in the South, colored people weren't supposed to have any say. They were supposed to cower or grin when it came to talking with whites for fear of their lives. Papa would do neither.

Papa wasn't the usual colored person. He felt that Mr. Larry was a farmer, just like he was. So, he spoke to him, farmer to farmer.

Mr. Larry grew angry.

"We'll just see about that, Campbell!"

That night, a group of Klansmen dressed in white sheets, came to their house. One of them put a wooden cross in the yard and set it aflame.

"Come on out of there, Campbell! We want to talk with you!"

Papa was so angry that they had come back to his home that he grabbed his rifle and headed for the door.

Big Mama Dee, who only came up to his shoulder, stopped him.

"Now what do ya 'spect to do with that gun, Papa?"

"I 'specta take as many of 'em down as I can, that's what I'll do!"

They had just started a home, and she wanted to have a family, to live in peace.

"No, Papa, I'm puttin' my foot down. We's gonna stay inside here this night and pray that the Lord sends them men away," Big Mama Dee reasoned.

"Then we'll leave early in the mornin' to go someplace where they cain't bother us!"

Her gentle voice won Papa over. It was a miracle that Mama Dee got Papa to listen to her. He invested a lot of time and money in cultivating and planting that field.

With much regret, early the next morning, they got everything they could gather loaded up in their wagon and took off.

"I got work on the railroad. I decided to drop 'Camp' and just became 'Bell,' so's they couldn't locate us. That's how we ended up in Bessemer as the 'Bell' family."

The syrupy sweet voice of one of the boys with cockeyed teeth broke through my reverie.

"Ya might as well put them books down, y'all ain't gonna make it to school this mornin'."

He proudly displayed his crooked teeth with a grin. They appeared to tumble over each other as if they were all trying to escape his mouth at the same time.

My heart sank. The beautiful beginning of my first day had gone up in smoke!

We might have made it to school if I hadn't taken a few extra minutes to reapply my lipstick.

I stared at the boys as they looked us over with contempt. Maybe they thought we were better than they. In some ways, I figured, we were.

The ragtag group of boys, who now faced us and eyed our nice clothes, wore frayed overalls and no shirts. The ones with shoes had soles that were flapping. Perhaps that's why they couldn't bear to let us pass.

Colored kids dressed nicely were a curiosity, and we were dressed better than most. Matthew and Luke wore new blue jean trousers with crisply pressed shirts and hunter's jackets.

My movie star-styled hair set off my starched, white cotton blouse and brown corduroy skirt. No one could tell me I wasn't sharp!

By looking at us, they couldn't have figured out how hard pressed we were to make ends meet at home.

We wore new-looking clothes because of the work Big Mama Dee and Mother put into remaking the cast-offs my Aunts Alice and Thelma brought home from their domestic work.

Mother and Big Mama Dee put many hours into remaking those castoffs. First, they'd check to see if the fabric was in good condition, with no moth holes or rips. Then, they'd either alter them, or remake the garments into something nice.

Mother was an expert mender. She'd close up rips using a piece of fabric she'd cut from the seams of the garment so that the fabric would match. You'd need a magnifying glass to find where the rip had been when she got ahold of a bad place!

Mother wove the moth holes in tiny stitches that would escape notice unless you ran your hand down the fabric to feel for the rough spot.

We stood there in our mended, reworked, clean, hand-me-down clothing with these boys staring at us in envy. We did look like we had more than they did. We didn't really.

"Soap and water are cheap," Mother would always say.

She got that mindset as well as the desire to have her own house from Big Mama Dee and Papa. Mother said that having a house of her own was a big dream that she and Daddy worked hard to make happen.

Mother and Daddy found a plot of land down the street from Mama and Papa. It was 1927 by the time the house was finished.

I was only four years old, but I remember how excited Mother was to be moving from her parents' house into her own place.

Papa and Big Mama Dee had a big, two-family home that we lovingly called the "home-house." The six of us shared a common kitchen and dining room with my grandparents.

Because we had only one bedroom for the boys and girls, Sherrie Lee and I had slept at the head while Luke, Matthew and Tommy had the foot of the bed.

I often giggled at the thought. We were like a can of sardines, lying head to toe like that!

Our new place had three bedrooms. Sherrie Lee and I finally had our own bed, which we shared with the little ones, Florence, Thelma, and Alice.

After a while, we had a lot more space because they slept on a little bed near the foot of our bigger bed.

"We're going to be the first ones in the neighborhood with electric lights, Clare!"

Daddy had proudly spread the builder's plans on the dining room table in Papa and Mama Bell's house.

"Look, Mama! It's even going to have hot water and indoor plumbing! The children will be able to take a bath in the bathroom!"

Big Mama Dee had sniffed and spat a chaw of brown tobacco into the black, metal spittoon that sat in the corner of the kitchen. It rang with appreciation of her aim.

"H.P. Douglas! Yo' gonna spoil them chil'rens with all that. My Lawd! Be raisin' a bunch of babies needin' hot running water to take a bath in 'fore long!"

Mother had laughed, holding her sides. She did that less often these days.

It was rare to hear her lusty laugh. It made everyone within earshot laugh along with her.

She knew not many people called Daddy "H. P." and got away with it.

It was a nickname he'd earned while playing baseball on the sandlot with the men in the area. They started calling him "high pockets," because his baseball uniform's pockets would sit high on his hips. Mother, Big Mama Dee, and close friends were the only ones who could get away with calling Daddy that to his face!

A thought suddenly occurred to me. Maybe we did have more. We had parents who worked hard to care for and feed us.

We had a new house with hot running water and electricity. Our family had the only telephone on the block. Folks came from all over to hear the Joe Lewis fight on our radio.

It was about ten years before that my parents had started to scrimp, save, and sacrifice until they were able to build their dream house. Their many thrifty habits had paid off.

My family knew how care for each other. They knew how to make do.

Luke's voice cut into my thoughts. He was cordial and calm.

"If you don't mind, we'd like to go on our way."

I don't know how he mustered up that smile. Maybe he smiled to show them he wasn't afraid.

The stocky boy with bad teeth tried staring down my brother. He was shorter, so this took considerable effort.

"You in my neck of the woods, boy. How you 'spect to get by us?"

This black-haired boy drew his words out like the salt-water taffy we made around the fire for Papa's evening story times.

The boy was right. We had to walk right by Bessemer High to get to Dunbar.

I felt sick. I had never run into anyone from Bessemer High these past years because we left very early.

I figured Matthew was right. I resolved that I'd never be late again!

Back when I first started going to Dunbar, Sherrie Lee and the boys had told me there might be trouble. I tried not to worry.

Matthew laughed at my expression. I guess I looked pretty scared.

"If there's any trouble, we'll finish it," Matthew reassured me. His eyes flashed with conviction.

It was true. My brothers were very good at handling themselves and weren't afraid of anything.

My brothers had a reputation in the area as good fighters, too. I knew that Luke boxed at Deacon Jones's since he was five. He'd been on Dunbar's boxing squad. And Matthew was one of the school's best wrestlers.

Without a doubt, in our family of eight, you'd better be able to take care of yourself! There were only six seats at our table and two of them were for Mother and Daddy. The eight of us would have to jockey for position every night to see who'd be left standing instead of seated at the table.

Matthew stepped forward and eyed the boys just as sternly as Daddy looked at us when it was time for a whippin'.

"Be ready to run for the corner and stay there until we've finished this."

Luke spoke so softly, I wasn't sure if I'd heard him correctly. I nodded, too frightened to say anything.

My brothers stepped forward. The three boys in our path took a tiny step back, almost imperceptibly. They regrouped.

"So, tell me, Luke, where you headin'? Didn't y'all graduate?"

The black-haired boy attempted a congenial smile. But since his expression was something between a grimace and a grin, it wound up twisting his face grotesquely. The other two stood by, menacingly.

"Seein' my sister off to school, Clyde. Ain't you goin' to be late, yourself?"

They knew each other's names! How was this possible?

They stared at each other for a good, long time.

Everything was held in the balance at that moment. I had sucked in my breath, ready to run.

Clyde took a step toward us. His henchmen were right behind him. However, Luke and Matthew held ground, not the slightest bit intimidated.

"I was fixin' ta clean this sidewalk with the likes of ya, but seein' that it's y'sister who's off ta school, just count yourselves lucky!"

"Sounds good to me, but we'll catch you later."

As Luke and Matthew slowly walked past, Luke nudged me to walk up ahead of him. My feet felt like lead.

When we were a good number of feet away, I overheard one of the boys say, "Why'd you let them n— pass, Clyde?"

"They's both good fighters, I didn't want to tussle with 'em just yet. There'll be another time when one of 'em are alone."

Luke and Matthew hadn't even flinched, but kept their same stride. It was as though they hadn't even heard the conversation! Their eyes were focused straight ahead.

When we were out of earshot, Matthew made a dismissive grunt.

"They talk mighty tough once we've passed their sorry asses. Shoulda taken 'em up on the challenge."

"And all that woulda done was made Lil' Sister run late."

"Yeah, I didn't want my clothes messed up, either. Come to think of it."

Luke and Matthew chuckled as they stepped up their pace.

Groups of white students were beginning to show up as we passed the Bessemer High area. Some stared at us. Others tossed taunts and mean comments at us.

"Dark clouds are passing overhead."

"N—!"

My face burned as I thought how mean they were being to us. Didn't their mothers and fathers teach them better?

Matthew and Luke marched along without looking back at the hecklers. They kept their heads high and looked neither to the right nor the left.

But I noticed something else. Something I hadn't seen before that lifted me above my current circumstances. My brothers were courageous.

They were walking me to school, unconcerned about the riffraff, shoulders squared.

My parents taught us that school was the one thing that would make a difference in our lives. Maybe that's why nothing could stop them from getting me there.

I often prayed for that kind of courage. This day, having seen how it looked, I was encouraged. I steeled my body and walked with shoulders back, too.

Maybe this run-in was meant to help me release my fears. I hoped this was the year I'd gain more of that type of courage, too.

CHAPTER 6

TIME TO FESS UP

"What do you mean, 'goin' to the city?'" Adam exploded.

Charles didn't know how to break the news to them any other way. To his father and Adam, his announcement came across as a capricious thought, sudden and out of the blue.

But after attending the tent meeting, this moment was drilled into Charles's consciousness. He was resolute. He had chosen the Sunday morning's drive to the sawmill as the time to begin hoeing that row.

"You mean to tell me you'd leave me, Henrietta, and Martha with all of the farm work to do without so much as a 'by your leave?' And me, still recovering? How could you be so selfish?"

Charles bowed his head. His brother's harsh assessment was anticipated, but hurt nonetheless. He prayed for the right words.

"Martha and Henrietta picked the same amount of peanuts yesterday as I did on Friday. At this rate, we should have most of the acreage cleared by in the next few weeks. Besides, I can come back to help y'all with getting' it to market."

Ben rode along in silence, mulling over Charles's news.

"This has been heavy on my heart for some time, Adam. But at that tent meeting, one minute I was accepting the Lord, and the next thing I knew, I had this strange understanding. It was only then that I was certain it was the right thing to do."

Charles's eyes glanced to and fro. The countryside's rich, dark green foliage mixed with golden shades of autumn beneath the beautiful, blue Alabama sky was restful.

But, today, it did little to salve his soul. It gave him no answer as to how he could handle this situation.

As they neared a juncture, several people passed by on foot. Some were farmers who walked with their families in their Sunday best, apparently on their way to church. All of them were oblivious of the drama playing itself out in the Stevenses' wagon.

The day began as many other Sundays, with the men sharing one of Ben's breakfasts. Ben cooked his spread at five, in preparation for a long day's work at the mill and to give Mama Edna time to prepare for church.

Grits and fresh eggs, fried chicken and buttermilk biscuits with freshly churned butter. Sorghum syrup flowed freely as each man ate his breakfast in silence.

After Ben hitched the mule to the wagon and drove it to the front of the house, Adam continued the drive, taking the men down the deeply rutted path from the house to the dirt road.

This morning, he drove in order to return home in time to take the women to church. The three men had taken this road many a day in the past to go to the lumber mill on Swift Creek. Ol' Bess knew it by heart.

Charles had been filled with a mixture of dread and expectation as he watched a few trucks and wagons passing them along the dusty road.

How was he going to tell his father? Now, he'd have to share the news with Adam, as well.

That promised to be a risky venture. He didn't want to make this any harder than it already was.

At that moment, Adam had chuckled, noting Charles's quiet demeanor.

"What could it be? Some girl? Ain't much like you."

"Guess I must be rubbin' off on Charles."

Charles felt himself relaxing. He grinned in relief at his father and brother's mild teasing.

"Guess so."

He had paused, thinking perhaps this was the opening he had waited for. With his father and brother in good spirits, was this the time? Had the Lord heard his plea?

"Lord, please guide me and give me courage," he prayed.

At that moment, Charles felt a peace descend upon him. So much so, he made up his mind to dive in.

He cleared his throat and spoke up.

"Daddy, I've made up my mind to go to the city this fall. I feel that's what the Lord is calling me to do . . . instead of farming."

After the initial shock of the announcement, Adam had simmered for a long while.

"So, now you're saying the Lord told you to do this? He wouldn't want you to shirk your responsibilities and leave the family, just like that!"

"I hope you can understand that I believe there's something else out there for me to do. That the Lord has prepared a different future for me," Charles tentatively offered.

His father cocked his head at Charles.

"Have ya figured out how yo' gonna survive out there, Charlie? Seen many a country boy get eaten up and spit out by them cities. Jim Crow and all.

"Ya just turned twenty. Ya gots a lot of learnin' to do, about life and the ugly places outside of Billingsley—a lot of people outta work in them cities."

Adam said nothing but shook his head and muttered to himself about Charles going off "half-cocked."

Charles paused and considered his father's advice.

"You right. But, Daddy, what better way to learn? Besides, I can stay with Cousin Viola and Bert, or at Aunt Lonnie's like you did. They both got a couple of extra rooms, I'm sure.

"Most likely they'd be happy to have me rent one of 'em. In the meantime, you know I'm not afraid of hard work, Daddy. I figure that there are jobs out there—if a person applies himself."

Ben continued on in silence for a stretch of time. Charles knew his father well enough to not argue his point any further. It would only seem as though he were more desperate than resolved.

Losing Samuel in the mill accident sixteen years earlier was a terrible blow to his father and mother. While Cora was never the same, emotionally, Daddy Ben never mentioned his oldest son's death. They all knew that it left Ben with an ache only the Lord and time would heal.

Adam's recent accident amplified the dangers of working at the mill. Charles thought it might have hit a still-raw nerve in his father.

"Well, 'spec you better visit yo' mother and the rest of the relatives, first. Come winter, it'll be hard to get back down here, with these roads."

Charles looked at his father in surprise as much about his agreement as he was in the mention of his mother. Ben hadn't often spoken about Cora.

"Yes, sir! I will," Charles said, quickly recovering.

Adam interrupted, "You gonna let him up and go? Just like that?"

Shaking his head, he finally asked, "So, how soon you planning on leaving us?"

Charles let the air out of his lungs, not realizing he'd been holding it in. He shot a glance at his father. But Ben kept his eye trained on the spot just above Bess's ears as he did when he was the driver.

"Uh, I'll leave at the end of next week, after visiting Mama, Adam." Charles paused and offered, "Aunt

Nellie always says she wished she could see her sister. I'll invite her along."

Daddy Ben nodded.

"It's almost three hours one way on the bus. She'd probably want to visit her relatives in Mobile, too. You best spend the night with 'em, son, fo' headin' to Bessemer. I'll talk with her."

Charles thought a couple of weeks was a good length of time to complete the task and take the peanuts to market. He mused what this yield would be.

They would need funds for new corn or cottonseed. Later on, he would come back to help Adam and Henrietta finish the harvest and prepare the pods for market.

Whatever the yield, it might provide payment enough for several months of the farm's mortgage. Charles hoped that it would be a hedge against the winter months. That way, he wouldn't feel so bad about leaving.

"I first have to finish most of the harvesting, Adam," Charles offered. "You know, at forty-six cents a bushel . . ."

Adam waved him off.

"I know. I figure it'll yield about two thousand dollars."

Adam had always been fast with calculations. It impressed Charles that he had picked up that skill up from Daddy Ben.

Ben made sure that his children were able to manage every aspect of farming. Adam had certainly picked up the business side of it.

"Right, that'll give you the money toward your cotton seeds or fertilizer."

Adam spat between his teeth over the side of the wagon.

"Just about take all of it . . ."

Ben chuckled.

"'Spec you're gonna need it fo' y'self a bunch more than we will, son. How about ya take half. We have some money saved up for the shortfall."

"Thank you, Daddy, but I couldn't . . ." was all Charles could get out.

"Ain't asking you, son."

Charles bowed his head in thanksgiving. In God's miraculous way, the peanut crop was paying his way to this new freedom!

Lord, he prayed silently. *What do you want me to do when I get to Bessemer? I never wanted to be a financial burden on my family. That money is a sacrifice for my father.*

Adam stared at Ben with disbelief.

"You going to give half the entire yield to Charles?"

Ben gave Adam a quick grin. "He planted it. Bought the seeds with his peach-pickin' money. 'Spec we can spare a portion of it, don't you think, son?"

He turned to Charles. "Just use it like you ain't got none. Money ain't so plentiful these days, 'specially around in the city. With Jim Crow, you have to pay for everything under the sun, and then some."

Charles nodded in silent agreement. His father was a man of few words, but he always spoke the truth.

He would have to earn enough to take care of everything that came with leaving home; bed, board, and even if and when he wanted to take out a young lady, those would be hefty expenses. Jim Crow laws made it harder for colored folk, but the Depression made it twice as hard.

But Charles decided he would have to make a go of it, no matter the cost or the number of obstacles that would be thrown in his way. It gave him comfort that he was taking the Lord's leading.

"That's going to be a tough haul, Charles."

"Just like you always tell me, Daddy, 'the Lord will provide.'"

Ben grunted his agreement.

But then what? Charles eyed the fields along the roadside, continuing his silent prayer.

By the time they reached the Swift Creek Mill, Charles felt he had lived several lifetimes. He had gotten it out and was none the worse for wear.

Charles knew Adam had not finished with him. Once Adam got ahold of something that didn't sit well, he wouldn't let it rest without a fight.

After Samuel died, Adam took his responsibility as the eldest seriously. He felt that it was his charge to take care of his siblings, too.

"Charles, did you really think this through? I mean, thoroughly?"

Charles could see that Adam meant well. He was clearly worried about the future of his younger brother.

"Yes, Adam. Fact of the matter is I had this idea when I was working in the peach orchard, four years ago."

The peach orchard was the summer job they took to pay for their room and board for high school. Because their school was in Clanton County, friends of the family provided extra rooms for them for a fee.

After times got hard, Ben gave Charles the bad news that he'd have to forgo school to help out on the farm.

It hit Charles hard. But, little did he know at that time the calamity was the impetus for this very seed of an idea to grow. He kept picking peaches to fuel the idea.

"I figured that if I took some time off to work in the city, I'd make a lot more money working there than I would working here."

Charles figured that besides the distance, it wouldn't be any different for him to stay with his Cousin Viola or Aunt Lonnie. He had gotten used to staying over at someone's house when he attended school in Clanton.

At the sawmill, men were beginning to unload a rail car filled with pine trees. Charles jumped down to help pull the ropes that were tethered to the logs held aloft from their flat cars.

It was tiring work, as the logs had to be held up until the driver of the wagon pulled up. Once they were lowered onto the wagon bed, they had to be transported to the mill. Some of the men shouted greetings at the Stevenses.

With a wave, Adam turned Bess around and led her to the horse trough before starting back.

Ben, agile in his forties, jumped up on one of the wagon beds to join the team loading logs. Although many men were half his age, Ben helped to wrangle the logs from the train's flatbed.

Charles was going to miss working alongside his father. There was always great camaraderie and enthusiasm when they teamed up. Ben seemed to pass his joy for working hard on to those around him, colored and white alike.

Charles was relieved that his father did not make his leaving Billingsley become an added emotional burden. He knew Ben to be a practical, thrifty man who liked the fact that Charles had created a sound financial plan for his departure.

Charles turned his attention to the job at hand. The men worked tirelessly with the riggers, pulling ropes that brought each log aloft while the foreman guided its descent on to the truck's bed.

It took ten hours to pull a shift and they happily drew a total of $10.50 cash for one day's work. It was good, honest, hard work.

They knew that this money would help keep the family well within the margin of paying off the farm. The peanut crop would have helped to put them ahead of their financial goal to make ends meet when he left. For all of Ben's optimism, Charles knew that there was more to pay other than the bank loan.

In his heart, Ben was a cotton farmer. He'd go back to planting cotton as soon as he could despite the fact that fertilizer had gone up in price and the boll weevil, which dug its heels deep into the soft Alabama soil, favored cotton.

The pest had been around for more than thirty years. Both the boll weevil and the cost of fertilizing the fields worked together against Southern farmers like Ben. Farmers had been looking for years for ways to rid themselves of the blight it caused to their cash crops.

Ben had to remortgage the land when the Depression hit. It was right after the Spanish flu and before learning that the dustbowl in the Midwest made times hard for that part of the country, too. It was a rough time for farmers around the country.

But with that said, Ben was willing to plant cotton again. The simple truth of it was the market for cotton was always strong, whereas peanuts hadn't yet found same level of demand.

With a loud hoot, the gas whistle broke Charles's musings. Lunch break came with shouts of joy from the men on the crew.

"Hey, Joe! Your Aunt Nellie's got any more of that hooch for sale?"

He looked up to find George McLucas, the resident funny man of the crew, standing nearby. He gestured as if he'd thrown a jar of moonshine over his shoulder.

Charles grinned at his coworker. He was another Billingsley native who had grown up with Charles and Adam.

Charles and his brother were different, however. Charles knew Adam didn't enjoy joking around with George, but Charles was a lighter touch.

He needed a break from his consternation. Besides, he always enjoyed jibing with McLucas.

"Not to speak ill of my aunts' product, but I think you'd do yourself a heap of good if you'd steer clear of that stuff, George . . ."

"Heck no! Friday's only five days away and I want to have some stored up before she gets a run on her supplies, my boy!"

Ben walked up. George knew better than to ask the stoic Ben Stevens. Ben never approved of his sister-in-law's commerce.

"I've got to go there in a short while. If I can remember, I'll place an order for you."

Charles had no intention of talking about moonshine with his mother's sister. But as this kept the conversation lively, he played along.

"On the other hand, we might need you next Sunday, and that stuff will lay you too low to recover in time."

"What? You know I can handle her shine, boy!"

Charles's smile was slow and easy.

"Come to think of it, I could use a double shift, so I'll bring you twice as many jars!"

The men laughed good-naturedly. The Vincents were an integral part of the small community. Everyone knew

Nellie and the Vincent family. Their family was said to be relatives to the white Vincents who lived in the next county.

Aunt Nellie was such a colorful character and well-known in the area as much for her shine as her prowess with a rifle or knife. Her many rows with Uncle Harold were legendary.

Later, the ride to the house was equally quiet. Adam offered no other conversation about Charles's announcement.

Charles didn't know if it was because Adam's disgust had dissipated, or if he knew that after a day's work, both men would be bone-weary. They all were eagerly anticipating one of Mama Edna's Sunday dinners.

Ben cleared his throat, throwing a side-glance at Charles.

"I spoke with Mr. Crane while you and George were goin' at it."

Charles's head jerked up sharply. Adam stared at Ben incredulously.

Mr. Crane was the foreman. He and Ben had a quiet appreciation of each other, despite their racial differences. Both men were solid, family men.

"I mentioned that you'd be headin' to Billingsley in a few weeks and asked if he could keep an ear open for any work you might land."

Ben paused a long while. Charles had to break the silence.

"Did he know of anything, sir?"

Ben's face was unreadable in the waning rays of the sun. But Charles caught something that looked like the glimmer of a smile spreading across his face.

"Well, ain't you the eager one for a man who's willin' ta throw everything ta the winds—or into the hands of the Lawd!" His laugh was unmistakable in the night air. It's rumbling began like a thunderstorm.

"As a matter of fact, God did answer yo' prayer! You know Crane's a good man who loves the Lord. So, he says you should check out a meat-packing place his uncle runs.

"He'll put in a good word for ya. Good thing I raised a bunch of honest, hard-workin' chil'ren. Cain't promise anything, but at least it's somethin' to check out when ya get there."

Charles smiled broadly. His father was not a talkative man. For him to speak to Mr. Crane on his behalf displayed his concern for his son.

"Thank you, sir."

With the money from that job, and the peanut crop's yield, he'd be starting off with on a stronger footing than most young men his age.

Who knew? Maybe he could even start looking for the woman who'd become his wife.

He wondered if there were someone out there who'd he spend the rest of his life with. Someone who'd love him and help raise his children.

"Jes' don't get tied up with none of those city women. They'll take you to the cleaner!"

Charles grinned at Adam. It was as though his brother were reading his mind. But he could tell Adam was coming around, offering brotherly advice.

Some years ago, Adam and he had taken a break in picking peaches. They sat under a tree and bit into the juicy flesh of some of the sweetest peaches that grew in the county.

Their talk drifted to women and how they were going to live once they got married. Because Charles missed his mother and the family that they might have had with her around, all he knew was he wanted to have a family that would be together, with God at its center.

Adam warned him before about the fast women he had seen in a trip to Bessemer. Glamorous ones that looked so lovely but wanted to be shown a high life of dancing and drinking, like he saw in the movies.

"Better to find a country gal, Joe. If you do go to the city, don't be lookin' around there for a good woman. Just make enough money to hightail it back to Billingsley, brother. Do y'self a favor and find a country-bred, church-going woman."

Charles grinned to himself. Maybe that's why his older brother was so concerned about his taking off for Bessemer.

Adam would soon learn that he could certainly take care of himself. At this time, he had no intention of taking up with some sweet-talking, fast-living, city girl. His sights were on one that had faith in God.

He remembered having asked his father about women one evening while sitting on the porch. Charles remembered how huge the sun had been at sunset that evening.

It had been after a school dance and several of the girls had kept their eye on him, giggling.

At first, he had been baffled by their behavior. It wasn't long before they all had been swimming together in the creek.

The changes had come quickly to all of them. He looked down at his hands, tracing the veins and hairs that had grown more prominent along with his facial hair.

These and other changes made him realize that starting a family of his own wasn't some remote idea anymore.

"Daddy, when you found Mother, how did you know you'd picked the right one?"

Ben adopted the far away expression he had when he thought about Cora. Solemnly, he rubbed his jaw.

"It was the one that looked into my eyes and I saw our dreams were the same. That's the one I kept. That was yo' mother."

CHAPTER 7

PAUL LAWRENCE DUNBAR
HIGH SCHOOL

Paul Lawrence Dunbar High School had more than three hundred students and that morning, it looked like every last one of them was outside by the time we got there.

The students milled around the enormous, red brick structure. Within the entire area of the school grounds, there was a high level of energy. This was going to be the best year ever. Maybe that's what had my right eye twitching!

I was in such a hurry to get my senior year started that I absent-mindedly hugged my brothers in a hasty goodbye.

Matthew stood there, hands on his hips, with a wry smile.

"So that's how it is, Lil' Sister?"

Matthew's loud proclamation, which drew attention to us, caused me to cringe.

"Hey, we made a great protection crew for you, Lil' Sister!"

I grinned and gave both of them a kiss on the cheek. This time, I realized that I actually enjoyed their teasing.

"There. You know how much I appreciate y'all!"

After all, they had safely walked me through a dangerous area. My brothers were very dear to me.

A few students passed by giving us inquisitive glances. Matthew bashfully stepped away. Luke covered his embarrassment by becoming gruff.

"Just wait on this side of the street, we'll walk you back—to make sure Clyde and his friends aren't looking for an easy mark."

Entering the school's corridor, I gazed about, reminiscing about my first days in Dunbar. How far I had come in just three years!

"Jesus Christ and the Holy Spirit!"

I cringed. Reverend Marshall always told us that a person who used the Lord's name in vain put their soul in danger of hell fire. Who could be so careless?

Spinning around, I found my first and best friend, Harriet, staring at me. You'd have thought I had grown two heads!

It was plain to see that Harriet had called upon the name of the Lord to help her cope with the shock. With her, it was a statement of praise.

I gave her a big hug and teased, "Better close your mouth or you're gonna catch a fly."

I knew full well what was goin' on in her head. After all, just a week had passed since we'd last seen each other and I had been wearing braids.

Harriet, with her hair in bangs and pigtails, wore the same burgundy plaid shirtwaist with its white, starched collar that she wore the first day I had met her. While Harriet was always bandbox fresh, I knew that she only had three dresses and a couple of skirts.

Glancing down at my new outfit, it dawned on me that this was the first time I had ever put the entire package together. I was just a day shy of getting used to it myself.

"Honey, hush! Where'd you get such a sophisticated look, DeLois Ann? I swear, I mightn't even known it was you if it weren't for that old crazy-lookin' book bag of your'n!

I laughed. The book bag was made from some leftover fabric from my blue serge skirt and Mother's old flour sacks. She sewed them together into a neat patchwork and fashioned it into a book bag using Luke's purchased bag as her pattern. Mother was very talented in doing things like that.

"Harriet, this is the new me." I fluffed my hair and tossed my head, striking a movie-star pose.

Just then, I noticed that several girls were enviously staring in my direction. I smiled and turned away.

What made it funny to me was I had not changed, really. I was the same person they had walked by so many times the last semester.

They hadn't given me so much as a second glance. What on earth had gotten into them?

It was as if I were suddenly one of the popular girls. Not that I held any false hopes of ever becoming one.

People were fickle. No matter who was in today, it'd be someone else tomorrow. That, I knew for sure.

"Don't tell me you're gonna wear your hair like that all week!" She eyed my hair with curiosity.

"More like, all senior year! I'm tellin' you, Harriet, this is just a few more steps than wearing my beady-balls to bed and braidin' my hair up every mornin'!"

Sherrie Lee had started me on that practice. She and Mother would twist and pin their hair up in four topknots and go to bedtime wearing a scarf. I discovered that my hair grew longer that way.

"Every boy on the football team is gonna want ta take you to the prom, Dee Dee! Honey, hush!"

Harriet was the truest kind of friend. She always made me feel beautiful, no matter how dreary I felt or looked.

"That would be funny!" I shrugged her comment off as too unbelievable to entertain.

"Harriet, you wouldn't believe it, but this style'll last all week! Mother pressed it on Sunday. All I have to do is bobby pin it up and wrap my head with a scarf at night. I can wear this style clear to Saturday without it frizzing up and looking bad!"

I saw such yearning in her gaze. It touched my heart. For a moment, I thought she'd just burst with wanting the same look.

"If you want, she could do the same for you . . ."

To my surprise, she looked as though I had spit on her or her sandwich or something. She shook her head, bottom lip quivering. Catching her breath, she struggled to regain her composure.

For a moment, I had forgotten how proud she and her family were. When the Depression hit, her father lost his job at the steel mill. He took day-labor jobs but wasn't able to make the same amount of money he once had.

When it happened, Harriet told me that her family made ends meet by skipping meals.

"My father says that we're never to take handouts of any kind from anyone. He always says, 'I ain't goin' back to no slavery times!'"

Now Harriet's gaze locked with mine. Her eyes became fiery and distant. Perhaps she was thinking about that comment.

Pulling herself together took a lot of effort, but when she had, her eyes softened, and she took my hand.

"Thank you, DeLois Ann, but I never could do that without being able to pay your mother back for her time."

I let it rest as we walked in silence to our first class. My father almost lost his job, too.

If it weren't for the fact that Daddy was the only one able to fix and repair the factory's conveyor belt for the billet machine when it went out, he might have ended up on the street looking for work like Harriet's father.

As it stood, the factory just cut his hours back to eight. Until we adjusted, and Mother was able to pick up laundry clients, we struggled during that time.

We took turns catching fish and frogs from the branch. Mother fried frog legs periodically. On other days, we lived off of hens' eggs and the salt pork Papa had smoked the previous fall.

Out of the corner of my eye, I caught her glancing at my hair. Suddenly, she reached out and touched a few strands.

"It's so soft and nary a bit of grease on it!"

Amazement was evident as much in her eyes as in her voice.

"Tell me, how did your mother do that?"

I loved Harriet as much as a sister. I was hoping to share as much as I could without making her angry. I felt I had to try, just one more time.

"She always said that my hair took more pressure than heat. I guess it has something to do with the way she lets her Madame C.J. Walker hot comb glide through it. Then, she does something like this."

I swept my hand down and, quickly, flipped it up. Harriet focused on this demonstration of Mother's technique.

"You could always come over and visit with me when she does my hair. That way you can learn her styling tips. I know Mother wouldn't mind."

Harriet shook her head resolutely.

"Thanks, but I'll show my mother your Bette Davis picture and ask her to do it to my hair, too. But, I swear, your hair looks just like a white gal's. I think you just have good hair."

Good hair was what many colored girls wanted, but that was one thing I didn't have. It just didn't need a lot of heat to set it.

I had kinky hair. It wasn't the straight or even slightly wavy hair that white girls had.

Mother and Sherri Lee had that hair. Mother's hair was so long she could sit on it. Some nights, Mother would let us take turns in helping her to brush it down her back.

Big Mama Dee said I'd a much better grade of hair before I got typhoid fever. The fever caused it to fall out.

She warned Mother not to cut my hair off. But it looked so bad Mother felt she had to. It never grew back the same.

I figured that type of hair must've come from Papa Bell's side of the family. His father was half-white.

But just like the caramel color of my skin, I was happy with my grade of hair, just as it was. It was what the good Lord gave me.

Before I could reply, we had gotten to class. The bell was just ringing when we slid into our seats.

I looked about the room and noticed many eyes on me. It was unnerving. Sherrie Lee hadn't warned me about the courage I'd have to have to carry this look off!

One set of eyes had me curious. Bill White was the captain of the football team. He stared at me as if I had dropped out of the sky.

I tried to appear nonchalant and studious, burying my head in my notebook. But at that moment, someone tugged one of my locks, mussing my hair!

"Ow!"

A deep voice behind me said, "Hiya doin', Dee Dee?"

It was Darryl, the one boy that had started off being the biggest bully of Dunbar before he transitioned from junior varsity to linebacker on the football team. He had slipped into the chair behind me while I wasn't looking.

I turned around and slapped his hand, giving him a stern look.

"Darryl, don't you do that ever again!"

He grinned sheepishly and looked off in the distance as though he had done nothing. I turned back around, rearranging and fluffing my hair to hide my embarrassment. My face felt like it was burning.

Later, Harriet told me that he did that because he liked me.

"That big bully?" I was shocked at the idea.

Harriet laughed. "How did you ever come up enough courage to slap his hand?" She gave me a quizzical glance.

"I can't believe you did that! Not many would have that much nerve!"

I don't know what had gotten into me, either. The boy was over six feet tall and almost as big as Papa Bell. He was bigger than most boys going to high school.

I suppose I'd been raised with two older brothers, a tough big sister, and had been crazy enough to tussle with the three of them when they got my goat.

Maybe instinct had kicked in.

Whatever the case, I became aware that his comment and my reaction had caused the class to turn around to give me a gander.

One of those people was Bill White. The most popular guy in my senior class was staring at me, again!

Then he did something that I never would have imagined. He gave me the chin up sign. I needed that. It didn't hurt at all that it came from Bill!

I determined that I would own this new look. I knew I had to get out of my shyness. I wasn't about to have a bully put me back into that poverty of spirit. I'd enough of that with Matthew's earlier comment.

With my chin up, I fixed my gaze on Miss Trudeau, who had finished writing the date on the chalkboard.

"Today, we'll take a look at one of our poets, Langston Hughes."

Miss Trudeau gathered a stack of mimeographed papers.

"Now, I want these back after the class is over, which is why I numbered each copy."

She indicated the purple-ish number on the right-hand side of the pages.

"These copies are expensive to make, and many more classes will benefit from them if you return them after class." Miss Trudeau paused. She peered over her wire-framed glasses, which had slipped down her nose.

"I'd like you to copy the poem into your notebooks, and then write your own impressions or a poem of your own. Tell me, what music do you think inspired Mr. Hughes—gospel or jazz? You have twenty minutes until the bell rings."

It was the type of assignment I enjoyed. What I did not enjoy was the actual process of writing.

I never liked my penmanship. It wasn't rounded and easy to read like Mother's, or carefully printed like Daddy's. It didn't help to have my brothers laugh at it, either.

"Looks like chicken scratch, Lil' Sister!" Matthew had to imitate the hens scratching for food, as though I had forgotten how that looked.

I pursed my lips and tried my best to keep each letter formed perfectly. I could go a lot faster, but then, the writing would go cold on me. I had to be able to read it later!

As I read the poem, I felt that Mr. Hughes's poetry was more jazz-like than like the blues.

I had heard some warm, thick strains of jazz leak from the radio, late one evening. We were all supposed to be in bed, but I couldn't lie there when I heard that music.

I had sashayed along the thin strip of floor between our bed and the wardrobe. It was easy to imagine myself in a nightclub in Harlem.

The music was hypnotically smooth and laced with rhythm. It seemed to answer an unfulfilled question from deep in my soul.

Mrs. Trudeau continued to lecture as we copied the poem.

"Mr. Hughes wanted to share and build on the common experience of colored folk with others—even those of other races. He wanted to build us up from our base. Even using the cruel history of slavery as the mold to pour this poetry into.

"All of this gives the reader a more universal and jubilant, creative experience. By a show of hands, do you agree that Mr. Hughes has succeeded in this?"

I raised my hand, too. But found that a poem of my own had bubbled up in my mind. I hastily wrote some of it down on the back of my page.

Langston Hughes had published his piece in a time of fear and ugliness. He lived during bad times too. Maybe worse.

But he worked with the events of the time and wrote something of beauty into existence. Maybe I could do that, too.

Eating with Harriet, I commented on the class assignment, "You think that she's gonna grade us on length or on our impressions?"

Harriet chewed on her biscuit for a bit. Her face scrunched up the way she did when she was considering something.

"I heard that Miss Trudeau likes short and sweet explanations. I heard she lives with her family and needs to finish her teacher's work in order to help her mother with the sewing she takes in."

I hadn't thought of the teachers doing anything other than teaching. But these were hard times; I guess they were making ends meet just like us.

How different the first day as a senior was from the first time I had entered Dunbar. Back then, I was very reserved about being around others.

Mother had made me go to school wearing my wet underwear. She became upset with me as it increased laundry loads. She had a lot of linen to wash on the scrub board, not to mention that big mattress she'd take outside, replace the old cotton then clean and air it.

I knew she was upset because she would threaten me each time with more severe punishments. At first, I thought she just didn't like me.

But then Big Mama Dee suggested an ancient remedy to Mother of sleeping with a dead rat around my neck! While many of Big Mama Dee's remedies worked and were powerful, even Mother thought that was too much.

I had an accident every week from the time I was in grade school all the way up until my first year in high school. What seemed to work was to keep to myself. That way, I didn't have to worry about being talked about or worse, laughed at.

Children acted just like the Rhode Island Reds that Mother kept in the chicken coop. If they found one chicken that was doing poorly, they'd just keep on pecking on that bird until it was dead.

But Harriet was different. I thought about the first time we met.

I had always chosen a place in the far corner of the lawn area, near the street, to eat my lunch. This left lots of room for me to slip out if it got too crowded.

I had carefully arranged my books so that I created a barrier between me and where the next person could sit. That way, I didn't have to worry about anyone getting too close or having anyone see what I was eating.

Mother always packed me two cold biscuit and salt pork sandwiches. Actually, since the Depression, I didn't care what Mother put in my lunch bucket. Everything she fixed for us was delicious, especially if you were hungry!

I had noticed that some of the students were reading or doing paperwork that day. They probably were covering for the fact that they didn't have food for lunch.

The grassy area had filled in quickly. I must have been really enjoying my cold sandwiches because it took me a minute or two to realize that there was someone standing next to my books.

"Would you mind if I joined you?"

I had looked up at the young girl, not knowing she would soon become my best friend. Harriet couldn't have been any older than myself. She had on that same plaid shirtwaist dress with a white collar. Her shoes were well-polished and her hair combed neatly into two braids.

"My name is Harriet, mind if I sit next to you?"

I didn't have the heart to tell her she was making a big mistake. It would have looked rude to turn her away. She waited expectantly.

I finally shrugged and moved the books onto my lap. Suit yourself, I thought.

I knew she must not have had lunch money either, because she immediately began studying one of her books. With some quick thinking, I offered her my second biscuit sandwich.

"I'm full and my mother told me not to waste good food," I said truthfully.

It wasn't a lie. I couldn't eat knowing that she was hungry. It took some persuasion before she'd taken it.

Reflecting about our first meeting made me curious. Throwing Harriet a side-glance, I decided to finally ask a question that had bothered me for three years.

"When we first met, Harriet, did you know I had a problem with bed-wetting?"

She looked at me in surprise.

"You did? I guess I never would have known because of my adenoids. I can't smell much. Sorry."

I guess that's why we became best friends. I thought that people wouldn't want to associate with me because of how I smelled. Harriet, for good reason, didn't care. God had taken care of it!

CHAPTER 8

BEGINNING THE JOURNEY

Packing for the trip to Bessemer was not difficult. The small valise contained his Bible, two shirts, and a pair of good trousers, along with underwear and socks.

Charles didn't have a pair of dress shoes, but he wasn't worried. Bessemer was sure to have an ample supply at good prices. When the need arose, he'd have to find a pair. Until then, he'd have to make do with his work shoes.

Quickly glancing around the corner of the room where he slept, Charles became acutely aware that he wasn't leaving much behind. What he was leaving was a sense of permanence and safety.

"Charles! Yo daddy's gonna be pullin' up the drive with that aunt of your'n any minute!"

Charles chuckled. There was little love lost between Mama Edna and Aunt Nellie.

He touched his bed sheet one last time.

"Simplicity," he said, as if to remind himself of his mission.

Charles wanted this statement to become his standard. But most importantly, while in Bessemer, he didn't want to be behind the eight ball in his finances.

What had worked for his family in the country would have to do in the city. In time, with hard work, he'd have more of the comforts of life. But for now, he prayed for God to supply his needs.

When Charles entered the kitchen, he found Mama Edna putting on the top on his lunch pail, an old bait bucket that had been repurposed. She looked from him to the valise.

"Guess yo're all fired up an' ready to leave?"

"Yes, ma'am." Charles took in his grandmother's expression. Her high cheekbones, which were even more pronounced when her dark, long hair was pulled up in a bun.

She went back to dusting the chicken pieces with her secret mix of herbs and spices. The aroma of fried chicken filled the entire front room, as did the fragrance of biscuits and gravy.

The greasy fragrance was captured in Charles's jacket. It made his stomach rumble. He hoped that she had prepared enough for him to eat on the road and have some for later.

Noticing her stern expression, Charles knew he was in for another grilling about his decision.

Adam must've given her the second shift, Charles thought wryly.

"Yo's a man of God, now, Charlie! Ya got to take on a heapa responsibility, here, not in that city. 'Specially with Adam bein' hurt and all."

Mama Edna was nearly seventy, but she never missed a beat. She was as shrewd as she was wise.

Charles thought back to the conversation he'd had with his grandmother the day before. Sunday had been filled with highs and lows. But that evening, after Charles had shared his thoughts with her, Mama Edna waited until Daddy Ben had given the prayer for supper to have her say.

She peered closely at Charles. Her gaze was as intense as her words.

"I see ya gots yo' mind made up. I know you always doin' some dreamin' or plannin' or whatever ya want to call it, but we gots to be practical. The only way to keep this farm is for all of y'all to work it."

"Thank ya, ma'am! That's just what I said!"

Adam paused when Henrietta patted his hand, signaling to let it go. But Adam plowed on.

"Ya got dreams. We all got 'em, Charlie. Just make sure that ya got all ya i's dotted and t's crossed before you start off. That's the best way to go into any plan. Tell him, Daddy."

Charles remembered how Daddy Ben sat silent, taking another bite of his drumstick. Would his father stand up for him?

Martha glanced from Adam to Charles to Ben. She had been keeping a close eye on Charles's reaction to Mama Edna's grilling with a mischievous grin.

Charles attempted to address Mama Edna's concerns.

"You know I always have a plan for my future and dreams, Mama Edna. I figured that we got this year covered. But I plan on sending money back to help out some . . ."

Charles didn't want to say too much at the time. Truth be told, the plan wasn't as tight as he would have liked. It was his father's generous offer that seemed to be the Lord's way of confirming his decision.

What he did know was that Dr. Carver's comments about the opportunities of industry in the city were like goads in his sides. The US of A was growing in so many ways, and he was chomping on the bit to throw his hat in the ring, too.

The city seemed to offer him the future and the hope that he had been looking for. He was saddened to see how the path his heart was set on so strongly impacted his family.

It must have hit Adam the hardest, especially after Samuel's tragic death. Charles was too young to recall what happened, exactly. He only remembered the funeral.

But no one could have stopped Samuel from taking Adam's shift that day. His oldest brother's death had an effect on all of them.

Charles just knew it was time for him to leave. How was he to find his own way if he stayed on the farm?

Mama Edna's and Adam's concern were evident. Mama Edna had been a vital part of Ben's business sense, upbringing, and success.

Adam had stepped into Samuel's shoes and began to pattern his life after Ben's. But that was Adam's choice. Not his.

"You got a good mind. A lot of people wished they had the smarts and land you got for farming!"

Mama Edna clucked her tongue derisively.

"Too many young folks go to the city without a plan and take up with them fast women. Cousin Viola's seen a mess of 'em up and around yo' Aunt Mamie's boarding house. You ain't got time for that kind of nonsense. You listenin' to me, Charlie Stevens?"

Martha laughed; she was attempting to break the tension. Mama Edna's tirades were a common occurrence. She was just happy it wasn't her turn at the receiving end.

"No, Mama Edna, he ain't listenin'! He's gonna wind up bein' some kind of jitterbugger! You wait and see!"

Charles had laughed. He chose that moment to get up from the table to dance over to Mama Edna. Putting his arms around her, he pretended to steal a kiss.

"You know you're the only gal for me, Mama Edna. The way you make biscuits and fried chicken? You spoiled me!"

"Hmmph! You been spoiled afore I got ya! Get outta here, boy." She fended him off, stifling a giggle.

"Just clean up that plate so's I can wash it. Ben, beat some sense into ya boy's head. You see he's got no good on his mind!"

With that, Mama Edna gathered up the empty dishes and left the table.

After a while, Daddy Ben stared up at Charles from under his brows. It was his leveled, signature look. That time, however, it held a slight twinkle.

"I raised the family with the Lord's help. Now that these boys are men, there ain't nothin' more I can teach 'em.

"We cain't hold onto them forever, Mama Edna. Son, as long as you bring home your fair share and keep your mind on the Lord, you'll do fine . . . wherever He takes you."

At that moment, before anyone interrupted, Charles had time to speak with his grandmother. He wanted to clear the air.

With his departure eminent, Mama Edna regarded him for a long moment. Surprisingly, her eyes watered.

Charles was stunned. He hadn't expected Mama Edna to get worked up over his departure.

Mama Edna was as hard as flint, seldom showing her emotions. She prided herself on her steely gaze and accurate assessment of a situation.

But at that time, he felt he witnessed remorse and deep emotion that only a few would ever see. It was as if she knew he wouldn't be returning to the farm once he left.

Charles almost set the valise down to hug her. But the moment passed.

Mama Edna roughly brushed at her eyes as if a fly had gotten into the room and straightened her back.

"Ya got so much goin' on for ya here, Charlie. I tell you, honey, the world out there ain't kind. Ya know that there's been no trouble here in Chilton for over thirty years, but that there Jefferson County is a whole 'nother matter all t'gether!"

Charles nodded. Everyone knew that beatings and lynching had been part of Jefferson County's history regarding his people since slavery times.

Some folks credited the Klan's lack of activity around Billingsley to the fact that over the years many colored people in the area began owning rifles. Others had said that the Depression knocked the Klan down a peg or two.

Every now and then, a colored traveler would speak at the church about a cross-burning party they had heard about or witnessed. Charles was relieved that most of them were in areas near the Mississippi side of the state.

He didn't really know how he would fare in Bessemer's Jefferson County, or the world, for that matter. What he did know was he'd have to develop enough faith to trust God wherever he went.

He also knew that his God was much bigger than the Klan and would travel with him outside of Chilton County. Whatever the case, his faith had diminished a great portion of his fear of the future.

He felt that it was for this moment in his life that everything was coming together—the die was cast.

"I'll just trust that God will take care of me, Mama Edna."

He cleared his throat, gaining more strength in his conviction.

"I know that if things don't work out right away or if times get hard, I have a family and a home that I can come back to. But, for right now, this is what I believe the Lord is guiding me to do."

He hugged and kissed her on the cheek. Mama Edna held him in her grip and steady gaze.

She did a quick check to see if he had the same resolve in his eyes that he seemed to have in his voice. After a few seconds, she seemed satisfied on both accounts.

"Charles, ya remind me of yo' mama, sometimes, head in the clouds. No small wonder she ended up in that home!"

Charles was taken aback. Up until then, he'd never heard why his mother had been placed in Mt. Vernon.

But Mama Edna, oblivious of the harshness or provocative nature of her comment, continued her thought.

"I'm gonna be prayin' fo' ya." Her voice wavered, which surprised Charles. "Take care of ya self."

Charles knew that the subject had been broached and sealed at that point. Mama Edna had turned away to add a small, cloth-wrapped package of biscuits to the bucket.

She handed it to him with a pat on the back. He took it, perplexed. But Charles knew better than to press the point with his grandmother.

He lifted the top of the bait bucket. The aroma of fresh, fried chicken filled the air. It buoyed his spirits.

"You sure know the way to a man's heart, Mama Edna!"

Mama Edna had laughed. It was a husky, yet feminine chuckle.

"Get outta here, boy! Y'all still got to make it in time to catch that bus!"

Charles could see the wagon in the distance. But upon stepping off the porch, a movement caught his eye.

Adam emerged from the barn, wearing a somber expression, hands in pockets. Charles steeled himself, imagining that Adam would carry on the questioning that he had just gotten from Mama Edna.

"Was hopin' to catch you 'fore you took off." Adam slowly withdrew a handkerchief-wrapped item from his pocket.

"Knew you always admired this." He handed it to Charles.

Charles pulled back the corners of the white, blue-striped cotton to reveal a worn, pearl-handled pocketknife.

He looked from the knife to Adam in amazement. He knew that the knife had been Samuel's.

Upon his oldest brother's death, it became Adam's favorite whittling knife. Adam always carried it with him.

"I can't take the knife, Adam." Charles offered it back to his brother.

"Naw, it's yours, Charlie. Figured it's useful and it's a little somethin' that when you see it, you'll think about home. That's all."

The wagon with Ben and Aunt Nellie pulled up in front of the house. Adam clapped Charles on the back, spun on his heel, and headed up the porch steps.

Charles watched after him, stunned by his brother's generosity. He wiped his eyes.

"We ain't got all day, son," Ben called from the wagon. Charles hefted the knife and stuffed it in his pocket.

He gave his Aunt Nellie, a tall, strongly-built woman, a kiss on the cheek.

Nellie looked more Choctaw than mulatto, with her fair complexion and pearl-gray eyes. Her sandy-brown hair, which now had streaks of salt and pepper, was parted in the middle and platted into two silky braids.

To see his aunt dressed in a long skirt and feminine blouse was an unusual sight.

"Doncha be standin' there gawkin' at me! Ya know I gots to look sharp goin' to see my sister!"

Nellie's usual, rough-woods garb was brogans, overalls, and a man's shirt. This was a special occasion.

Charles threw his valise in the back and leaped up to join her.

"Well, Charlie Stevens. Follerin' after y'pa and y'brother, are ya?" She waited with a smile playing around her lips. It was as though she expected him to deny the accusation.

Charles patted Aunt Nellie's hand.

"It ain't about leavin' Billingsley, so much as it's about followin' the Lord, Auntie."

"I heard ya brother say somethin' similar when he and Henrietta were in Tuscaloosa. One day I bet he's gonna turn up in Bessemer, too, all citified."

Charles had to laugh. The description didn't fit his brother to any extent. Adam always saw himself as a farmer and loved the land.

"Times are different, now, Auntie. People are goin' to the city to make ends meet. You know how tough the cotton crops have had it these last few years."

Charles knew his family would rib him. Deep down, Aunt Nellie and Mama Edna were concerned about his leaving.

The one person he wasn't worried about when it came to saying his good-byes was his father. They seemed to have had a general understanding.

While Ben was a man of few words, both men knew that they'd continue to pray for each other while apart.

"How's Uncle Harry getting along?"

Nellie spat a chaw of tobacco and hit a fence post. That was her only reply.

Keeping the talk light, Ben began reciting a list of instructions.

"Now, your Aunt Nellie figured that since the Vincents' have got people in that area, you'd best stay overnight to get an early start in the morning."

Aunt Nellie nodded.

"Yep, Mt. Vernon's a good piece from Mobile, but theys got a bus that takes y'all to the city from that hospital."

Leaning over to Charles, she whispered loudly.

"Now, my kin ain't saints, like ya Daddy here. But one night'll be okay for ya, young man. Lots of liquor flowing around Mobile with them longshoreman and sailors in and out of their boarding house."

For a few moments, Aunt Nellie was lost in old memories. Ben regarded her with a wry smile and shook his head.

"You'll both need to catch the early bus to Montgomery. But, son, you'll continue on to Bessemer."

"Aunt Nellie, you want me . . ."

"Now, Charlie, I'll be fine coming back on my lonesome. Harry is fixin' ta pick me up tomorrow, you'll remind him, huh, Ben?"

"Yep. Didja bring y'Bible Son?"

"Yes, sir."

"Good. Ya trip is the long one. It'll take three hours to get to Montgomery, but Bessemer's gonna be at least seven more."

Charles knew that it was going to be a long trip when he saw the size of the chicken bucket Mama Edna had made for them.

It was good to have as a comfort. He wanted to be sure that he was in the right spirits as he watched the landscape change from rural to cityscape.

Feeling the excitement rise within him, he turned to his father.

"Was Cousin Viola expectin' me tomorrow? What if it takes a longer time? Seems like I'll be rollin' in around four or five."

"Just be sure to catch that six o'clock bus. She works the night shift, so you'll be just fine."

Aunt Nellie shifted her packages around, seeming to break through her period of reflection.

"We'll be leavin' that there home right after we have lunch with Cora."

She mumbled, "That'll probably be about as long as I can stand that place."

Charles reflected on what she meant by that but knew better than to ask. Aunt Nellie had a temper. She could be sweet one moment and cuss a person out the next. She had a tongue like a sailor and was just as salty. She was also an excellent shot.

Charles had witnessed many occasions in which she'd shot out of her cabin window and dusted some unsuspecting person's shoes if they dared to approach her place without proper notice.

He figured that in her line of business and living out in the woods, she had to be as tough as nails.

Cutting a glance at his aunt, Charles wondered at times how his mother and Nellie could be sisters. He chuckled to himself as he basked in the love that he felt from both his father and aunt.

The road became more populated. It could only mean that they were coming near the city of Montgomery. The bus stop would only be a few minutes away.

Charles pondered what it would mean to leave his mother at the residential care home and start a new life in Bessemer. Each visit held the potential of being the last one.

Aunt Nellie must have been on that same train of thought. She spat a chew of tobacco at the city's signposts as they passed.

"Why'd they go and have her put in Mt. Vernon makes no sense to me. Bryce is a perfectly good hospital and it's in Tuscaloosa!"

"You know that's for white folk, Nellie. No need in sawin' that same ol' piece of wood, now."

Ben threw a quick glance at Charles. His son's morose attitude seemed to deepen after this exchange.

"Son, she's comfortable and cared for in that home. They do more than any of us can do for her, in her condition. She's always been delicate."

Charles dropped his head in reflection. His father had spoken of how the hard life of the farm hadn't agreed with Cora. These comments brought a new series of dark thoughts to Charles's mind.

He wondered if Cora Stevens would remember him. What if it took him a long time to return? Would her health hold up until he was able to come back? Worse yet, would his mother even be alive at that time?

At the bus stop, Charles gave his father a handshake. He held it for a moment, with his feelings welling within him; he wasn't sure if he ever wanted to release it.

He watched Ben walk away and wondered if the day would come when he would be able to put into words to his father all the confused thoughts he'd suppressed.

CHAPTER 9

PENNY HEAD, BILL, AND MR. WILSON

The bell rang. Harriet and I began collecting our lunch gear. Harriet lingered.

"C'mon, Harriet, we've only got five minutes!" I urged my friend as she paused to look over my shoulder.

"Say, Dee Dee, when was the last time you saw ol' Penny Head?"

I stopped and gave her a quizzical glance. Before I could ask why, a pair of well-worn shoes stepped into my line of vision.

I looked up to see Penny Head Howard leaning toward me. He stared soulfully into my eyes through his thick, horn-rimmed glasses.

I hadn't seen ol' Penny Head since the beginning of my junior year. His tall, slight frame looked even gawkier as he had outgrown his last year's pants by two inches. His boney elbows poked through the holes in his sweater that he'd patched himself, with big stitches, several times.

Penny Head's real name was Cleophus Howard. He picked up the nickname Penny Head from day-one because his hair was copper-colored like a freshly minted penny.

I really don't like nicknames. However, his was the only one I felt comfortable using. It fit him to a tee.

"You're looking mighty lovely today, DeLois."

At once, I was repulsed. I didn't know if these feelings erupted because of his unwavering gaze or due to the cloying tone of his voice or his attempt at charm.

For the first time in my life, I wasn't sure if I wanted to be cordial. If I were, it might've encouraged him to stick around.

It wasn't in my nature to be mean. I prayed for the Lord to guide my answer and give me a kind spirit.

"Thank you, Cleophus. I'm sure you've met my friend, Harriet?"

Penny Head nodded, but barely glanced at Harriet.

"Yes, nice seeing you," he said as he continued staring at me.

I could trace Penny Head's attraction to me back to when we were ten years old. He'd had a crush on me since we were "play married" six or seven years earlier in a Tom Thumb wedding.

Aunt Thelma coordinated the event as a fundraiser for Saddler's Chapel. Everyone got a big kick out of our awkward exchanging of vows and tinsel rings. It turned out to be one of the church's most successful events.

After that Tom Thumb wedding, my brothers had never let up teasing me. To this day, they said ol' Penny Head never knew we weren't really married.

"I was wondering if I could ask you if you were goin' with anybody, yet? Seein' as it is our senior year and all . . ."

I must've looked aghast because even Harriet stifled a snicker. But to her credit, Harriet rallied to my defense.

"Dee Dee, we've got to hurry . . ."

I was stunned by his boldness. It was almost as though someone turned the page on a perfectly good first day and when the page turned, there we were—me staring at Penny Head Howard and him with his question.

Certainly this was not the man I had prayed for! Why would the Lord bring Penny Head into my first day as a senior to torment me with the question of dating?

"Dee Dee, may I walk you to our next class?"

I looked up and found, standing next to Penny Head, Bill White. It created such a picture of contrasts—awkward effrontery and Southern gentility—that I smiled.

It took all I could muster to keep from laughing out right. I took Bill's offered hand, smiling graciously.

"Good of you to ask, Bill."

We left as Harriet and Penny Head looked on, one with an expression of amazement and the other with one of disappointment. Another page had turned. This time, in my favor!

As we walked into the building, Bill put his hand on my back. I thought he might've been a bit forward, but shook off the thought. I decided that this charade might add a bit of spice to the drama.

Perhaps Bill was just being chivalrous. But along the way, I began to feel uncomfortable.

Then, his hand dropped to my waistline. I cringed and moved away from his touch.

Bill looked at me in surprise.

"I thought you might be needing a rescue."

It wasn't so much what he said, it was the way he said it. It was as if he had come to my aid and expected me to be happy to have his hand on me.

What I chose to do next came as a surprise to both of us. I smiled and stepped toward the girls' restroom.

"If you don't mind, I'll meet you in class, Bill."

Bill was instantly apologetic, realizing his error.

"Uh, okay. I'll see you."

I quickly went to the basin and mirrors. I had to check to see just who was this newly confident, beautiful young woman? Somehow, she had taken over my life!

The hairstyle and makeup took me to the next level. Now, I was in charge of my life. Sherrie Lee was right!

Just as the tardy bell began to ring, I made it to my next class, American history. Harriet had saved a seat for me. She gave me a fleeting look, then focused on the door. Before I could thank her, the teacher had entered.

He was a small man, with skin the color of coffee. He sat on the edge of his desk and surveyed us carefully.

The lenses of his round, gold-rimmed glasses obscured his eyes, but when he turned away from the large, high-paned windows, the bright sunlight revealed an expression of great intelligence, and eyes that seemed to catch every movement.

Then, clearing his throat, he spoke. His tone was clear, but a bit rapid, as if there were something urgent he wanted to share before the bell rang again.

"This is American history and, I'd like to add—current events," he stated. His well-trimmed mustache arched with every syllable, but he had a strange accent. His spoke very well, but he enunciated in such a way that if I had closed my eyes I would have mistaken him for a white man.

"My name is Hubert Wilson. I am originally from Chicago, Illinois."

I sat up in my seat. I had heard a lot about that city. My uncles had friends who were Pullman porters. One had given them a Chicago Defender.

The newspaper was owned and published by a colored lawyer and had photos of well-dressed colored people shopping at stores standing next to and, in some cases, even in front of white people!

I would love to visit that city someday. It seemed like another world compared with Bessemer.

"While this class deals with American history, we're going to take a look at subjects with new eyes, of how these past events have shaped our lives today.

"These events are still shaping our tomorrows! So, we're going to take a closer look at the effects and challenges that you're feeling, personally, in this day and time.

"In keeping with this theme, I will be reviewing the national and some world news through our local newspaper.

"However, before we start, I have a question that is aimed at students new to our lovely campus."

Harriet and I took a quick glimpse at each other. Then, looking around the room, I could see that many of our classmates were as surprised as we were. Was he going quiz us on something that first day?

"What will your role be in our history? Or, another way of looking at this is—are you going to be a taker or a giver?"

With that, he stopped and surveyed the class for a raised hand. No one flinched.

"I know it's a hard question. But that's what life is about. Hard questions have even harder answers. But that's why you're here—to think."

Mr. Wilson walked up and down the aisles. Every now and then, he'd stop at a student's desk to look at their books.

"It appears that you must have taken all of the basic classes for the past three years. I'd like to give you my book, but we only have twelve. There are forty of you.

"Our state has allowed the education of the white student thirty-seven dollars per pupil while the Jim Crow status of our schools only merit seven dollars per pupil. Thus we have an arithmetic problem a grade school child could do.

"Needless to say, while there is a shortage of books, there is never a shortage of knowledge if you're willing to work to gain it! You'll have to be resourceful in finding this material and keep up with the readings. But more about that later."

I couldn't figure out what was going on with this teacher. Mr. Wilson was not at all like the other teachers I'd ever had at Dunbar. He seemed to be talking to himself, and was quite happy with his own company. I just prayed that he wouldn't stop next to me!

"This year will mark the first year that your minds will be challenged and your desire to strive for a goal will be strengthened. Your faith in your ability to succeed will be realized. All I ask you to give me is your unwavering attention; I'll give you the tools to acquire the rest."

As I stared at this man, I found myself holding my breath. For the first time, since I first arrived at Dunbar, I was awestruck.

This teacher had, in five minutes, hit upon the very thing that had motivated me ever since I'd started reading.

Up until then, I had only envied smart people. Luke, in particular, was the one I most wanted to be like.

But now, I was hearing that I, too, could succeed, that I could be smart. I needed this class at this time in my life. I only wondered why would the school administration have waited until senior year to offer it to me?

Mr. Wilson had made his way back to the front of the class. I leaned forward, eager to find out how he planned to do this for all of us.

"This is my first year at Paul Lawrence Dunbar High School. So, my only request is that you remain alert.

"The manner in which intelligence is imparted in this class is for you to have sharp minds and be ready to dissect the news we'll be reading.

"I ask you to read everything you can get your hands on and look beyond what you might have been told by your mamas or your daddies and especially the chronicles that are being presented by the white establishment's newspapers here in Alabama." He paused.

He was amused at our young faces. We wore shocked expressions. Nobody had dared to speak so openly about the conditions that we lived under. Did this man value his own life?

"Not that all of the colored papers are correct, either. And, no, I'm not going to ask you to take part in any insurrections," he chuckled. "That would be counterproductive to both us and the next generation."

It was humorous to me that he thought we all knew what he was talking about.

"What I am saying is that when you examine all forms of documentation, you're lifted above the fray. You are able to see more of the full picture of history, and not just the fringe or obscured portion that you've had access to in the past.

"I want to direct your attention to the realities of history. Personally, students, I want you to see through the veil that has been thrown over history by those who may have less interest in portraying it accurately.

"I'm passionate about this because history is a science. Its foundation isn't up to a casual, convenient, or well-meaning interpretation. Sometimes, one can look at an event that happened in the past where an interpretation occurs in error because sometimes it's interpreted wrong on purpose.

"However, most times, it's done by those who would like to obscure the contributions of people around the world, specifically in our case, the contributions of people who hail from the continent of Africa. Why else would Egypt be stated as the Middle East when it resides on that very continent?"

Mr. Wilson chuckled to himself as he walked to the front chalkboard. He wrote the word "patterns" in big letters.

"Students, I want to show you a series of patterns. A method of improving your minds, conditions, and fortunes in these United States of America.

"This country has been a refuge for many over several centuries. Folks have come here from around the world, some freely, some indentured, and some by force of slavery. Collectively, however, we have built this great country.

"It is a remarkable country where many have built fortunes and legacies. They did so because they didn't accept defeat. That was not an option!

"Students, there is a larger reality outside of our present time and this great state of Alabama. As you become more aware of our history, you'll become capable of growing to your full potential."

Mr. Wilson picked up a heavy, battered book. I could barely make out the title.

"While world history marked the beginning of your quest, American history will quite literally guide you to your futures.

"Just remember to question everything and to believe only what can be substantiated by a number of firsthand sources."

Mr. Wilson grinned. The smile was even more surprising than what he had just said. He had nice, even teeth that were white and perfect.

He must've eaten a lot of apples. That's what Big Mama Dee said would make my teeth straight and strong.

"Ladies and gentlemen, welcome to American history and current events."

The bell rang. Standing slowly, still a bit stunned with the tirade of information we had received, I moved toward the door.

For a moment, I had completely forgotten about Harriet, Bill White, and even ol' Penny Head. This was my dream of how high school should be!

Harriet caught up with me.

"What was that man talking about?"

"A lot of things, Harriet. But, I can safely say this is going to be one of my favorite classes!"

Harriet gave me a puzzled glance.

"Let's get a pickle from the corner store. My treat!"

"You must be feeling good, Dee Dee!"
She didn't know I was walking on clouds all the way to the store.

Harriet and I were like a couple of chickens, we chattered without stopping on the way there! We found that we had a sewing class together, too.

We were excited and talked about all the nice dress patterns the teacher said she would help us construct. The teacher assured us that even with a shortage of funds, we would be able to do fundraisers in order to purchase our fabric.

"By spring, we should have at least two to three dresses ready for graduation parties!"

Harriet was beyond excited. I knew she must have been planning to create her prom dress.

Last year, our conversation on that topic had been a sad one. She told me that her family would not be able to afford any new clothes for her this senior year. She was blue about not being able to go to the prom because of this.

"We'll earn enough money, Harriet, I'll make sure about that! Don't you worry none!"

Harriet gave me a hug. It was easy to be supportive of her. She was my best friend, after all.

At the store, I bought two pickles and gave one to Harriet. They were two for five cents. I felt I could splurge and use my ironing money, with this being the first successful day of school!

I wondered more about who would take me to the prom than which dress I'd wear. Mother had already begun altering a dress that Aunt Thelma had gotten from the Lewis family.

It was a cocktail gown that Mrs. Lewis said she could not wear again, as it had been seen too many times.

"Mother's already begun altering a dress for me. At first, I thought she was going to have me wear one of Sherrie Lee's old dresses. That would have been too emotional for me."

Harriet gave me a supportive hug.

"I know, Dee Dee. I know."

I was saddened into silence at the thought. Oh, how I wished my oldest sister could have seen how much I'd grown this senior year!

To perk myself up and not dwell on our loss of Sherrie Lee, I considered what a blessing it was to have Aunt Thelma in my corner. She had presented this new, sea foam-green taffeta with a fitted bodice and wide tail to Mother for me.

There were little pearls sewn along the net bodice. The back was pretty daring. It scooped pretty low—but the netting kept my back from being too bare. We were all excited about its possibilities.

"Hello, Dee Dee."

I was surprised out of my reverie by Bill White. He stood at the store's entrance, with Darryl and other buddies from the football team.

Harriet and I were so caught up in our conversation and pickles we didn't even see him.

"Oh! Hi, Bill. Hi, Darryl."

It was the best I could do. I tried to hide my shyness, but he made it difficult, the way he kept looking me up and down.

Darryl just stood there shaking his hand and rubbing it, while grinning. He enjoyed acting as though the slap I gave him earlier still hurt.

"A bunch of us are going to the juke joint next Friday. Want to come along?"

I was buoyed by the thought of being asked out by Bill White. But the juke joint was another thing.

Not that Mother and Daddy would have allowed it, even though it wasn't far from our house. Big Mama Dee said the name itself told the tale.

The word "juke" was Geechee for "wicked."

Matthew often told us of the fights that took place there. Mother attributed it to the free-flowing moonshine that one of our neighbors made.

"I don't think so, Bill, but thank you for the invitation."

"If you ever change your mind, just let me know and I'll go with you. Y'know, to keep you safe."

He threw a quick glance at his buddies, who smiled widely. Somehow, their smiles didn't feel very reassuring to me.

I was perplexed as we walked down the street.

"So what's up with you and Bill White?"

I cast a quick glance at Harriet, then turned away. I didn't want her to see my embarrassment. My face felt flushed.

"Harriet, I can't honestly say. He didn't give me a second glance last year."

"But that was before you got to be a glamour girl! Look at you! What guy wouldn't want to take you out?"

"My folks would never allow me to go to that place."

I didn't tell Harriet that I did feel a certain temptation to go there. Its music was always enticing.

It was said that the Joint's owners always got the latest swing records. They were the first in Burstall to get a jukebox. Tales of its loud dance music had spread throughout the neighborhood, if not the whole of Jefferson County. I'd love to hit that dance floor!

Although we were in the middle of the Depression, people in our community loved dancing. I did too. It kept my courage and spirits up. Many a night I'd listen to the music coming from Daddy's radio and practice alone in the kitchen after I'd finished the dishes.

I could imagine dancing with the man of my dreams, who'd be tall, dark, and handsome, as Sherrie Lee had teased. We laughed and thought about all the many shades of brown there were and how our particular dream man would look.

But as alluring as dancing at the juke joint was, Bill White was not the person I'd want to be with when I went there.

Something about him didn't set well with me. I didn't know what it was, but I decided to trust my feelings.

CHAPTER 10

MOUNT VERNON

"C'mon, son! We gots to be goin'! That bus sho ain't gonna wait for us po' colored folk!"

Aunt Nellie's banter broke into Charles's reverie on Daddy Ben. He had surprised Charles in many instances and made him wonder what other unexpected discoveries awaited him on this journey.

Absently, he reached for Aunt Nellie's basket, but she swatted his hand away.

"My arm ain't broken. Y'all just grab those jars of shine in that other sack. I'm gonna try to sneak 'em in for her attendant.

"Be surprised how much nicer people'll treat m'sister when they get a little happy, if ya know what I mean." Aunt Nellie winked and poked Charles in the ribs with an elbow.

Charles laughed. It lifted his mood and put him in good spirits to have his maiden aunt as a traveling companion.

When they were growing up, there were times when Mama Cora would have the three of them stay with Aunt Nellie and Harry as well as her other sisters and brothers until she was feeling better. Generally, they made their rounds among Pappy and Grannie Vincent's family.

And as long as he could remember, Aunt Nellie had been into developing her distillery. Ben would sometimes ask her how could she, as a child of God, be in that business.

While Charles had never been a fan of her liquor, he knew it was her livelihood and tried not to be critical. Picking up the three cloth sacks, each with a jar of clear liquid, he figured that he would help her out "toting the booze," as this was her only request of him.

They paid for their tickets at the Colored Only counter. Waiting until all of the white passengers boarded, they headed toward the back of the bus where the Colored sign designated their seats.

But as the bus began filling up with white riders, the bus driver got up and moved the Colored sign back two more rows of seats.

"I ain't gonna move for no mo' white folk, Charlie. Hell, my own mama is half white. Why should I move?"

Charles nodded at that comment. Anyone looking into Granny Vincent's bright blue eyes would be hard pressed to say she was a colored woman.

He chuckled at the irony. Growing up, he knew that no matter the color, people could be either kind or mean. His father taught him that a person's skin color didn't make them any better than the next person.

Daddy Ben would always say, "God don't see no color, son."

"Les' just sit here," Aunt Nellie said, pointing at the second to the last row of seats.

Charles moved their belongings to the rear and gave his aunt a seat near the opened window.

The trip to Mt. Vernon was early enough in the day to beat the heat. Nellie watched the bus fill up and shook her head. Eventually, there were no more colored seats available.

Charles stood and offered his seat to an older woman, who took it happily. Even though the bus hadn't gotten very hot, standing made it a harder ride on the elderly.

Aunt Nellie continued to talk to Charles in a voice loud enough to be heard over the diesel engine and by anyone within a few feet.

"Now, what I was gonna tell you back there on the ride in was they coulda had all the colored folk stay at the Bryce Hospital. They had both races at that place until about thirty years ago. Seemed to be doin' all right then!"

Charles looked around and saw that several colored bus riders were amused by her comments, while others looked away in embarrassment.

Charles's interest and sense of humor got the best of him.

Nellie was entertaining. He knew she would continue the conversation, unruffled by either response.

"So what made them move our folks out?"

Bryce Hospital was only half the distance from the family. It rankled him, too. Had the hospital kept their colored population, he would have been able to visit his mother every weekend.

Nellie was about to spit, but realized her spittoon was nowhere nearby. She put the spittle in a piece of newspaper, balled it up, and stuck it inside her pocketbook. The woman sitting next to her hid a chuckle with a cough.

"They say it was gettin' too crowded, but what they meant was they was gettin' too crowded with colored folk!"

Charles understood the impact this would have had on the institution and the white families coming there.

"I think they didn't want us ta have the same nurses workin' on both races. Think how that would look. Colored and white insane sitting up there eatin' and talkin' together, 'cause they don't know no difference anymo'!"

Aunt Nellie chuckled. Several of the colored passengers laughed outright. They were enjoying her tirade.

"They put all of 'em on a train and transferred 'em out ta Mt. Vernon after they cleaned it up a might. Hear tell it used to be a Civil War army jail." She took another bite of tobacco.

"Kept Geronimo there. Now what is my sister doin' in a jail that they had to put Geronimo in?"

Amid the chuckles, Charles shook his head and let that fact sink in. He had no answer for his aunt, not that she expected one.

He watched the trees and small houses rush by. The smooth, two-lane asphalt road was lightly trafficked, allowing the bus to make good time.

Finally, several hours later, they rounded the bend and were able to see the long, twelve-foot-high red brick wall that surrounded the residential care facility. It was a fortress.

Off to one side, Charles could see a white mansion complete with antebellum columns. He pointed the building out to his aunt.

"Tha's right. Y'all too little to remember mosta this. Somebody said an ol' white family gave their place to some religious folk . . . a charity. Now it's part of the home, too."

The bus pulled into the parking area to the right of the building. They disembarked with a small group of colored and white workers. Some of the riders made their way through the admissions' gate along with Charles and Nellie.

Ben had paid the fee for his wife's care a year at a time. It meant long hours at the sawmill and pulling double shifts. He wanted Cora to have the best, even if he couldn't give it to her.

They went through the huge double doors of the facility and entered the vestibule. The receptionist, a brunette with bright red lipstick, greeted them politely.

"Cora Vincent Stevens? She's in Room 108, just down the hallway. Y'all have a good visit, now."

Nellie sniffed her reply. Charles knew Nellie wouldn't bother to return the white staff's pretend politeness.

But Ben taught him that it didn't hurt to practice kindness to all of God's people. He tipped his hat and thanked the woman for both of them.

"I hear they still don't treat our folks right. Wish I could be a fly on the wall to see what's what," Aunt Nellie said.

She leaned close to Charles as they walked down the hallway.

"One time, they fed these folk some bad cornmeal mush. Bunch of 'em got sick. So's I told the orderly to make sure my sister got the same food they feed the workers.

"Anyhow, I know it's the colored staff that take care of Cora. That's why I gots to do what I can do to make sho my sister's doin' well!"

Nellie swapped the cloth bags Charles carried containing the liquor for the basket of food. She cradled the hopsacks like babies.

Charles took in the smell of antiseptic and the general cleanliness of the facility. It didn't look too bad, just very old.

The paint was peeling around the window seals. He also noticed some cracked panes and a few stuffed with newspapers to keep the wind out. The white and black speckled linoleum was worn, but waxed to a high sheen.

They passed several open doors revealing their occupants either lying down or sitting up in bed. He noticed that the rusted, metal-framed beds had threadbare covers, but some had bright-patchwork quilts.

"Families that come a lot make sho they families git good care. What yo' got to do is pop in and check to see what they's doin'. Surprise 'em! Those visits are the best ones, Charlie."

Room 108 had its door closed. Charles steeled himself before entering, but Nellie swept in without a knock or a moment's hesitation.

It had been years since he had been able to get away to see his mother. He made no excuse for himself, other than acknowledging that it was a day's travel.

His father had always told him that in her condition, Mother Cora wouldn't know if they were there or not.

"There was nothing the family could do for her, son. Mt. Vernon helps her much more than we ever could."

Charles knew it was his father's way of coping, emotionally, with the distance. Mustering up a level of resolve, Charles entered the room.

A colored orderly was chatting with Nellie. The man smiled broadly.

Charles could see that he was now carefully holding one of the sacks that Nellie had had him carry.

"Y'all knows we take extra special care of yo sister, Miss Nellie. We get her the best food and if'n anybody don't follow up on doin' things like sponge bathing her or combin' her hair, they hear from me somethin' fierce!"

Charles approached his mother's bed. It had a neatly stitched patchwork quilt folded at its foot. He could see that Cora was covered with a clean chenille bedspread.

She was sleeping. He took in her keen features, tiny nose above small mouth and her creamy skin, free from wrinkle or frown.

Charles pushed back a silken lock that had worked its way loose from her bun. Her brunette hair was streaked with silver.

He found himself heaving a sigh relief. It appeared that his mother was relaxed and unconcerned.

This was in stark contrast to his earlier memories. Instead of running around, looking frantic and lost, she lay calmly in bed, unworried about her circumstances. Charles kissed her forehead.

Her eyes fluttered opened at his touch. Cora searched his face for a long time, vacant of any remembrance.

"Mama? How are you?" were the only words that Charles could utter.

"How am I?" Cora looked from Charles to Nellie, who took her hand.

Charles searched his mother's face expectantly. Was she able to converse with him? It would be such a blessing to have a conversation with his mother at this time in his life.

"Nellie? Who is this man?"

Charles's hopes gave way to despair. Nellie rested her hand on his shoulder.

He held it, struggling to pull from his reservoir the strength to keep from shedding tears.

Nellie whispered in Cora's ear.

"This'uns yo' son, Cora, Lil' Charlie! Sweet Sister, he's Charles, yo' youngest son."

Cora looked confused. She wiped at her eyes, as though trying to lift the veil of uncertainty.

"My son," she said with a tremulous voice. "My son is a lil' boy. My son Charles's only six years old."

Her eyes took in Charles's broad shoulders, his shadow of a beard and mustache.

"This'uns a man, Nellie. This ain't Charles. My Charlie's a lil' boy . . ."

Charles held his mother's hand and whispered, "I am Charles, Mama. Haven't been to see you in a while and I grew up to be a man. I'm still your Little Charlie!"

Cora stared at Charles, straining as though trying to understand and believe his reassurances. Finally, shaking her head, she lay down again.

"My Charles is a boy. A lil' boy."

Charles looked at his aunt in despair. She touched his shoulder.

"She don't rightly know anymore, Charlie," Nellie whispered softly. "She done kept you as a boy in her mind for the last fourteen years."

Charles's shoulders sank. He felt crushed by dashed hopes. He had longed to share his new faith and dreams with his mother. Now, they would have to remain locked in his heart.

Later, as they picnicked on the lawn with Cora in a wheelchair, Nellie spoke in soft tones with Charles.

"Yo' mama, bless her heart, was the funniest woman! Beautiful and full of life! I remember when she stood on the porch and started singin' like an opera star after hearin' one of those ladies on the radio!"

She chuckled in remembrance. Aunt Nellie faced Charles.

"You got her spirit of fun. Seen that when you were a little boy! Knew no strangers white or colored. Remember how Romano's girls used ta pull ya along in ya cart? Sayin' they got a cute little baby boy!

"Hell, we all loved takin' care of y'all when she wasn't feelin' good. Nothin' so nice as havin' chilluns around the house!"

Aunt Nellie took Charles's hand. Her brow furrowed.

"I told Ben to get y'all kids out here more often." Aunt Nellie almost spat the words out.

"It's that Mama Edna who always tied him in with her sayin' he couldn't leave the farm . . . that he had to work. Y'all did what you could with the farmin'."

"But she was always pressurin' him to work hard to pay off that land early. He never felt like he had the time to visit this here girl. He said his biggest job was to make sure that she was 'well taken care of.' Between the farm and that mill she wouldn't let the man take a break!"

Charles shook his head as he chewed his sandwich.

"Mama Edna cain't be that mean, Aunt Nellie . . ."

Nellie smoked her pipe silently for a few minutes. When she did speak, it was with measured tones.

"She was always mean towards ya mama. Couldn't stand the fact that her boy, Ben, had found him a girl without her say in the matter. And a beautiful one at that!

"Look at her, and tell me ya Mama Edna weren't a trifle jealous? I think she made it her business to make Cora's life miserable!"

Charles had never heard his aunt speak so unkindly about Mama Edna. It was disturbing.

He took his mother's delicate hands and helped her hold a sandwich. As she took small bites, the ugly memories began to surface.

He frowned, struggling to suppress them.

"Ben's only a man, Charlie. He been used to followin' what his mama said since he was a little somethin'. I like Ben, Charlie, but he jes' puts one leg in his pants at a time, jes' like me. He's jes' a man, and a man can make mistakes ev'ry now and then. Jes' like any other man."

She eyed him as she took another draw. Aunt Nellie blew a stream of white smoke over her shoulder.

"I cain't fault him, none. But I still think it was a mistake only bringin' y'all out here ev'ry once in a while. Cora's mind couldn't keep up with ya growin'."

Nellie's eyes softened. "I jes' hope you don't hold it against her nor him none."

Charles shook his head and cleared his throat filled with emotion.

"No, Aunt Nellie," he said hoarsely. "I don't hold nothin' against no one. Just the way it turned out, I guess."

Nellie put a hand on Charles's arm and leaned over. She looked him in the eye.

"Ya certain ya gotta leave us, Charlie? I knows yo' mama ain't aware of much, but I believe, in my heart, she's gonna be missin' ya raggedy butt." She squeezed his hand and grinned. "I guess I will, too, son."

Charles hugged his aunt.

"I think if she were in her right mind, she'd awanted me to do my best to follow the Lord's leadings, Auntie." Charles paused, got up, and kissed his mother on the cheek. He held her hand.

"Mama always said, 'jest do His will,' and that's what I believe I'm doin'. I feel doin' what is right means that I'll help Daddy out with her care and all. I just want to make sure she gets to hear my voice every now and then."

Charles took his mother's hand.

"I know she woulda been proud of me followin' the Lord."

He noticed the wistful expression his mother had as she watched him speak. A tear escaped his eye. Charles ignored it, focusing on his mother's attentiveness.

"And I promise, from now on, I'm gonna follow Him in everything, Mama. Just like you wanted me to."

CHAPTER 11

BOOK SCAVENGER HUNT

My head was buzzing as I walked home from school with my brothers. Their banter and jesting didn't have its usual effect.

It only took Penny Head stopping by to say hi to them. His long, soulful glances my way were all they needed to get started on me, stirring up a mess of old jokes about our "love" and the Tom Thumb wedding. I knew my effort to counter their teasing would just throw fuel on the fire, so I just kept silent.

My thoughts were still on Mr. Wilson's American history class, not to mention my unsettling conversations with Harriet about Bill.

To my relief, I found that as soon as I stepped inside the house, my attention was redirected to the tasks at hand. Mother would be home soon, and I had promised that I'd have my little sisters and brothers ready for dinner.

First, I took the sheets down from the clothesline. It was a treat to sniff their lovely, fresh smell. They had basked all day in the hot sun.

Mother and Big Mama Dee's washday was Monday. They started as soon as we were off to school. Mother was at Big Mama Dee's ironing their customers' shirts, which meant I still had a bit of time to make the hot-water cornbread and greens before she returned home.

I pulled out the big cast iron skillet and Mother's medium-sized crockery bowl. Rolling up my sleeves, I put on an apron and got started.

Later, as I cleaned little Mae up for dinner, my mind returned back to Mr. Wilson's class. Having so few history books troubled me. I just had to keep up with my assignments!

"How in the world am I going to get that book?"

Mae looked up at me and shrugged her shoulders.

"How'm I supposed to know?"

I laughed and absently handed her a cornbread from my freshest batch.

"I know, dear heart. I was just talking to myself. I'm giving you a piece of my world famous hot-water cornbread, but only if you promise not to tell anyone! And—if you stay cleaned up, you might get a little buttermilk before dinner!"

With a big grin, she scampered away as though I'd given her a sugar cookie.

I was happy to see her enjoying it on the back porch, talking to the chickens that miraculously appeared. She tossed them a few crumbs for which they eagerly scrambled.

I sighed. Life had been so simple when I was her age. Now, I was facing bigger challenges.

Would I be up for them, as Mr. Wilson had asked? Absently, I picked up a piece of bread and munched on it, trying to unravel my mixed feelings.

At the end of the school day, as Harriet and I walked to the place where Matthew and Luke would meet us, our pace had slowed. We were deep in conversation about this challenging book task.

Neither of us had spoken about it during school, but both of us had been troubled about how we were going to do our homework without that history book.

"Where do we find it, Dee Dee?"

I shook my head.

"He didn't say. I'm surprised he didn't give us any hints as to how we could find it. But I'll never forget its cover!"

It was almost as though he wanted us to go on a scavenger hunt to find it. He seemed to be the type of teacher who wanted us to find the book by using our wits.

"For the life of me, Harriet," I said slowly. Then, a spark of an idea popped in my head.

"Maybe we can go to the library?"

Harriet's face lit up then clouded over.

"The colored library probably won't have it, Dee Dee. And you know we can't go into the Bessemer Library . . ."

We exchanged a knowing glance. The colored library was in my old grade school at Saddler's Chapel, right across the street from me. It had only a few copies of books, cast-offs donated by white families in the area.

But the Bessemer Library, even though it was on 19th Street and on our way home from school, was off limits to colored people. This made me sad, because the entire building was filled with books of all kinds.

"Whatever we do, we've got to find it fast! How many other students are looking, just like us?"

"I'll go into Saddler's Chapel library, anyway, as soon as I get home, Dee Dee."

I kept thinking about the white library. I was sure they'd have all the books that we needed. But nobody colored could get a card; nobody colored was even allowed inside.

Suddenly, an idea came to me. I turned to Harriet, eyes bright with excitement.

"Where do you think Mr. Wilson got those books, Harriet?"

"Probably from the Bessemer High Sch—" Harriet broke off and stared at me, aghast.

"Yes! Let's go right after school, on Friday. School'll be out for a half a day, and we probably won't run into to any white kids if we can get in and out."

Harriet almost stopped in her stride. She held my arm.

"But, Dee Dee, that's too scary! You know how they make all of those comments when we walk by their stupid school! Who knows what they might try to do to us if we were to go inside! And if we went in, would they even give us the books?"

I could see Harriet was just as frustrated and fearful as I was. But while I couldn't explain it, something had gotten into my spirit.

How could I let the one class that meant the most to me, become my worst one just because I didn't have the history book?

Many of the other books we used had come from Bessemer High School. They were usually dog-eared and had torn pages. But they were better than nothing. We had to try!

"Look, Harriet. I'm sure Mr. Wilson'll give us a note to take to their principal. He might even give us extra credit if we can get more than a few of them . . ."

"But what will Luke and Matthew say? Your brothers will keep us from going there, Dee Dee! I don't know if I even want to!"

I rested a reassuring hand on Harriet's shoulder. Maybe the courage that I'd seen in my brothers earlier that day had taken root in me. Whatever it was, I was sure that we could do this.

"I'll let my brothers know that we've a few errands to run in Bessemer. That way, they won't feel as though they have to walk us home. It'll be the truth. But, let's keep this between us, Harriet.

"My brother Matthew would be sure to broadcast it, and then my Mother and Daddy will be upset!"

"Yep! And they might just tell my folks, too. After that, I'll be sure to get it!" Harriet interjected, rubbing her backside. "But, I'll only do it if Mr. Wilson says, yes!"

We had scurried over the railroad tracks to where Matthew and Luke planned to meet us. It was one of the first times we had ever walked in silence, both of us lost in our own thoughts.

Harriet touched my arm.

"But on another topic, Dee Dee, I think that boy has the biggest crush on you! You see the way he couldn't take his eyes offa your red lips?"

I had. It was something that I was trying to forget. That, coupled with the way he kept staring me up and down, didn't set well with me. It reminded me of the uncomfortable feeling I had when he had walked me down the hallway after lunch with his hand on my back.

"You know, Harriet, I really didn't like his attitude. He seemed to believe I would jump at the chance to go out with him.

"So what if he's the most popular boy in our class? Because he is a football star? So was Luke two years ago. I didn't see Luke strutting around like he was God's gift to women!"

Harriet's eyes widened. She hopped around the sidewalk, whooping and laughing.

I wondered what had come over her, behaving so silly. Finally, she bent over, gasping for air.

"Listen to you, DeLois Ann! He's really made an impression on you, sistah! I think you are interested! Why else would you be getting all worked up?"

Once again, she laughed so heartily, she had to hold her sides. I felt my face heating up.

Several hours later, it still had me a bit embarrassed. I threw myself into the housework, of which I always had a lot. I knew that it would distract me.

In addition to the cornbread, Mother had asked me to cook the turnips and mustards before she got back with the catfish that Aunt Thelma had caught earlier.

Mother loved to cook in a clean kitchen. Actually, she demanded it. So, I made sure I cleaned up after myself before starting on my ironing in the den.

The clothes were in neat, smooth balls in the wicker basket. I had sprinkled them with water before starting the dinner chores. Now, they were ready to be ironed.

The garments represented my makeup and hat money. We never had allowances. After Sherrie Lee passed, Mother let me help her out with the ironing.

Sherrie Lee. I chided myself for almost forgetting to thank God for her example!

Big Mama Dee had taught me that if I ever were saddened by something, I was to give a sacrifice of praise.

"Best way to chase away the blues, chil'," she said.

Singing always helped to lift my spirits. I started singing one of my favorite songs. As usual, Big Mama Dee was right. I perked up right away!

Looking at the mounds of clothes reminded me of the ironing lessons I had received from my older sister. They weren't necessarily fun, but looking back, I found I treasured every reprimand later.

"Not too much water, Dee Dee, or they'll sour! Now, make sure that the iron is not too hot. Don't make any cat faces on that blouse!"

She would hand me an old feed sack that she had draped over the ironing board and a clean soda bottle filled with water. The top had little holes from pounding several penny nails into it to make it a sprinkler bottle.

"Test it on this sack. If they need more water, sprinkle 'em with this. Better than scorching someone's clothes! You'll end up paying them for the damage instead of getting money for it! I'll show you how to apply the starch."

I liked making the starch water. It was a lot like cooking. We mixed the white Argo cornstarch with water until it was creamy white. Then, we cooked it until it was like syrup.

She'd apply a dab of it to a garment to test its consistency. If it was okay, then we'd apply it to the collars, cuffs, and shirtfronts of our freshly washed garments.

I didn't start out too well when it came to ironing. It seemed like I was all thumbs and had no fingers. The large, heavy iron seemed to have a mind of its own.

I was thankful that it wasn't like Big Mama Dee's old iron. We had to put hot coals inside and then change them periodically when they grew cold. I said a silent prayer of thanksgiving for Daddy getting us electricity!

One thing about ironing, it gave me lots of time to think.

What were those feelings that caused me to feel repulsed when I considered both Penny Head's and Bill White's actions, earlier today?

Penny Head was just silly. But Bill was just a boy who, last year, wouldn't give me the time of day. But this year he seemed to be smitten with me.

I had read about that happening to a heroine in one of Mother's romance magazines. I'd seen a movie once where a woman had been an ugly duckling, only to emerge later as a beautiful swan.

But was that all that it took to turn someone's head? Just a little makeup and a new hairstyle?

"Oh my!"

I looked at the blouse of Banker Lewis's daughter. I had just pressed a cat face into its shoulder! Quickly, I rewetted the cheerful, yellow cotton piece before placing it in the bottom of my clothes' basket. I pulled out one of the plaid dresses.

"Lil' Sister! Flo won't let me play with your doll baby!"

I glanced over at Alice and Little Thelma who were holding a couple of articles of clothes for my old doll.

It was a well-loved doll with composition head, made with pieces of pressed paper that had been modeled and heat-hardened into a lovely doll with curly brown hair.

Her pink legs and arms were sewn onto a stuffed, cloth body. The girls loved that her eyes opened when she was held up and closed when she was laid down.

My only peace when ironing came when the three girls were able to take turns playing with it. Alice, Thelma, and Flo even let Mae have a turn. Each one could have an opportunity putting on and taking off her clothes. They held her as if she were a real baby.

"Maybe you all could play rock teacher, instead, for a while? Go and get Little Brother and let Tommy start the game with you."

The girls reluctantly placed the doll in her cardboard-box crib with a cotton-filled flour sack and ran off to find the boys.

"I'm first!"

"It's my turn to be first!"

I called after them, "Do eeny, meeny, miny, moe, catch a tiger by its toe!"

I could then hear the group of them giggle on the back porch.

Tommy was a great rock teacher. He held out his two fists to Alice to see if she knew which hand held the rock. She thoughtfully chose his left hand.

With a big grin, Tommy displayed that the rock was in his right hand. Peals of laughter met this revelation.

"Ya won't move up to college that way, Alice!"

Their game gave me time to check on the turnips. They were almost done.

I was congratulated myself that I had accomplished all of my chores just as Mother walked in!

There were a lot of balls in the air, but I felt that I had to prove myself as capable as Mother and Daddy wanted me to be. Plus, I really loved having the extra money.

"DeLois Ann! Did you feed Mae, yet?"

"Yes, Mother! She ate a piece of bread and had some buttermilk."

"I wouldn'ta believed it the way this chil' is standin' around askin' for more bread!"

I chuckled as I peered into the kitchen. Sure enough, Mae had her sweetest expression as she held out her hand for another piece of hot-water cornbread.

"You must've sho put yo foot in this batch, Lil' Sister!"

I giggled. Mother didn't often compliment me, but I wanted to make sure that everything went smoothly this evening. Tomorrow would be a day of challenges!

"I'll get the fish ready. Ya homework done?"

"Not yet, Mother. I'll start on it right now."

My homework. I had to work on the writing assignments for all of my other classes. Mr. Wilson had given us an option, since we didn't have the book, to complete our reading assignments by reading current events in the newspapers and commenting on them.

Perhaps by Friday, I'd not have to worry about having the material for that class anymore. I was sure that my plan would work!

CHAPTER 12

RELATIVES AND RECOLLECTIONS

After visiting Mt. Vernon and Mobile, the bus ride from Mobile to Bessemer was a welcomed transition for Charles. The nine hours would give him plenty of time to collect his thoughts.

Charles sat in the cramped rear of the bus that smelled of packed bodies, diesel fumes, and Mama Edna's fried chicken. But even with that stomach churning mixture of aromas, he was able to relax in the realization that he was finally on his way!

Aunt Nelda's people, distant relatives of his, were reservoirs of news about the developments around the Mobile area. They lifted his mood with their light-hearted conversation.

"Hey, Charlie! Good to meet cha!"

Willard Thompson pumped Charles's hand with a firm grip.

"So this is the little rascal y'all been tellin' us 'bout! A heartbreaker, too! Watch out, Bessemer!"

"From your lips to God's ears!"

Aunt Nelda and the Thompsons' laughter was good medicine for Charles. He knew he was in for a lively evening.

Nadine and Willard, both near seventy, seemed ageless. Willard was a robust, chocolate-brown, compact man who had slicked back his gray hair.

He sported a grizzled beard but had no mustache. The beard whipped around his jawline like that of most of the sea-faring folk of the area.

Willard had a habit of stroking it often, especially when emphasizing a point or when caught up in a fit of laughter. The latter happened quite often.

He was proud of the fact that he still worked alongside men half his age on the docks of Mobile. They hauled the crates of cotton that came straight from the cotton gin mills of Montgomery and loaded the cargo into the belly of ships headed up north.

Nadine was a dark brown woman with a shock of white hair pulled back into a loose bun. She retained much of her earlier beauty despite a few wrinkles and an ample figure. Her large, expressive eyes amplified a quick wit.

As soon as Charles and Aunt Nelda arrived, the couple ushered them over to a table already prepared with a hot meal.

"I hope y'all forgive the simple fare we put together. This is fish fry night, and some friends are gonna stop by in a bit," Nadine apologized.

Charles stared at the bountiful plates of fried catfish and okra, candied yams, turnips and mustards with pickled beets and succotash. These lovingly prepared foods said "home" to Charles.

After saying grace, Nadine quietly slipped away from the table. She disappeared into the kitchen.

"Now what is that woman up to?"

Willard chuckled as he thoughtfully stroked his beard. When she returned with a platter filled with rounds of hot corn muffins, Willard gave her a big kiss. Everyone clapped. Nadine curtsied.

While enjoying the meal and light conversation, Charles gazed around their home. It was a shotgun-styled home with a large front room, remade into a living room and dining room. The kitchen was in the rear of the house with each room leading to the next, straight back to the door that opened to the backyard.

Willard had added three small bedrooms on the right side of their corner lot. He was able to retain a small yard enclosed by a picket fence that contained a pen for their chickens.

After the meal, a group of friends began arriving and soon, the Thompson house was packed. While it was impossible for Charles to sort through all the names, he did his best.

For the most part, they were a merry bunch. Cards were produced and the high-spirited group settled in for a night made livelier with Aunt Nelda's "shine."

As Aunt Nelda dealt, conversation meandered to the current state of the economy and jobs.

One man leaned toward Charles with a huge grin.

"Jobs are boomin' down here! Charlie, you can get a job easy at the docks as a longshoreman. No need to go all the way up to Bessemer!"

Willard patted Charles on the shoulder.

"Hey, look here, Charlie. Bessemer is still a good shot. The metal and coke theys loadin' now is goin' straight to Bessemer. They makin' lots of steel up in that area."

Darryl Johnston, Willard's coworker, shook his head.

"That's 'cause there's a war a comin'."

Darryl was thin, dour-looking man in his thirties. One would have thought him to be much older from his demeanor.

"But that don't matter none to us colored folk. We ain't even gonna be able to join no white man's army as long as Jim Crow's around. A po' man cain't get ahead no matter how hard he tries."

He sat back in his chair with his arms folded. Darryl appeared to enjoy soaking up as much attention as possible.

Aunt Nelda glared at him under hooded eyes. Charles wondered how long it would take her to shut down his act. He knew she didn't take kindly to folks bringing up the sorry state of affairs in the South into an evening of fun.

"My folks still stuck in Mississippi sharecroppin' fo the same white family that been they's parents' owners! Still pickin' cotton to this day!"

"Well, Darryl, you seemed to be getting' ahead mighty well, here in Mobile. Only thing gettin' in ya way is that alarm clock. Keeps messin' wid ya sleep! Darn thing is always tryin' to get ya up in time for work!"

Amid the laughter, Willard took a closer look at his hand of cards, seemingly unperturbed by the eruption of merriment his teasing had caused.

"Don't think that white man got anythin' to do with that!" Willard remarked as he threw down a card.

Darryl grew sullen.

"Y'all know what I'm talkin' 'bout. Cain't get ahead by joinin' the Army. And tell me why we hafta leave the South to get a better deal 'stead of stayin' here an' being treated like trash? It ain't fair!"

His last query hung in the air like a bad odor. The mood of the evening had temporarily been broken.

But Charles connected with Darryl's comment. "It" meaning the Jim Crow way of the South, simply put. It remained a sore spot for all of the colored folk he knew. He wondered if the North held a better promise for him, someday.

His father, however, seemed to be unfazed by the oppressiveness of Jim Crow. Charles wondered how Ben was able to keep his bearings in the face of constant mistreatment and fear.

Charles paused by the entrance of the lumber mill one Saturday. He had brought his father a lunch and sifted through the men to locate him.

A large group of men were on their way to the lunch area. Bringing up the rear was his father.

The white workers were typically allowed to line up in front, to be the first out for lunch with the colored men following behind. Charles shook his head.

Burdened by this practice, Charles spoke with his father about it that afternoon.

"This just doesn't make any sense, Daddy. These men are all doing the same work! We work side by side at the mill. But the colored man's paid half their wages, if that. And we still have to take a place at the back of the line?"

Ben quieted Charles with a slight gesture.

"Son, we're only in this for a spell. The land's gonna be paid off in no time. 'Sides, what good would it do to ruffle feathers?"

At that moment, Ben had paused over his pork and biscuit sandwich. They had chosen a favorite spot for their break. It was on a fallen log near an outcropping of saplings at the water's edge. The scenic beauty of the woods and the gurgling stream soothed Charles's spirit.

Ben glanced around at the other colored workers. They all sat in the same area, downstream from the white workers, who had use of the company's picnic area.

"I know it can be hard on a man's pride, but think about it, son. Does any of this kind of stuff really matter? Look, they payin' us to become self-sufficient!

"If we take care of the farm, the farm'll take care of us. The way I sees it, we come out on the top of this deal!"

Ben had chuckled and took another bite of his sandwich. Charles nodded his head. His father's wisdom, once again, made a lot of sense.

However, this and other images stayed with him. He had seen men of lesser skills, jiving colored men at the watering hole, the latrines, and during breaks.

The colored men smiled and took their cruel comments without a word, knowing the consequences would be harsh. There was always the possible loss of their jobs, or worse, if they were to voice discontent.

"Look, young feller! Nobody can control yo' thinkin'!"

Aunt Nelda had taken the opportunity to step in and give Darryl a word to the wise.

"A man can do anythin' he put his mind to do." She paused to spit into Willard's spittoon.

"But it takes some gumption and grit to get it done no matter the bumps in the road!"

Aunt Nelda eyed Darryl. Everyone could tell she wouldn't take a negative reply kindly. Charles didn't know many men who would have the nerve to gainsay her or have the last word.

But Darryl shook his head again.

"Now, Ms. Nelda, they cain't all make shine like you do . . ."

As if on cue, Nadine brought Darryl a big piece of apple pie topped with her homemade ice cream. Darryl brightened at the sight of it.

It was the first smile he'd let escape the whole evening. High spirits returned.

Aunt Nellie eyed Darryl as he scooped down the dessert. Charles held his breath, not knowing what was on her mind, but prepared for some type of retort.

Only he sat close enough to hear her mutter under her breath, "Needed somethin' to put in that piehole o' his!"

Later in the night, the good conversation and apple pie began to take effect. Nadine's sharp eyes caught Charles nodding off. When he caught himself, he turned to see her hide a smile.

"I thinks this young man could use some sleep. 'Specially if he's goin' on that nine-hour bus ride in the mornin'. You gots to be sharp if ya gonna be lookin' for that job in Bessemer as soon as ya lights off that bus!"

Aunt Nellie cut her eyes over at Charles.

"You fadin' that fast, Charlie? Let the old heads beat you to a pulp? I got enough left in me to play another hand!"

"Not to be disrespectful, Auntie, but you got a reason to keep your eyes open," Charles gestured at her pot. Aunt Nelda was an expert at bid whist.

"Don't want to scare you folks, but she'll be here 'til she fleeces everyone!"

Laughter filled the air. Aunt Nellie waited until Charles leaned over to kiss her good night to swat him on the behind.

"That's for givin' away my secret strategy!"

The gulf breeze caused the curtains to flutter in Charles's room. The sultry air did little to bring relief.

As he lay awake, Charles could hear Aunt Nellie's distinctive laughter over that of the others through the thin door that separated his bedroom from the dining room. It helped to lift his spirits, if only momentarily.

Later, while on the long bus ride, Charles had time to review the many thoughts that had swirled around in his head after visiting Mt. Vernon.

All he had planned to do was to visit the home, see his mother, and share his newfound faith. But his visit opened old wounds; wounds he had not felt in years and had thought were healed.

Charles rubbed his brow. Perhaps his mother would have recognized him if had he visited a couple of days each year. Should he have simply taken a few summer days' pay from his work in the peach orchard or the mill to pay for the ride down to Mt. Vernon? The thought had occurred to him, but he hadn't acted upon it.

He could have picked up the reins of Ol' Bess and made a regular visit to the home. Even that would have been better than nothing. What had kept him from doing something so basic and yet so essential?

Seeing his mother reminded him of the panic and fear he had seen in her eyes when he was three years old and the pain of the memory, which he felt at that moment was undoubtedly the cause of his failure to visit her more often.

The bus to Bessemer stopped at the railroad tracks. The Gulf, Mobile, and Ohio's forty-odd cars passed by at a leisurely pace.

The clacking of the wheels, the loud sound of steel against steel, took him back in time. It reminded him of when he was jarred out of a nap by the clanging of pots and pans.

"Stop naggin' me! Ima workin' as fast as I can!"

Cora's voice was high pitched and angry over the loud banging of pots and lids. He could tell she was at her wits' end by her wide eyes and the heightened crescendo of noise that came from the kitchen.

Peeking around the doorjamb, Charles saw Mama Edna with her hands on her hips, watching Cora walk swiftly from the sink counter to the table.

"It jest ain't fast enough! Them babies are gonna be up and hungry, what you been doin'?"

Mama Edna smirked and tossed her head, as if mimicking Cora. Cora tried to ignore her mother-in-law as she sliced potatoes for the stew pot. But against her will, Mama Edna had her attention.

"Brushin' yo' hair, like you got all day to doll up for Ben. Well, only thing Ben wants to see when he gets in from a double shift is his food! Ya ain't at home in dat big house ya grew up in, Miss Prissy!"

"I know where I am! I'm doing the best I can—now, will ya let me finish dis meal?"

Mama Edna was relentless. Her eyes narrowed and her nostrils flared.

"I bought dis farm with Ben—and he brings you here! Well, you can be a mother to his children, butcha ain't the woman of this house! Dis is my farm, too. And I ain't about to let ya ruin my son's mealtime!"

Cora tried to get past Mama Edna to put salt on the meat, which sat on the counter. Mama Edna pivoted and put her body between Cora and the pot.

"Mama Edna, would ya please step aside fo' I can do my cookin'?"

With a quick motion, Mama Edna stepped on Cora's instep, causing her to howl in pain.

Charles put his hand to his mouth, in surprise and fear at his mother's anguish. But he dared not say anything.

Charles felt that his presence could only help his mother if he stood by quietly, as a witness to this unfolding ugliness. He had to be there to protect her by watching, recording everything with his eyes, especially if Daddy were to ask him what happened in that kitchen.

"Whatcha gonna do, tell Ben? He ain't gonna believe ya!"

At that moment, Cora looked up and stared straight into Charles's eyes. They both understood what had to be done—escape.

Cora rushed out of the room, grabbing Charles by the hand and calling for Adam and Martha.

Martha, who'd been playing with a doll out on the porch, came inside. She stared quizzically at her mother. Before she could ask a question, Cora grabbed her by the hand and dragged her back outside.

"Get the wagon ready, Adam! We're fixin' to go to Grannie's house!"

As they sped down the dirt path, Mama Edna yelled at Cora from the farmhouse doorway.

"Every kettle's got to sit on its own bottom! Ya cain't always run away!"

As the train clacked past, Charles thought deeply about the images collected in his mind from childhood. They had been buried in the recesses of his memory until now.

Had Cora been thrown into a panic because of Mama Edna? Would Ben have believed her?

Worst of all, was he, Charles, just as responsible? He had never told his father.

As uncomfortable as it had been, he forced himself to have a conversation with Aunt Nellie about it on the way to Mobile.

It helped to focus his energy on the central cause of the pain they had all experienced as a family. A huge portion of their stability as youngsters was wrenched away when Cora was placed at Mt. Vernon.

Was Mama Edna the only one who had played a role in Cora's confinement? This was a potential viper's pit that he'd have to cross with his father.

While Charles respected his father's decisions and knew they were based on well-thought-out reasons, Charles feared what Ben's answers would be.

"I ain't gonna meddle into his affairs, but you're old enough to know what's gone on with ya mother."

Aunt Nellie had taken Charles's hand in hers. The bus that took them from Mt. Vernon to Mobile was nearly empty.

Without inquisitive ears nearby, Aunt Nellie continued, "Yo is ya own man, now, Charles. Y'all entitled to come up wid yo own thoughts and direction on this. Life's about facing the pleasant and the foul and learning how ta handle both."

Charles had gripped his aunt's hand firmly. He thought back to how his mother needed his help with something as simple as eating. It filled his heart with both sorrow and love.

"It would make me feel a lot better being able to do something for her, after all the years of her doing for me, Adam, and Martha. I'm just sorry I waited this long, Aunt Nelda."

Aunt Nellie clucked her tongue, regarding him for a moment.

"Ya's good people, Charlie. I sense somethin' different about ya, now. Pray over this. See where the good Lawd leads ya. But he might be leadin' ya to talk with yo daddy about the questions ya still have, truth be told."

CHAPTER 13

THE DIE IS CAST

"You've got to take responsibility! You've got to decide to climb this mountain on your own!"

Mr. Wilson did his customary walk up and down the classroom rows. But we were taking notes and too busy to see if he was standing by our desks or not.

"There is no excuse! Education is the key to everyone's future, young people." Mr. Wilson gazed over his spectacles.

"With it, you can not only climb those mountains, you can leap over valleys and soar above oceans! But you've noticed and taken part in this school's many opportunities. Some of you have taken vocational training, and others of you have accepted our college prep courses.

"With the clear thinking skills we're teaching you in these classes, they will propel you to higher levels of success, thus giving you a financial base. You'll need these to enter college. However, to get there, you must hunger and thirst for wisdom!"

My head shot up. His choice of words sounded like Reverend Marshall's at Saddler's Chapel. Did they talk with each other?

Mr. Wilson smiled at the attention this phrase brought him. He enjoyed saying things that made us stop and think.

"Yes, your ministers preach about how you must yearn for righteousness. In the secular world, this right-mindedness combines knowledge, wisdom, and understanding, just as the Bible states, as its base."

As I listened to Mr. Wilson, I reflected on all the places outside of Bessemer that were waiting for me to explore!

Up until Mr. Wilson's class, my thirst for escaping the ordinary had come to life through books. I read everything I could get my hands on, but mostly fiction.

I found fiction allowed me to escape the ugliness of life in the South. Since I'd always had an active imagination, making up stories, like Papa. It was a way to remove myself from dwelling on what was going on around me.

After a while, it came naturally. Movies were a great escape, too.

But Mr. Wilson was broaching a subject, an idea about something very different. A new way to look at the world!

"Students, you might say you have no money to go further than high school. I had the same problem. But to claim your birthright, your place in this nation, in this world, you have got to be creative! Seek what has been proven to work in the past and avoid what has failed!

"What is that? You will find out once you read the autobiographies of other great people and by researching the eyewitnesses accounts of history!"

Our eyes were wide with amazement. Prior to this class, history had been a boring subject. I never linked it with my future success.

His speech made me more determined to have that book!

As Mr. Wilson lectured, I took notes. But while my hand was moving, my mind was already contemplating how to approach him. What would be the best way to ask Mr. Wilson for permission to go to Bessemer High School to pick up those textbooks?

"Throughout history, men and women around the world have engaged in the pursuit of knowledge. When they couldn't afford it, when it was outside of their economic grasp, do you know what they did?"

Mr. Wilson paused and sat on the edge of his desk, gazing around the classroom. None of us raised our hands. It was very quiet. We all wanted to know!

"Through prayer and a steel-minded determination, they obtained that which they sought! But it always takes hard work, young people! And this hard work, in particular, requires grit!"

There was that word! Sherrie Lee had told me never to lose my grit! At that moment, I was sold on our going on a quest for those books! It was the right thing to do!

But along with those feelings, I sensed that Mr. Wilson's emotional lecture was based on something that he had personally experienced.

"Students, I feel deeply for you, if not having the funds to pursue an education is your plight." He paused and wiped off his glasses.

"You see, I could not afford to go to college either. My parents were humble folk. They could provide only for my food and shelter, not my schooling. Do you know what I did?"

My classmates and I looked at each other, clueless of how he might have gotten a college education. I leaned in, knowing that the answer would help me too.

My Daddy believed in our having an education. He said that he would mortgage the house and sell all his stock in the rolling mill to make sure each one of us got a college degree! I wanted to do what I could so he wouldn't have to go into debt.

"I worked on the railroad as a Pullman porter and in between stops, I did a correspondence course and read books that I knew would elevate me, the classics, which I'll share with you later."

He glanced around with a big smile.

"I'm only telling you what has worked for me, students, because I'm here to help you succeed! My mission is to inspire you to do so!"

The answer to my concern, how I could frame my request, came at that very comment. He wanted us to succeed. How could he refuse us?

"So, there you have it! You must have courage and perseverance, my friends! It takes a confident courage to believe you can make it! Such courage can take you on the quest of a lifetime. It will change lives, futures, and establish an unending legacy for your families!"

Mr. Wilson even stated that it was a quest! I wanted that legacy! I knew that I had the courage to seek after it!

Finally, class ended. I was excited instead of fearful at the thought of asking Mr. Wilson for permission to pick up the books from Bessemer Senior High School.

As everyone else filed out, I caught Harriet's eye and motioned for her to follow me. Reluctantly, she did so.

Quietly, we reverently approached Mr. Wilson's desk. We were awestruck. This teacher had opened the door to our future.

He had opened his briefcase and taken out an apple. My eyes widened. I knew it!

Carefully setting today's lecture and notes inside, he glanced up and noticed us for the first time.

"How might I help you young ladies?" he asked, smiling.

"Sir," I began. I looked down at my feet, suddenly shy. But Harriet gave me a pinch, which drove me into action.

"Oh! Sir, we would like to know if you would help us continue our search for knowledge. We want to have that legacy you mentioned." I took a deep breath and saw that he was nodding his head. This encouraged me to plunge ahead.

"If you would give us a note for permission to pick up a few extra copies of our American history book from Bessemer High School? We walk right by it every day . . ."

I was out of breath, trying to get all of my jumbled thoughts out fast. I didn't want him to say no.

"We have the courage, Mr. Wilson!"

I was really shaking. While I prayed for courage and faith to flood my mind and settle my nerves, in a way, I felt we already had both.

Mr. Wilson seemed more amused than surprised. He stared at the ceiling. He rubbed his chin and tucked the other hand under his armpit, as was his thinking stance.

"Well, young ladies. That's an admirable task you've decided to take on." He gazed at us sharply.

"And it will take much courage, too."

He paused to let that sink in. Then, he motioned in the direction of the school.

"Bessemer High is not, one may say, our territory. Yet." He smiled at this thought.

Mr. Wilson often made comments that were strange to us, the humor of which only he understood.

Suddenly resolved, he nodded.

"All right, the die is cast! I shall write that note for you! I think it is a good idea to wait until Friday," he began.

"I will accompany you and possibly make a case to the principal of that fine establishment for at least ten more books. Because there will be a whole day of school for Bessemer High, and a half-day for us, it will allow us to get in and out before their school day is over. Yes, that would be wise."

Harriet and I exchanged glances. I could see the relief on her face. The Lord was certainly looking out for us!

"That would be wonderful, Mr. Wilson. We just didn't want to fall behind on our assignments, once we begin the book studies," I offered.

Mr. Wilson smiled broadly.

"Fine students! I had been perplexed about this dilemma myself. I had decided that I would spend the first few weeks on several foundational assignments before we dove into our text. I don't want to take precious time away from all of the other stories and history I wish to impart that may not be included in the schoolbook.

"This is the proper thing to do, to go to the very school that is our source. And your presence will put a face to our school's shortage."

He folded his arms and looked at us, beaming.

"Yes! You young ladies have a lot of courage. Mind you, it will not be an easy mission. But we will succeed together, as a people with an enormously rich history of grit, forbearance, and knowledge of how to get things done!"

Harriet and I made sure that we were as cool as cucumbers around Matthew and Luke, so as not to arouse any suspicion about our Friday mission. I thought of a perfect solution for us. One that would give us a great excuse for walking home on our own.

I decided that I'd just casually mention that we had a half a day of school on Friday.

"Harriet and I have an errand to run on Friday, so we won't be needing you boys to escort us home."

The fact that I didn't explain where we were going must've made Matthew curious, but to his credit, he didn't say anything. He just raised an eyebrow before returning to his conversation with Luke.

Luke, on the other hand, didn't let it go quite so easily.

"You don't want us to accompany you?"

I gulped to keep from looking guilty about our plans and quickly stated, "No, we'll be fine. Just going through town. Maybe to do a little window shopping."

He nodded in acceptance. I had selected the right excuse! There was no way that my brothers would want to follow along on what they considered a girls' activity!

Matthew, on the other hand, kept talking about the classes he had the following week, as he was starting a new semester at seminary.

"I even may preach my first sermon by Thanksgiving! Can you imagine that?"

"You might want to preach about how we can't soar on our own strength!" Luke nudged Matthew.

We all laughed. Everyone in the area had heard tell of how Matthew tried to fly holding on to a sheet and jumping off the top of Mr. Moody's barn.

Just before jumping, he'd proclaimed he was Superman. He fell to the ground and broke his arm. Matthew never tried that stunt again!

Luke poked him in the ribs.

"Yeah, you fell like a sack of potatoes, Matthew! That'll keep everyone in stitches. Maybe you'll wind up not havin' to talk for the full hour!"

"Hey, that was my shining moment! A moment of truth!" Matthew cut his eyes at us.

"That I, yours truly, found I could not fly!"

Harriet and I were in tears of mirth when we parted. Laughter was surely the best way to take away the tension of the mission we had ahead of us.

Friday came quickly. I made sure that I had my best school outfit on, my first-day-of-school clothes. I didn't want to arouse Mother's attention, so I wore a modest amount of makeup. Just enough to look presentable.

Arriving at Dunbar, I thanked Matthew and Luke for walking me to school that first week. I made sure they remembered that since we had a half day, Harriet and I would be fine walking home afterward.

Luke watched quietly.

"Just don't dilly dally around. Papa wants us all to get a jumpstart on picking his pole beans," Matthew bellowed.

I flushed, not wanting my fellow students to know that I had farming duties awaiting me that afternoon. My attire was anything but that of a farmer!

But I knew in my heart that we were all blessed by Papa's farming. I, for one, enjoyed eating pole beans on Sunday with my fried chicken!

Harriet rushed up to me. She was dressed, bandbox fresh. Her plaid dress had its white collar starched and her only shoes were polished. She had even added ribbons to her braids.

"Sorry, I'm late, Dee Dee! I had to put a load in the laundry pot before I left."

Luke's sharp eyes took in Harriet's garb with a slight bit of suspicion. But as Luke and Matthew left, they only said, "See y'all, later!"

We sailed through our first four classes and waited eagerly by Mr. Wilson's classroom door, our fifth period class.

He emerged, dressed very neatly, as usual. He wore a gray suit with a starched white shirt and a dark blue bow tie. Mr. Wilson smiled at our appearance.

"You girls represent our case very well. I may be delayed a bit as I must make sure that our principal has contacted Bessemer's principal.

"If you would like to meet me in front of the school, I should be there shortly and will accompany you."

Harriet and I nodded. It was our plan to go to the school directly after classes, but we decided to first make sure that Mr. Wilson was still going.

It was always best to double-check in times like these. Big Mama Dee always told us never to jump into anything head on but always feet first. I wanted to be sure that Mr. Wilson hadn't fallen ill or that something else unforeseen had come up.

"Yes, sir. We will see you at the school!"

Harriet was quiet as we walked down street into the white area. The crisp autumn air and chirping birds gave us a boost of cool courage.

No one seemed to give us a second glance. The only people walking along were day workers and delivery people.

"I only hope that we can do this and be gone before that school lets out, DeLois Ann!"

I grabbed her hand, hoping that some of my courage could be transferred to her.

"We'll do this, Harriet! Have you been praying for the Lord's protection?"

"Yes, I have! I've been praying ever since you had this crazy idea!"

She gave my hand a squeeze.

"But after hearing Mr. Wilson's lectures and knowing that I don't have to go there alone, I believe that the Lord has given me some more courage, Dee Dee. A lot more than I had earlier this week, that's for sure!"

We rounded the corner. Bessemer Senior High School loomed in front of us.

Harriet and I paused, staring at the impressive, two-story brick building. We exchanged a glance, and I knew we were thinking the same thing.

Whatever might lie before us was the unknown, a scary mystery. We only hoped and prayed that we would be protected as Daniel was before he stepped inside of the lion's den!

CHAPTER 14

BESSEMER

Bessemer had made a name for itself during the 1890s because of its iron mining, coal, and limestone deposits—all needed to make steel. It had become one of the modern leaders in the steel industry by the 1980s, and was then a bustling metropolis, flexing its muscles with renewed energy.

As the large silver bus crossed a network of rail tracks, Charles wondered whether any of those trucks led back to the sawmill in Billingsley.

Suddenly, Billingsley was a place of comfort. This thought startled Charles.

Too late to second-guess my decision, Charles shook his head, as though erasing the image out of his mind.

It conflicted with his current mission. He knew, deep in his soul, that he had made the right choice.

He wanted a better life. The minister at the tent meeting had said that the Lord "knew the plans" he had for Charles. Charles desperately hoped that those plans included a good job and meeting a wonderful woman who would become his wife.

CHAPTER 14

BESSEMER

Bessemer had made a name for itself during the 1890s because of its ore mining, coke, and limestone deposits—all needed to make steel. It had become one of the modern leaders in the steel industry by the 1940s, and was then a bustling metropolis, flexing its muscles with renewed energy.

As the large silver bus crossed a network of train tracks, Charles wondered whether any of those tracks led back to the sawmill in Billingsley.

Suddenly, Billingsley was a place of comfort. This thought startled Charles.

Too late to second-guess my decision. Charles shook his head, as though tossing the image out of his mind.

It conflicted with his current mission. He knew, deep in his soul, that he had made the right choice.

He wanted a better life. The minister at the tent meeting had said that the Lord "knew the plans" he had for Charles. Charles desperately hoped that those plans included a good job and meeting a wonderful woman who would become his wife.

Gazing out of the bus window, Charles knew that his dream would have to begin in Bessemer. He needed a job that paid well.

The city had a combination of green parks and many red brick and concrete buildings that lined up close to its wide sidewalks. It seemed to be a prosperous place by the number of cars, trucks, and horse-pulled carts he saw moving along its busy streets.

But Charles could also see that while most of the people were white folk, many were without. Hoboes, drifters, and people who were down-at-the-heels wandered the streets.

He saw some of these men pause, every now and then, to ask passersby for a handout, only to be refused. They continued on, approaching others.

With this many white folk wandering around without jobs, what kind of a chance do I have? Charles mused.

Charles squared his shoulders and told himself that he was about to embark on a new adventure. Everything he had ever known about the world was about to shift. This realization gave him both a sense of excitement and purpose.

I'm setting up a new future, something other than farming. It's gonna be a new life, even if it means goin' into a foreign land.

I have a different calling. I'm going to let the Lord take care of me. I'm just a traveler like Abraham, he thought.

Charles silently thanked God for the resolve to leave his hometown. On the bus, he read the Bible. It put his mind firmly on God's plan for him. While reading, Charles happened upon Abraham's journey to the promised land.

He chuckled to himself.

I'm praying and reading the Bible! Would wonders ever cease?

Abraham's story reminded Charles that even though no specific directions had been given to him directly from God, he was following God's lead. He knew that as long as he walked in faith, he'd have the Lord's covering.

He had to rely on his faith that the Lord would provide more for him, even in this industrialized area of the South. He was no longer tied to the whims and ravages of the boll weevil.

Reflecting on his future in Bessemer took his mind off of the situation he had left behind in Billingsley and Mt. Vernon.

It was difficult to run the events of the day around in his mind. He still felt guilty that he had not been able to help his mother so long ago.

But Charles finally reasoned out that he had been just a child. There was nothing he could have been done to change Mama Edna's taunts or save his mother from the misery she endured.

Charles would have to wait to speak with his father. He supposed Daddy Ben also had great remorse about the decisions he'd had to make difficult decisions regarding Cora.

He knew only that his father's feelings for Cora were strong and that he still loved her. He could tell by the way Ben's face lit up whenever he spoke of his wife.

That the past was sealed was a surety. Yet while Charles couldn't do anything about the past, memories of his mother's anxiety, those bitter memories, would surely surface every now and then.

But now that he was an adult, he could help out. That thought brought peace to Charles's mind. With a sigh of resolve, Charles prayed for peace in his and the family's life.

With that prayer, the conflicting thoughts were, at least temporarily, laid to rest.

Maybe Bessemer will hold some of that peace for me, Charles thought.

It was a crazy idea. Could the busy town of Bessemer in Jefferson County have a remote chance of being a peaceful setting for him? Somehow he felt that with prayer, it was possible.

The bus depot was across the tracks from the train station. The signs on the side of a building offered Coca Cola for 5 cents. A newspaper boy called out the headlines to those waiting at the depot's crosswalk.

Charles waited patiently for the other passengers to leave the bus. He had taken one of the last seats in the colored section. It allowed him to stretch his legs and watch the other passengers come and go.

He observed a few of the white passengers as they gave colored riders looks of disgust if they got too close to them while disembarking. A mother pulled her little girl protectively to her side when a portly, kind-looking colored gentleman bent over to peer out her window.

When the man saw her searing glance of contempt, he straightened, suddenly, as if struck from behind. He quickly apologized and took several steps back.

Jim Crow laws made life demoralizing for his people. He could see its effects, and the lack of love for one's fellow man, vividly.

Charles knew the city would harbor many folk who'd have that attitude of mind, but he didn't want to dwell on it. He had a mission to accomplish that wouldn't allow thoughts of defeat or feelings about a group of people's hatred to hold him back, physically or emotionally.

Dr. Carver said, "Fear of something is at the root of hate for others, and hate within will eventually destroy the hater."

Charles knew that his father supported this belief. His daddy had told them that a man makes his way based on his own work. He had taught his children to always put in an honest day's work.

"It's in the Bible, son. If a man doesn't work, he don't deserve to eat! It also says somewhere that we supposed to work like we workin' fo' the Lawd.

"That way, nobody can say that you ain't worth your wages. And as long as yo' honest and treat people with kindness, no way ya be broke or jobless!"

Charles grabbed his valise from the dwindling pile of suitcases on the overhead racks. He stepped out onto the streets of Bessemer with the awareness that this was the beginning of his new life.

He was going to start his adventure in the industrial age to which Dr. Carver had referred. This age would soon hold no one back because everyone would be needed to move the country ahead, to get through the Depression.

With a smile, Charles approached the portly gentleman he had seen on the bus. The man stood on the local bus platform, smoking his pipe.

"Sir, could you tell me how to get to 555 Third Avenue North?"

"Son, you've got me hungry just askin'."

The man chuckled and his belly rippled with each bit of laughter.

"That'll be Czarnik's Meat and Grocery Store. Boy, they have the best wieners in Bessemer—probably all of Alabama."

"Is that right?"

"As sure as this is Monday! Used to have a cart right here near the bus depot selling wieners on buns. Hot dogs. You've brought back some great memories, my boy!"

Charles's smile widened. This was good. The more well-known the place, the better his prospects were of getting a job. If what the man said was true, this meat shop needed good workers to continue its progress.

The man gave Charles directions to the store. He also made Charles promise to buy a pound of pork sausages for himself, just to see how good they were.

Charles shook the man's hand and promised to do so before heading out. He walked with a quickened step to what he hoped would be his first job in Bessemer.

He passed a large Baptist church and took note of how many people in need he saw in its soup line. Others were standing around with hats in hand by banks, restaurants, and grocery stores. Burly policemen moved them along, brandishing their billy clubs.

Their fate doesn't predict my future, Charles prayed as he passed by these groups. *I have great skills and opportunities are waiting for me.*

Charles arrived at the store on Third Avenue North. The name Czarnik's was painted across its window in large red and black cursive letters. The store's red, white, and blue awning gave shade to another group of people clearly in need of a job.

Suddenly, an uneasy feeling overtook Charles. With so many out of work, what if his job had been taken?

I hope Daddy was right about Mr. Crane's puttin' in a good word for me. I pray I still have a chance!

Charles pulled out his Bible and read Jeremiah 29:11 and 12. He prayed silently, gathering his thoughts and resolve. He knew he had to put away any doubts he might have before crossing the threshold. He felt that the Lord could make a way when there was no way, if he had faith.

"This job is mine! I believe that the Lord brought me here for a reason, and I claim this promise, today!"

Prominently displayed in the front window, Charles saw the old wiener cart with the name Czarnik's on its side. Strings of plaster sausage were draped across the window, and plaster sides of meat were pegged up on either side of the display. Czarnik was a businessman, and he capitalized popularity of his pork sausages.

It was easy to see that while this was a butcher shop, Czarnik's predominant business was meatpacking. Only the front of the long, white building served as its store.

Inside, customers milled around the cases and in the aisles, perusing the many food items of this well-stocked store. Fresh produce and canned goods were neatly arranged on the shelves of each aisle.

The front of the store had the checkout and meat displays. Felix Czarnik ran the show. He wore a white apron with the big black and red Czarnik's right across his ample belly.

The big man wore his salt-and-pepper hair cut short and sported a walrus mustache. Mr. Czarnik enjoyed his work.

Charles took a place at the rear of the line. He got a chance to hear the many orders for Czarnik's pork sausages and Mr. Czarnik's repeated, but not unkind, admonition that they were properly called 'wieners.'

"In the old country they are called wienersnitzels. But here, in America, 'wieners' is okay!"

When Charles arrived at the front of the line, he ordered a pound of pork wieners. Mr. Czarnik glanced up at him, somewhat surprised by his clear speech and lack of country twang.

But when he took in Charles's valise, he made a dismissive gesture. He shook his head, leaning over the counter.

"No jobs! How many times do I have to tell people that? You want I should put a sign in the window or something?"

Charles was taken aback, but then quickly regained his composure.

"Hello, Mr. Czarnik, I'm Charles Stevens. I believe that your nephew, Bobby Crane, mentioned that I was a good worker and would be comin' here.

"If he did, I'm sure he told you that I'm not just someone looking for a job. I'm the person who can help you keep making and selling these great wieners to more people."

Mr. Czarnik looked at Charles in disbelief at his boldness. But, seeing that he had Czarnik's attention, Charles continued.

"I just came in from Billingsley, but already ran into folk that told me you have some of the best meat in the state. I'd like to be a part of making your quality product, sir."

Mr. Czarnik's frown turned into a smile. He began laughing.

"Ya, I did hear about your coming from Bobby, but he didn't warn me about the amount of smooth talkin' I'd be hearin'."

He paused, wiping his hands absently on a towel. After a few thoughtful moments, he beckoned to Charles. Charles leaned toward Mr. Czarnik.

"Look, Charlie, I like you. But I do have a bunch of fellas comin' by every day lookin' for work. What makes you a better worker?"

Charles prayed silently. He took a deep breath and launched into part two of his sales pitch, which he had hoped would show Mr. Czarnik how much he wanted to work for his company.

"Well, Mr. Czarnik, I'm a hard worker and an honest man. You'd never have to look over your shoulder wondering if I'm pulling my own weight and then some. I worked two full-time jobs, farming and at the lumber mill, while going to school at the same time, before I was fourteen."

Charles took a deep breath.

"You see, I learned a lot about farming from my father and what it takes to be a valuable worker in the city from Dr. Carver."

With that, Mr. Czarnik paused his cleaning of the counter. He grew very interested in Charles.

"Do you mean Dr. George Washington Carver? He was the man who started this part of the South on curing meats!"

He took a closer look at Charles.

"Do you mean to say, you met the man?"

Charles chuckled.

"Yes, sir. He spoke to me when I attended a lecture at Tuskegee with a group of Future Farmers. He's had a tremendous influence on my life!"

Mr. Czarnik shook his head incredulously.

"I never met 'em, but always wanted to go right up to Tuskegee and tell him what he's done for us meat packers!"

"Well, Dr. Carver taught us that 'if we learn to do common things uncommonly well: we must always keep in mind that anything that helps fill the dinner pail is valuable.'

"Right now, I'm eager to learn about pickling pork, creatin' wieners, and anything else you care to teach me. You see, Mr. Czarnik, I'm ready to start. I'm ready to fill that dinner pail!"

Mr. Czarnik began laughing. He wiped his eyes with the back of his hand.

"Okay, I won't make any promises, Charles Stevens. But I will give you a chance, as Bobby doesn't stick his neck out for just anyone.

"You impress me as a smart young man. We'll put your sausages back in the cooler and you can set your valise down behind this counter. Grab an apron. I want to see what you can do."

"You'll never regret your decision, sir!"

Mr. Czarnik grinned.

"Let's hope not, Charlie. I've had that happen only a handful of times. I consider myself a good judge of character."

Charles stowed his valise and grabbed an apron that hung on a hook by the double doors.

As he followed Mr. Czarnik into the back of the store, Charles said a silent prayer of thanksgiving. He knew that his opportunity had arrived.

CHAPTER 15

OUT OF THE FRYING PAN

Harriet and I stood stock still, staring at that huge school. It looked ominous. Funny, I had never taken the time to gaze up at it even though I'd passed it every day for the last three years.

Through one of the classroom windows, I noticed a very surprised white student staring down at me. He wrinkled his nose and was about to put up a finger, when the teacher pulled down the window shade.

"We've got to pray, Harriet," I said, "big time!"

Harriet took a deep breath, swallowed, and nodded her head.

"You start, Dee Dee," she gulped and grabbed my hand.

"Dear Father God! You are over this world and everything in it. Please be with us today, dear Father, as we enter this school for white children. Be with us, protect us, and keep us from hurt, harm, and danger."

I searched for the words to express my mounting fears, but Harriet boldly proclaimed.

"You're our shield and protector, dear Jesus! Please, Lord, hear our cry! In Jesus's holy name, Amen!"

"I'm so happy that I made it here before you went inside, young ladies!"

It was God's perfect timing. Mr. Wilson walked briskly toward us. Just seeing him renewed our hope of success.

"I wanted to get you in and out before their classes changed." Mr. Wilson paused to glance at his pocket watch.

"Untimed, this visit may cause something of a disruption. Shall we go in?"

We scurried up the staircase behind Mr. Wilson's quick stride. He held the doors for us, and we stepped inside the dark interior.

The antiseptically clean hallways were painted army green and the floors were tiled with what looked like a single sheet of brown linoleum. However, the sides of the floor curved up to meet row upon row of dark green lockers.

So many lockers! Could there be that many students in this school? Our school was large, but this one was at least two to three times Dunbar's size!

Mr. Wilson hurried us to the door that had a wooden sign with the word Office dangling above it.

Inside, standing at a long, wooden, highly shellacked counter were several parents. Mr. Wilson asked us to sit on the bench across from the counter while he approached the line.

An office worker looked up at him, then over at Harriet and me.

"What are you doin' here?" she asked with a gruff, unfriendly expression. "The colored school is down the way . . ."

"I know, Madame. I'm a teacher from that very school, here to speak with your principal, Mr. Godfrey. If you would be so kind, I believe he is expecting me. Thank you."

The other parents turned to look at Mr. Wilson, then a few turned and spied us. Some of the expressions toward us were a mixture of surprise and disgust, while others seemed ambivalent.

Miffed by his comment and air of confidence, the woman abruptly left the counter and walked to the office door on the right side of the area. The door was ajar, but she still knocked on the doorframe.

"There's a colored fella out here, Mr. Godfrey. Says he's a teacher from the colored school . . ."

"Ah, yes. Thank ya, Sally," a deep nasal voice from the office preceded the emerging figure of Mr. Godfrey, a short, rotund, balding man with a friendly face.

He walked to the counter and leaned over to shake Mr. Wilson's hand. Mopping his forehead, he smiled congenially.

"Well, suh, tell me what can we do for ya?"

"My principal stated that you and he had spoken about my picking up some additional American history books for the seniors of my class at Dunbar High School." Mr. Wilson gestured toward us.

"Oh, yeah, our colored school! I remembered talkin' with him just a short while ago . . ."

He walked around the counter, briefly glancing at Harriet and me.

"Guess these two are your'n?"

I have to give my teacher credit. Mr. Wilson wasn't at all perturbed by Mr. Godfrey's casual nature. I'd have almost said he had expected him to be that way.

"Yes, Mr. Godfrey, they are my students. In fact, they were so interested in furthering their education that they asked me if they could help me find books for them somewhere, and I realized that you might have a few extra American history books. We'd like those taken out of circulation, of course, for use at Dunbar."

Mr. Godfrey rocked back on his heels, his hand on his chin in a thinking pose.

I wasn't sure what we'd end up with, if anything, at that point. I glanced over at Harriet.

She had her head down, bowed in prayer. I joined her in a silent moment of fellowship.

"I like that! C'mon with me, the lot of y'all! Just foller me! Sally, hold my calls."

The secretary looked affronted as she watched us walk out of the office behind her boss.

"Now, we got some books back here in our book room. I cain't promise y'all that I got those particular ones, but we'll take a looksee."

Harriet and I were jumping inside of our skins as he led us up to the second floor. While we felt somewhat secure walking behind the school's principal, we didn't know what type of problems we might encounter. All we knew was we had stepped further away from our escape route. Every time a door closed, we flinched.

At the end of the hallway was a small cupboard with set of wooden, Dutch doors. Mr. Godfrey unlocked their solid, brass lock with a large skeleton key and turned on the light.

The musty smell told me the small cupboard, about three feet by six feet, hadn't been opened for a long while.

But the room was crammed with books of all sizes. What a treasure trove!

"These are all we have of our overflow. Unfortunately, I cain't fit in there anymore," Mr. Godfrey said as he patted his ample tummy. He cut a glance over at Harriet and me.

"If you young'uns don't mind checkin' the stacks, I'll take your teacher to the library storage room to see if'n anythin's there."

Mr. Wilson gauged the situation.

"Just how far is the library from here, Mr. Godfrey?"

"Jesta coupla doors toward the staircase . . ."

Mr. Wilson turned toward us.

"Are you girls okay working here for a bit, while we look into the library situation?"

Harriet and I were not okay with that arrangement, but we had to draw upon our courage reserves. Mr. Wilson made us feel like adults, asking for our opinion.

My parents never asked how I felt. Any decisions would be made for me, and if I didn't do what they said to do, I'd risk getting a switching or an all-out spanking.

His thoughtfulness gave me additional confidence. I turned to see that even Harriet was nodding her head. I plastered on a smile and nodded mine, too.

"We can do that, Mr. Wilson. We'll work until you return."

"We'll be right here!" Harriet chimed in.

"Very fine. Mr. Godfrey, let us do this quickly as we don't want to disturb your classes as they pass. How soon will the bell ring?"

Puzzled by the question, Mr. Godfrey flipped open his pocket watch.

"Looks like we got about ten minutes or so."

"Then let us make haste!"

"Oh, okay, Mr. Wilson. My, you sound like my old drama teacher. Big on Shakespeare!"

Harriet dove in as soon as the two men turned to walk the other way. She whispered, "C'mon, Dee Dee! Let's make this snappy."

"I want to see which door is the library, in case we have to make a run for it . . ."

Three doors down the hallway, Mr. Godfrey opened a glass-windowed door, and the men entered.

"Got it! Let's see what's here!"

The books were stacked in precarious piles. Some were on shelves behind others that stood on the floor to form wobbly towers.

Harriet held some in place while I checked behind them. I had hoped that our books would all be together, and we could grab a set and be off.

No such luck, I thought.

After combing through one stack, I found three American history books. Harriet took this time to glance up at the hallway clock.

"Dee Dee! We've got all of four minutes to clear out of here! What should we do?"

I smoothed back my hair, which had gotten mussed from leaning over the stacks. The opposite side of the book room held a promising set of shelves.

As I scanned them, I could feel my hands beginning to sweat in anticipation. I had used most of our time on the messier side of the book room. I wished that I had time to take a more leisurely look through all of them.

"We might find two more, Harriet. Just think of how much Mr. Wilson would love it if we had almost all of what we need!"

"But we got to get back to Mr. Wilson, Dee Dee! What if we get caught out there in the hallway when classes change, much less when school lets out? If we leave now, we can be safe and on our way home before their last bell rings!"

I hadn't thought about the last period ending. We were now two minutes from the class change and another forty minutes from the end of school.

"We could always come back, Dee Dee . . ."

Harriet's logic clinched the deal for me. We hastily closed the door and dashed down the hall to the library holding our books.

The bell rang just as we dashed inside. We fell against the door, catching our breath.

We then found ourselves face-to-face with a crowd of white students.

CHAPTER 16

PROVING HIS METTLE

Czarnik's ran deep into the length of its block and ended in the next street perpendicular to Third Avenue North's alley.

Once behind the swinging doors, Charles was agape at the size of the building. A series of worktables creating three different sections of production filled the front section of the long, narrow shop.

Walking through the meat carving section, Charles took in the aroma of spices. Freshly carved sides of pork and beef were hooked on carts to be rolled into the refrigerator storage unit in the rear.

He was amazed at the high level of activity. It was as though he had entered another business, distinct from the small grocery store on the other side of the double doors. Mr. Czarnik's business was strong and vibrant.

Mr. Czarnik took in Charles's expression of awe and smiled.

"Okay, nothing is written in stone, Charlie. But I think you are a sharp young fella."

Mr. Czarnik nodded to some of the workers and waved at others. But Charles could tell that nothing escaped his keen eyes.

This man might be in his fifties, but he's as sharp as a tack, Charles thought.

"You see, I was raised on a farm, right here in Alabama. Hired a lot of my fellas, who are hard workers, from farms, too.

"Now, possibly, you're a good worker. I'm willing to see what you're able to do. I'm just hoping it won't cost me any lost time."

Charles laughed good-naturedly.

"I can assure you, Mr. Czarnik, you'll get more than your money's worth!"

Mr. Czarnik shot him a quick glance and laughed.

"You are a sharp one, Charlie."

He gestured toward a table of men dressed in white, brandishing long knives.

"Now, this here is my team for cutting select portions of pork and the sides of beef for roasting, braising, whatever the housewife desires for her evening meal."

Sharp knives made relatively very few movements to extract smooth slices of pork. It was easy to see that these blades were held and operated by professionals.

Charles noticed that Mr. Czarnik had hired colored workers too. This gave him a great deal of hope.

It said to him that Mr. Czarnik was primarily interested in having a successful business. Color didn't seem to matter.

"And this group is working on the sausages. Sausages make up most of my profit. "Soon they will be ATCW—'Amazingly Tasty Czarnik Wieners equals good eatin' in every bite.' That's my motto!"

He proudly gestured at the men working along an expansive table littered with parts of pork meat. They sorted through and pulled out the inedible pieces.

Every few minutes, the men would pause, discard the poor-quality pieces, and place the good meat in large, silver bins. One man collected the bins and shuttled them down the narrow aisles, shooing away flies, until he reached another section located behind a huge canvas tarpaulin.

Charles could hear a loud, continuous grinding sound coming from the area behind the tarp. As he and Mr. Czarnik cleared it, Charles saw the workspace was dedicated to a different type of product. An immense machine with a flanged opening on top and a nozzle that hung over a canvas-lined container was the centerpiece.

Three men worked the area. The older white man, who collected meat scraps in the silver bins, would dump the pork pieces into a large container.

A young, fair-complexioned man would pour in the spices and herbs, mix them into the meat, then shovel it down the machine's large opening.

Seated at the machine's nozzle was a tall, brown-skinned man who looked like a heavyweight fighter with a shock of wavy salt-and-peppered hair. He expertly held a casing on the nozzle and flicked the machine's handle controlling the amount of meat being extruded into the casing, which he held in with his other hand. At regular intervals, he would twist and knot each section off with just a few hand movements.

The younger man would remove the large crate of sausages, as they were finished, to a table. He would cut off lengths of the sausage for packaging. The links were uniform in size and weight.

Another worker would enter the room periodically to load the sausages into crates. He'd shuttle the flatbed of crates to the company's curing locker.

In the midst of his work, the young man glanced up at Charles with curiosity. When Mr. Czarnik paused to speak to the man with the bin, the young man gave Charles a quick, conspiratorial wink. A spirit of camaraderie was evident.

"Now, you see how quickly Buster tackles this side of our production? He can create about five pounds in fifteen minutes. That's a pound every three minutes!"

At that moment, Charles noticed that Buster looked about for his next bin. He looked at the younger man, who shrugged. They were both nonplussed that the older worker had not yet returned.

However, Buster didn't sit idly by. He turned off the machine's nozzle, removed and cleaned it and the housing of extra product that had caked up then, reconnected the parts.

By the time he'd finished, the older worker had returned with a new bin of pork cuttings. Without missing a beat, Buster resumed his work.

Charles noticed that the younger man's brow was furrowed. As he added the spices and herbs to the meat, he gave the older worker's retreating figure a sidelong glance.

Buster resumed his work.

Gazing around the vast expanse of the meatpacking factory, Charles wiped his forehead. He counted close to eighty men total working the different stations.

Charles thought about how much time it had taken Adam, Martha, and him to plant and harvest a farm with forty acres. While it took a longer period of time to produce results on a farm, he saw that this business was similar.

A certain amount of product had to be created in a given period of time in order to make a profit and pay everyone. Every worker was an essential part of the business's profitability. Time was money.

"Well, Charlie?"

Mr. Czarnik looked at Charles expectantly. Charles rubbed his jaw, searching for the right words. He bobbed his head in the direction of the older man who seemed to take his time walking to get more meat from the trimmers.

"I can see you need someone to keep the tables cleaned and that contraption filled with the pork pieces.

"That older fella has to walk back an' forth at least four times in an hour to keep the container filled with enough meat to keep up with that sausage-makin' fella. Looks to me like that poor man is gettin' clean worn out."

When he turned to face Czarnik, he found the older man struggling to contain his expression. To his credit, Czarnik quickly composed himself. Silently, he beckoned Charles to continue.

"Well, I can help out there if that makes it easier for you to keep those bins goin' at a good clip, Mr. Czarnik. I could start right now, if that's okay with you."

Immediately, Czarnik called the older worker over and introduced him to Charles.

"Carl Westharden, this is Charlie Stevens. He's going to assist you in collecting the meat pieces for the sausage production today. Now, you two work it out—I've got to mind the store."

With that said, Czarnik turned on his heel and quickly walked away. Charles could almost swear that the man's shoulders were shaking, as if he were stifling laughter.

Carl eyed Charles suspiciously.

"You hired by Czarnik?"

Charles shook his head.

"No, sir. I'm just working today. We'll see how far it goes from here."

Carl nodded his head, satisfied. He jabbed his bin into Charles's hands.

"Better get to work, boy."

Charles caught the glance of the young man packing wieners. He raised his brows as if warning Charles, without a word, then looked away.

It irked Charles to be called "boy," although he'd been the recipient of it many times in his life. Mostly, he had heard it when visiting large cities like Montgomery.

But it wasn't the words Carl used as much as it was the way in which he said them. His attitude was dismissive, with rancor and superiority.

Charles chalked it up to prejudice, with Carl being white. Besides, Charles mused; Carl was Charles's father's age.

Instead of resentment, he made a decision to treat the older man with respect. It would allow him to take on the job, if it were offered to him, and work with anyone. The possibility of his getting paid overshadowed Carl's importance.

Quickly, Charles began picking out the discarded meat pieces. In a city where no one knew him from anyone, he would have to work hard to prove himself. Eventually, he'd earn the trust of Mr. Czarnik for more responsible jobs.

He noticed that some of the meat cutters would rake the trims to the back of their table. Others would keep little piles of meat near them, clearing the table when things got congested.

Charles gauged how to work with each of the expert cutters as he filled his bins. His only concern was staying far away from their very sharp, quickly moving blades.

When lunchtime came, the men pulled off their aprons and grabbed their lunch boxes. At that point, Charles realized that he had grown hungry too. Mama Edna's lunch was eagerly anticipated.

His Mobile trip seemed so far away. It seemed ages ago that he had been struggling with thoughts of how to help take care of his mother.

Reflecting back, it warmed him that the interlude with his mother at Mt. Vernon had been buffered with an evening in Mobile.

What a blessing it was that Willard and Nadine had had us over for a fried catfish dinner. Sure made for a light-hearted end of the day with Aunt Nelda, he thought.

God is good.

He pulled out his old tin bucket and found a seat near the edge of the alleyway. He figured that it was the colored area, as many of the whites seemed to avoid sitting there.

Mama Edna had wrapped the pieces of tender fried chicken and flakey biscuits with waxed paper. This was an extravagance.

Mama Edna always counted the cost of using that new-fangled paper. When they returned from trips to the mill, she would wipe it down and hang it on the clothesline to dry before reusing it.

She had even hidden a slice of sweet potato pie under the biscuits, wrapped in a clean cotton napkin. He had no idea how that last piece had escaped getting eaten.

Charles said grace and took a bite of the chicken. Instantly, the taste transported him to that Billingsley kitchen. The aromas of hot lard, paprika, salt, and pepper were collected and intensified in the crispy chicken skin.

He just couldn't think hard thoughts about Mama Edna while chewing that morsel of chicken. She did her part in taking care of the family in his mother's absence. But, Charles wondered, at what price?

CHAPTER 17

AND INTO THE FIRE

Among the sea of angry faces, one boy stepped forward. We braced ourselves.

"What're you black ants doin' in a white puddin'?"

That comment made me angry. He was being mean for no good reason. That wasn't right!

I frowned at him as he came toward me. I didn't even think about moving out of the way.

He tried to bump me with his shoulder as he passed. I lifted my books to block him and was about to shove back, but Harriet pulled me back.

"Help me, Jesus!"

At that moment, the librarian, a pretty blond lady, briskly walked up to the door. Turning her back on us, she sternly addressed the white students.

"Boys and girls, you heard the bell! Hurry or you'll be late for your last class!"

They filed out, slowly, shooting glares of anger and disgust at Harriet and me. The librarian turned toward us.

"What are you-all doin' in here? This isn't the colored school!"

"We-we know that, Miss . . ." I stammered. I truly didn't know what to say. The shock of that encounter had just begun to register with me.

Before I could formulate a thought, her eyes sank down to the stack of American history books we were holding.

"Those books aren't yours! You've got books that are the property of Bessemer High School! I can see our stamp!"

With that, she snatched the books from our grasps and shook her finger at Harriet and me.

"What are you tryin' to do? Steal these books? I'll have to take you down to the office to call the police! You oughta know better than to come into our school and try to take what's not yours!"

The last of the students filing out grinned at our calamity. We must've looked like a couple of cats that'd just been dunked in a tub of water.

At that moment, Mr. Wilson and Mr. Godfrey approached.

"I'm glad you all found some mo' books, girls!"

Hearing Mr. Godfrey's kind voice was a relief. He smiled generously at our sad faces. He gestured toward Mr. Wilson.

"They's with this teacher, Miss Pearl!"

Miss Pearl attempted to hide her surprise.

"What? But I caught these girls tryin' to steal! These are our textbooks!"

At that moment, Mr. Wilson saw the books. His eyes grew large. He looked at us as if we had found the mother lode.

"Excellent, my dear young ladies!"

It was only then that we noticed that he carried a stack of seven books! We had struck gold!

"Well, I know it looks like that, Miss Pearl, but these two girls are with this here teacher and they came to our fair school for a handout," he grinned broadly.

He took the books from Miss Pearl and returned them to Harriet and me.

At that point, I wasn't sure if I still wanted to take the books, but I kept my mouth shut.

"Surely we can give the colored school children some of our cast-off history books, now, cain't we?"

Mr. Godfrey turned to us.

"Didja find all of 'em in the book room?"

"Well, sir, we found the ones we were carrying, but we didn't get to finish our search," Harriet got out.

Mr. Godfrey laughed congenially.

"Well, it still looks like you got a haul. Mr. Wilson, would that do ya for a while? It's gettin' late, and we don't want to turn this here school into an uproar havin' colored gals runnin' around our hallways now."

Mr. Wilson nodded his head yes, but we could tell that he was clearly focused on completing the mission. I had a feeling that if it were another time and place, he might have given Mr. Godfrey a lecture on the ridiculousness of Jim Crow.

But realizing that our welcome was coming to an end, he beamed at us and said, "Well done!"

Mr. Wilson glanced at the wood-rimmed clock on the library wall.

It read 2:45 p.m. I almost gasped. In fifteen minutes, school would be dismissed! I wanted to turn and run down the staircase and out the doors, at that moment.

"I believe we're very well satisfied, Mr. Godfrey. We shall be on our way, but could I bother you for one more favor?

"I would like you to write a receipt for these texts, just in case someone else might think the books were stolen."

His eyes slid to Miss Pearl, whose demeanor hadn't changed one bit from the time Mr. Godfrey relieved her of the stack of books up until that moment.

"We wouldn't want to be stopped again on our way out," he continued.

"Good idea! Just come on back to the office. I'll write you a receipt for all of 'em!"

We trekked down to the office. By this time, a group of ten parents had lined up to sign their children out of school early. The overworked secretary looked up in relief.

"Mr. Godfrey, suh? I was fixin' to call for some help! These folks want to get their children out before three and I need help!"

Mr. Godfrey turned to Mr. Wilson and gestured at the benches at the wall.

"Would you mind? I'll only be a minute . . ."

We turned frightened eyes toward Mr. Wilson. He nodded to Mr. Godfrey and gestured for us to take a seat. He sat next to us, his expression only slightly perturbed.

"Listen, young ladies. How about you go on home? I don't want you to run into a crowd of flummoxed white students, or run late in getting home if we should be delayed."

"But, Mr. Wilson, how are you going to get all of these books back to Dunbar?"

I turned to Harriet, who was clearly ready to leave.

"Maybe we can come back after school is out to help?"

Mr. Wilson gave us a patient smile. He clearly anticipated problems and didn't want us to go through any distress.

"You've already helped enough, my dear students! Now, please be on your way. I will manage. I truly appreciate everything you've already done!"

I glanced at Harriet. We both hesitated. It was definitely a quandary. He had given us permission to leave, but it just didn't seem right to leave him there with all of those books.

Mr. Wilson glanced back at the line, which was down to four parents, at over at the clock. It was 2:55 p.m.

"Time's a-wasting, young ladies! I'll see you on Monday!"

There seemed to be no other choice. So, we thanked Mr. Wilson and scurried off, out of the office and down the staircase of the school.

Running down the street away from that building, I took in a deep breath, feeling a huge wave of relief!

"I can't believe we made it outta there alive, Dee Dee!"

"Harriet, thank you for thinking about praying! I don't know what got into me when those bullies in the library started comin' toward us!"

Harriet hugged me. "It's the hand of God that protected us, Dee Dee!"

Giddy, from our narrow escape, we ran to the corner. I looked down the street and spotted Miss Minnie getting on the bus. She was carrying a small bag of groceries.

I turned my back and faced Harriet.

"We can't go that way," I stated quickly. "I'd have to explain to Mother why were down here instead of downtown. Miss Minnie'd surely tell her that she saw me!"

"Let's cut through the alley!"

"Good idea!"

We dodged into the alley between the school and a parking lot. The only thing on our minds was to escape the area and Miss Minnie before the bell rang.

As we cut around another corner, the bell rang. I was elated. We had accomplished our courageous goal and were on our way home.

That's when I ran straight into Clyde!

He had his hands on his hips. As he rocked back on his heels, Clyde shook his head in mock surprise.

"Cain't believe y'all had the guts to come to my ol' school! I saw y'all leavin' and ya didn't for one moment think ya'd see me, didcha?"

My legs turned to jelly. I hadn't believed I would ever see that bully again! Twice in one week was almost too much for my poor heart.

He was there without his henchmen. But what chance would we have in fighting him off?

He grinned, showing off his strange teeth as he rolled up his sleeves.

"I don't usually fight girls, but sense yo' brothers ain't around ta protect ya, it won't hurt none to give ya two a bit of a lickin'! Ya had some nerve comin' ta my school!"

"And that's the only way ya'd win, too, fightin' a girl," said Luke walking toward us with Matthew. We were so relieved. Harriet and I both wondered how many close calls we could endure in one day.

"Then, again, ya'd be surprised how well my sister can fight, when she needs ta!"

An equally surprised Clyde moved toward Luke, attempting to take charge of the situation.

"Yeah, boy, this is more like it. You'll do just fine."

Luke approached us smiling as he rolled up his sleeves, while Matthew kept an eye on the entrance to the alley.

He and Clyde circled each other, bracing themselves for the first blow. Clyde grinned and threw a punch.

It barely glanced Luke's shoulder, as he gracefully sidestepped it.

Luke blocked Clyde's second punch to the face and delivered a roundhouse punch to Clyde's midsection. We could hear the air go out of Clyde in a big "Ooof!"

Clyde bowled over and stared at Luke with a mixture of respect and anger. The school bell rang. He grinned wickedly.

"Seems like you might be in a stew, with my buddies headin' out to meet up with me. They won't take kindly to a n— tryin' to wup their leader!"

"Tryin'? How long we been at this Clyde? Two, three years?"

Harriet and I watched with dismay. It didn't look very good for our little group.

"Well, they might decide to go straight home, if you ask me," Matthew said. "Seein' as they ain't got the skills you got, Clyde!"

Luke stepped over to offer Clyde a hand up.

"Besides, it bein' Friday, I doubt if they'll even come lookin' for ya. Yup, they'd probably beat it back home if they got any common sense."

That was when I began to understand. Harriet and I had been so excited about going on the book hunt we hadn't noticed that my brothers were lurking nearby.

They'd been keeping an eye on us since we'd left Dunbar!

Admittedly, I was grateful for their protection.

Clyde eyed Luke and Matthew. Then, collecting himself, he looked at Luke's hand but decided to slowly get up from the ground on his own. He backed away from our group.

"Where'd ya learn to slug like that? The movies?"

"Naw, we been takin' lessons ever since we were five."

Clyde nodded his head, acknowledging the level of their skills.

Matthew rolled up his sleeves.

"We can show you a couple of steps, if'n you want . . ."

"I got ta go, now. Maybe I'll catcha later on, boys!"

"Any time!"

Clyde rushed past the school as students poured out. True to Luke's prediction, very few of them gave us any attention.

Matthew and Luke had a good laugh at Clyde's expense. Then, they turned to Harriet and me.

"So, you all goin' to Bessemer High School, now?"

"Dunbar ain't good enough for the likes of you?"

I felt a big lump in my throat as I panicked for an answer.

"Mother is angry with you, Dee Dee," Luke stated.

"Yes! She didn't know you were going somewhere after school. And certainly not here!" added Matthew, eager to have a say in the conversation.

"Coulda been a different ending of your day if we hadn't doubled back lookin' for ya!"

I was finally able to get out a few words.

"But we just came to help Mr. Wilson pick up our history books!"

"The problem is, you didn't tell Mother!"

"'Cause I thought she'd say no . . .'"

About that time, Harriet tugged on my arm. "We've got to go back, Dee Dee! Now, we can all help Mr. Wilson!"

I threw her a look of relief and love. Harriet was always so practical.

In haste, I explained to my brothers our need for their help.

"Why didn't you say so in the first place?"

We entered the office as the second bell rang. Mr. Wilson looked up in astonishment at our return . . . and at our reinforcements.

"That was mighty fine thinking . . ." he began, but broke off as a legion of students swamped the office. They ran up to the counter with various requests.

It took them only a few moments to see our troupe waiting on the benches.

One student walked right up to us.

"What is your kind doin' here? This ain't yo school!"

There were other unkind comments made. "I didn't know somebody's mammy sent 'em to this school!"

"What is that smell? N— hair oil?"

"I smell toe jam. Black toe jam!"

My face grew warm. I looked anxiously at my brothers. They kept partial smiles on their faces, looking over the heads of the smaller students.

Mr. Wilson was like a soldier, his face unreadable. None of us talked back to the students.

When they found that we wouldn't reply, they stopped their horrible comments and resorted to sending us malicious looks.

It seemed no one wanted to be in school on a Friday any longer than they needed to be. Pretty soon, they all filtered out.

Finally, Mr. Godfrey walked over with a piece of paper.

I was sure he heard their taunts. But he acted as if nothing out of the ordinary had happened.

"I hope you didn't mind waitin' for a while. The end of school on Friday is kinda busy."

He shot a glance over at my brothers, but didn't feel that it was worth his time inquire about them.

"No problem at all, Mr. Godfrey. We are very thankful for the hospitality your fine school has shown us."

Mr. Godfrey turned beet-red and by instinct, held out his hand to shake Mr. Wilson's. Before he could recover, Mr. Wilson shook it and tipped his hat.

"We hope to do the same for you, as the need arises."

Walking down the steps of the school, Matthew let out a loud whoop.

"I wish you'd been at Dunbar when I was goin' there, teacher! That was a beautiful thing to watch!"

Mr. Wilson bobbed his head shyly.

"Remembering that words don't matter if they don't hold truth is how we keep our heads above the fray, young people. It's the only way we can distinguish ourselves as formidable chess opponents and later, hopefully, as colleagues!"

My brothers took three books each.

"You should go on home, Lil' Sister. Mother is waiting for you," Matthew said with a raised eyebrow.

"We'll help you take these to Dunbar, Mr. Wilson," Luke said.

Mr. Wilson handed Harriet and me a book each.

"I hope you were not inconvenienced, young ladies, on running our mission." He had taken in Matthew's comment and my brothers' now somber attitude.

"These books are yours for the rest of the semester. You've certainly earned them!"

My heart was both elated and sorrowful as I walked home. I couldn't get my mind off of the chastisement I expected from Mother.

To go to Bessemer High was a decision that started off very frightful, but in the end, we were blessed with the courage to accomplish an impossible task. My only hope was that Mother could see it that way too.

CHAPTER 18

CAMARADERIE AND FAMILY

Before he could pull out his Bible, Charles noticed that Buster and the young man who spiced the wieners were walking over to his area. The men greeted each other.

Buster glanced over at Charles's lunch.

"You must be from the country!"

Charles, chuckling, wiped his mouth with the cotton napkin.

"You got me there. Yes, sir. I'm from Billingsley."

Buster smiled. It softened his hard features, revealing that he was a handsome man. His height and physique, however, made it evident that he was not one to be trifled with.

Buster nodded at the piece of chicken.

"Only a few people know how to cook chicken like that. I'm Benjamin Bell. Folks call me Buster, and this is Todd Johnson."

Charles wiped off his fingers. They shook hands.

"Charles Stevens, just got in. Hoping to get a job here and maybe settle down."

Buster and Todd exchanged a glance that Charles couldn't read.

"So, whatcha think of Czarnik's?"

Todd grinned amicably, displaying a gap between his front teeth. The twinkle in Todd's eye indicated his good sense of humor. He reminded Charles of his brother Adam.

"Great outfit," Charles said, with conviction. He turned to Buster.

"Say, how'd you get to be so fast at makin' those wieners?"

Buster shook his head modestly.

"My old man raises hogs. We have to do this every year, as a matter of fact, around this time. We call it 'hog killin'' time.

"We'd wrangle 'em, slaughter 'em, and butcher the meat for the smokehouse in one day. I must've made thousands of sausages over the past ten years. Just got a knack for it."

"You don't say?"

"You bet. We got a large family. Everyone had to find their place and talent, pull their share of the load. There was no time for wool gathering, if you know what I mean."

"If Buster's daddy was anything like mine, it was more like, 'spare the rod, spoil the chil'!'"

They chuckled. Charles imagined Buster's strength and speed had to have come out of necessity.

"Son, if you get hired, hang on to this job. Ol' Man Czarnik is tough, but fair. Most of the men workin' here are pretty good folks," Buster said, suddenly serious.

"Yeah, except for that Carl; he's a rascal," Todd said. He kept his voice low.

Buster shot Todd a glance. He scanned the area before leaning forward.

"Just keep to yourself and learn the work. You'll be fine."

They noticed that the men were cleaning up and going inside.

"He's big on promptness, too," Buster stated. "See you around."

With that, the two men quickly cleared their areas and were inside in short order.

Charles wolfed down the last bit of chicken. He repacked the pie and biscuit and followed Buster and Todd's lead.

Mr. Czarnik returned to the work area not long after lunch. He watched as Charles quickly cleared a table's meat trimmings before walking them to Buster and Todd's area. He also noticed that the men seemed to get along.

His eyes slid over to Carl, who continued at his laconic pace, unaware of Mr. Czarnik's presence. His routine was to stop and chat with friends at the meat-cutting tables.

One friend gave him a heads-up glance and motioned to where Mr. Czarnik was standing. Carl picked up his pace and continued his work.

Mr. Czarnik's jaw set. He called Charles over.

"Well, Charlie, I can see my nephew was right about you. Can you be here at six o'clock, tomorrow?

"We start at five, with the arrival of meat from the countryside—but if you can get here at that time, you'll be joining us just as the carving commences."

Charles smiled broadly.

"Yes, Mr. Czarnik. If you don't mind, I'll be here at five. Thank you for the opportunity!"

On his walk toward Aunt Lonnie's and Cousin Viola's, Charles's step was lighter than when first disembarking at the Bessemer bus depot. He was jubilant over achieving his first goal.

It was a warm autumn afternoon. The walk from downtown gave Charles time to review the events of the day.

He knew that the wages were sufficient. He'd be earning much more than what he made while working in the sawmill. However, he'd still need a boost in pay to go for his biggest goal—a house.

With property, he would begin to think about getting married and being able to provide for his wife and children.

Charles laughed at his planning so far into the future before he'd finished his first full day of work in Bessemer. It was an exciting thought.

"Thank you, Lord!"

"Hey, Charlie, wait up!"

Charles turned.

Todd was sprinting to catch up with him. He laughed and slapped his thigh.

"Boy, you a walkin' man! Yes, sir! A walkin' man! Been trying catch you for more than a couple of blocks!"

They stood directly in front of the steel mill's gate where a throng of people waited for the shift change. Todd gestured at the men.

"Who'd a thought that's where it all started for Ol' Man Czarnik?"

"You don't say!"

Charles regarded Todd with respect and surprise. This lean, young man with an easy smile also had the gift of gab.

"Yep," Todd continued. "Seems like he saw how hungry these steel mill folks can get around lunchtime and started selling the sausages wrapped in bread on a pushcart."

"The cart in the window?"

"Yep!"

They walked along sharing their pasts and home lives.

"I'm just fresh out of Tuscaloosa. But my aunt lives here, and I board with her. You need a room; she's got spares."

Charles shook his head.

"I've a cousin and an aunt here. If my Cousin Viola don't have a couple of extra rooms, my aunt will. She runs a boarding house too. My cousin's a nurse.

"None of us have seen each other in a while, but we're all family."

"You somethin' else, Charlie! Come to town and get hired the first day! Even got a place to stay!"

"Well, all I can say, Todd, is God is good!"

Todd pointed out several other landmarks and the key businesses of Bessemer. Todd then grew quiet for a few steps. Charles knew that he had something on his mind.

"What's eatin' you, Todd?"

Todd looked at him with a long face.

"Just keep an eye on that guy, Carl. He's what they call a good ol' boy, seems he's connected to some part of the Klan. Bad news."

Charles nodded.

"Seem like the Klan ain't doin' too well if they're made up with the likes of him."

Todd laughed, slapping his leg.

"You a ticket and a card, Charlie Stevens! But seriously, he ain't worth tanglin' with, if you catch my drift."

They had just crossed the train tracks when Todd pulled up.

"Well, this looks like where we part ways. But I got a question for you, Charlie—they were tellin' me about the grand opening of a new juke joint in a coupla weeks. Want to come with me to check it out?"

He winked his eye and clapped Charles on the shoulder. Charles grinned.

He thought, God is so great! He was blessing him with a new friendship, too!

"Bein' from Tuscaloosa, I'd a thought you were only lookin' at country women, Todd. You sure you want to waste your time in a citified juke joint?"

"Well, I'm not serious, yet, Charlie. Just lookin' for a little fun before going back and settle down. You know, there's gonna be lots of pretty women with lovely legs . . ."

Charles did not share with Todd that he had recently squared himself with the Lord. A juke joint didn't necessarily sound like exactly like the right place for him.

While he was searching for the right woman, Todd's pleasant invitation overrode his initial hesitation. After all, he decided, it was an opportunity to see more of the city even it happened to take him to a juke joint.

He grinned.

"Might just give it a go. I like dancing, and it wouldn't hurt to meet some local people."

Todd slapped him on the back.

"You said it! See you tomorrow!"

It was a short walk to Cousin Viola's house. Hers was a low-slung, bungalow house with a wraparound porch. The neighborhood was not as poor or shoddy as some that Charles had seen along the way.

His grandmother's niece had planted geraniums around the home in pots, and the yard was well tended. Aunt Lonnie's house, which sat on the corner, was the larger of the two homes with extra rooms added on for boarders. It, however, was in disrepair.

"Well, we'll see what's going on. Either way, I can't lose. Plus, I now have a third option!"

Charles knocked on his cousin's door.

"Cousin Viola, you here?"

The door opened.

"Hey, Charles. You sho' is a sight for sore eyes!"

Cousin Viola had an ample figure and a well-coifed hairstyle. Her nurse's uniform was still starched and crisp after a full day of work.

Not many could pull that off, Charles reflected. *She must've got some knack!*

Cousin Viola gave him a big, motherly hug. She held him back and regarded him carefully.

"You turned out to be some heartbreaker! The women here are gonna be fightin' over you, son!"

He grinned. "I don't know 'bout all that, Cousin."

Charles saw that the room was clean and neat. The sofa's cushions were worn and the curtains a bit frayed, but the house was well-appointed and homey.

The large living room had a sofa with an antimacassar draped over the back pillows and two other armchairs situated at either end of the room along with their own side tables. The coffee table had a couple of tatted doilies with pictures, knickknacks, and a candy dish filled with peppermints.

Charles picked up one.

"May I?"

Cousin Viola threw up a hand as though she were offended, then smiled.

"Of course, Cuz!"

Near the candy dish was a photo in a simple frame. Charles looked closely and recognized that it was a picture of Cousin Viola and Mama Edna. They stood stiffly, staring directly at the camera.

His brow furrowed in thought as he stared at Mama Edna. Perhaps her niece, Cousin Viola, might answer some of his questions.

"I took that picture with Aunt Edna at a church event, years ago. I had jes' turned five."

Charles grinned. "What was that, thirty-some years ago, Cousin Viola?"

She laughed, "And holding! Aunt Edna always was the strict one. She was so much older than my mama and always acted like my grandmama! That's why people called her Mama Edna."

She took Charles to his bedroom. There was a dresser and a double bed that had lamps sitting on tables on either side.

"I talked with Bert the other day. We figured we could let this be yo' room fo' the week. Then, ya'll have to board with Mama."

She gestured toward Aunt Lonnie's house.

"My sister Ida's comin' up here to look fo' a job too. I thought it's a bit safer fo' her to stay here with us."

Charles nodded. Aunt Lonnie's place catered to men, particularly those who were in and out for short stays. It provided a rough environment for women.

"The bathroom's across from us. Ya got to go anywhere early, ya best get cleaned up at night or be willing to use the cold water from the outside faucet."

"No problem." Charles set his packages down and slapped his head.

"Say, Cousin, I almost forgot. I picked up these wieners from Czarnik's. Think that this might serve as our dinner tonight?"

Cousin Viola shook her head in disbelief.

"I heard about them wieners. Heard tell they're mighty good. I think I got some beans I cooked up yesterday that'd go with 'em." Her eyes danced in anticipation.

Cousin Viola glanced out the window.

"I gotta keep an eye out for my girlfriend. She'll be by any minute with Gertrude."

She paused, choosing her words carefully. "You ain't seen Gertrude since she was a little somethin'. She's twelve now, but she ain't quite grown up in the head, if ya know what I mean. Be patient with her, Charlie. She's got a loving heart."

As Charles unpacked his suitcase, he heard someone knock on the front door. Women's voices filled with laughter and good-natured teasing mixed with that of a young girl made the house feel homey.

He knew he'd get along with Cousin Viola. Aunt Lonnie couldn't be that bad either, being her mother.

Gertrude, Viola's shy, pigtailed daughter, ate quietly while Cousin Viola and Charles shared insights on farm and city living. Every so often she would hide her beans under the rim of her plate.

Once, she looked up and caught Charles's eye, and she pretended to eat one, turning up her nose.

"Yucky!"

"You better eat ya dinner, young lady!" Cousin Viola chided, shaking her finger at the young girl.

"Now, tell me, how'd you get into Czarnik's? I curious to hear that story, 'cause I hear tell he ain't hirin' nobody. None of his people ever leave. Maybe 'cause he gives 'em the old meat products at the end of the week."

"No kidding! Nobody mentioned that to me."

Cousin Viola regarded Charles with a smile.

"You think he'd advertise free meat? No way! Just be the best worker you can and check it out. I'll gladly take ya leftovers!"

"That reminds me of the leftovers from Mama Edna I brought you all!"

Charles pulled out the pie and divided it in three pieces. They sat down and enjoyed their slices and talked family over cups of hot, Alabama coffee.

CHAPTER 19

THE COST

Not knowing what Mother's state of mind would be as I came through the door made me very nervous. How did she ever find out?

I didn't want my parents to know where I was going because I knew they would be upset. They would have told me no because they wanted me to be safe.

But safety wouldn't help me in getting my studies done without the history book. Only courage would work.

I figured that picking up that book without telling them made the task easier. That way, they wouldn't be worried about me. And I wouldn't be disobeying them. Not directly.

Matthew and Luke said that Mother told them that she'd "expected more" of me. That really hurt.

I usually followed my parents' rules. But this one-day's mission to Bessemer High School fell into what I saw as a gray area.

Also, I considered that Mother and Daddy kept saying that they wanted me to get a good education. That made getting the history book okay.

I walked through the screened-in porch, relieved that my brothers had decided to accompany Mr. Wilson back to Dunbar. I needed to get back home before them.

If Mother were going to be rough on me, I would rather take the punishment without an audience.

Mother glanced up at me from her seat at the telephone table and abruptly ended her call. That wasn't a good sign. Who was she talking to?

Her large frame seemed even more immense seated at that little table. Because the small arm that held the phone hung over the seat, Mother had to carefully extricate herself before standing up. Fully upright, she appeared big, invincible, and angry.

As children, we all knew better than to gainsay Mother. One slip of the lip, and we found ourselves on the floor, where she had slapped us down and gave us a spanking. Those memories were in the forefront of my mind.

But something was different in her expression. It confused me. I gave her a hug, as I usually did. Her body stiffened.

"Young lady," she began, looking into my eyes, "why were ya standin' on the street near that there white high school today, insteada comin' straight home aftah school been dismissed?"

I was shocked. Not only had she known where I was, she also knew that there was an early dismissal. Who told her?

I had so many questions. Who was the person on the phone? Miss Minnie? Had someone told her about Luke's fight with Clyde? How much did she know?

"Uh, I-I had a special errand to run, Mother." I tried to be adult about it. But truth be told, Mother was always ahead of the game.

"When I hear from neighbors that my chil'ren are doin' somethin' that ain't right . . ." She paused.

"It's upsettin' ta me. Go to yo' room 'til yo' Daddy gets in."

Mother looked away. Was that a tear? I didn't know why Mother would be so emotional about my stopping to get a book.

I felt compelled to tell her the entire story, at least my part of it. There was nothing to be gained by telling her about Luke. His beating up a white boy behind the school would put her over the top!

"I just wanted to pick up a history book for my studies, Mother. You and Daddy always stress how important it is to do well in school . . ."

"Jus' go to yo' room!"

I trembled as I walked to the bedroom. I hadn't even been heard!

Lying across my bed, I struggled to no avail to keep back the tears. I had not cried that hard since Sherrie Lee's funeral.

Sherrie Lee's funeral.

For the longest time, I wouldn't even allow myself say "Sherrie Lee's funeral." It made the fact that I would never see her on this side of life too final.

Everything related to her death—the ache, going to the church, all of the relatives and friends crying and offering their condolences, the exhaustion—suddenly memories came flooding back on a wave that crushed me.

As I lay there, crying, I felt very alone. Sherrie Lee and I would confide in each other at times like this. She became even more of a friend than a big sister to me that last year. Now, I had no one.

It dawned on me that for the past three years, I had tried to busy myself to keep all of those feelings at bay. I had given my extra energy to housework and getting ready for my senior year. All the activity helped to extinguish the pain.

I had seen Mother do that many times. Especially when Sherrie Lee died. Immediately, she gave each of us jobs to prepare for the funeral. No one had time to shed a tear!

What I hadn't realized was that the pain was still there, smoldering like a piece of coal. It was just waiting for something to land on it before it when up in flames.

At that point, I could do nothing to extinguish those powerful emotions!

Was it those feelings that drove me to throw myself into this mission in the first place? Was picking up the history book just another way for me to focus on something other than my heartache and loss?

There was a firm knock on the door that caused me to sit up. I hastily wiped off my tears and opened the door.

Daddy stood in front of Mother. As my parents took in my puffy eyes and tear-streaked makeup, they exchanged a glance.

Daddy wore a thoughtful expression. He put his hands in his pockets.

"I'll leave y'all to talk. Gotta get dinner on the table," was all Mother said. She briskly walked away. I could tell she was still angry with me.

"Well, Lil' Sister, ya caused ya mother a lot of worry, today. Yo brothers tol' us some of what happened with ya and that there history book. But I want to hear yo' side of the story."

I steeled myself and tried to gain composure. I took a couple of deep breaths to slow my heart's fast beating.

"Daddy, Harriet and I went to the high school and the teacher met us there. With Mr. Wilson and Harriet there, I didn't feel I was in any danger, for the most part . . ."

"Lawd knows we've drilled it into y'heads how important school is to ya future. But this is a troublesome time. We's tryin' to build ya up, honey. So's we try to protect ya from the kinda hurt we know ya pro-bly went through in that white school's office." Daddy rubbed his jaw.

"Lil' Sister, ya got to tell us ya plans. Don't go off wid out lettin' us know ya whereabouts," Daddy stated consolingly. "It's too dangerous!"

I could tell that he had given me the benefit of the doubt on my actions. Daddy still trusted me!

"Now, c'mon. Clean up and come ta dinner. But whatever ya Mother thinks is fitting punishment, I'm gonna back her on it. One hundred percent!"

Dinner was a tense production. Mother didn't speak a word to me as I helped set out the platters of food that she had had to cook without my help.

My late arrival home had thrown off her Friday plans. She mentioned to Luke that she'd had to give Thomas the responsibility of watching the children while she delivered her butter to the grocer.

"Glad to have at least one of ya older ones I can rely on!"

I didn't have much to say at the table. I ate in silence, remorseful about the distance that was growing between Mother and me.

But as the dinner stretched on, I found myself increasingly worried, panicked about Mother's punishment. What would it be?

It didn't take long to find out. I took the plates off the table, then saw her standing by, watching me, with a frown on her face.

"I'm not two minutes offa ya, young lady! Yo' Daddy seems to feel that whatcha went through in that there white school was punishment enough for going on that headstrong trip. A hard head makes a soft behind!"

It had been a long while since I'd had a spanking. Was that what Mother had decided?

"But ya gettin' too old to be goin' out and lookin' for a switch. Seems ta me ya got too much time on ya hands ta cook up schemes like this one. What it look like to me is ya need more responsibility."

That stung! I had more to do now than ever before, with Sherrie Lee gone! What other work would Mother see fit to give me?

"First of all, no more lazing around reading my romance novels. Yes, I knew ya found 'em under my bed. Well, they's off-limits now!"

How did she know? I was always so careful to put them back in the same order.

Just then I saw Thelma and Flo snickering off to one side in the dining room. When they realized I saw them, they ran away. Those rascals!

Before I could say anything in my defense, Mother went on.

"Since ya want to be makin' decisions on ya own, you's now in charge of the entire household, young lady! Want to be treated like an adult, ya get adult responsibilities!"

I had no idea what Mother meant by "entire household." I was already doing most of the housework and some of the cooking. Soon, the mystery was unveiled.

"Y'goin' to take care of yo' brothers and sisters, make sho they got they's homework done, keep the house clean, on the weekends, ya cook breakfast and supper and take care of the weekly general cleaning."

My mouth fell open as I gaped at Mother. It was so much work!

And this was my senior year! How was I ever going to handle my homework and all of that extra work, too?

"Up to now, I've been too easy on ya. When I was yo' age, I had the whole house ta take care of an' th' three of ya young chil'rens. So's now y'get a taste a'what it means to be grown and make ya own decisions! And ya better keep those grades up!"

It was a big blow. I had only wanted to get that history book. Now I was up to my neck in housework.

She tossed a dishtowel into the sink.

"Time to get started!"

With that, Mother walked out of the kitchen. I was left alone, wondering how I could manage it all.

Matthew entered with his plate and a platter.

"Well, Lil' Sister, there's a price to be paid for independence," he looked around and whispered loudly.

"We'll help you out when we're here on the weekends. Mother will settle down in a bit. You'll see."

I hugged Matthew and thanked him. He ducked his head, bashfully.

"Nothin' to thank me for. We're family!"

Luke entered the kitchen, shaking his head in empathy.

"Lil' Sister, just take it easy for a while. You know how

Mother is. You just got her goat by doin' that errand without first askin' her!"

I nodded my head. How much time Mother would need to get over my stunt was a mystery. I just hoped I could weather that time period without getting worn out with all of my new duties!

CHAPTER 20

BALONEY

The week had gone by quickly. Charles now had purpose, and things seemed to be working out for him at Czarnik's.

On Thursday, at 5:15 a.m. sharp, Charles and the other workers had suited up. They were putting on their aprons and hats when Mr. Czarnik walked in.

Mr. Czarnik gazed around the locker room with a twinkle in his eye. He rocked back and forth from the balls of his feet to his heels.

Buster and Todd exchanged glances. Todd nudged Charles, motioning to Buster.

Buster gave a wink and said in a low voice, "That's how Ol' Man Czarnik looks when he's got a new idea. Kinda like the cat that swallowed the canary!"

Todd grinned. "It usually means a whole lot o' work, too!"

"Always with a new project, a new, *hard* project!"

Charles wondered if his new friends were right. He liked challenges.

He felt good about working beside them, especially Buster, with his years of experience. Buster had wisdom and patience. Also, he was a good teacher.

Charles wondered if this new assignment might help put him on the same playing field with the other men. It might improve his stature with Mr. Czarnik, and maybe insure his position with the company.

"Okay, fellows," Mr. Czarnik gazed around joyfully, "today we're going to make a new meat product."

When no one asked any questions, he launched ahead.

"It's bologna! Or baloney, as most of the meat packers I know call it!"

The men exchanged looks of interest mixed with caution. Charles figured they were feeling overwhelmed in light of the busy schedule many were already handling. Mr. Czarnik saw to it that his employees were not idle for a moment.

"It first came from Bologna, Italy. The Italians had what they called mortadella. But when we got it, we added garlic, of course. Good for the blood!"

He thumped his chest and received some mixed expressions, from blank to slightly amused.

He nodded. "Well, now! Maybe this doesn't translate in discussion. You still don't know what I'm asking you to make. So, come this way."

Mr. Czarnik motioned for them to follow him into the store. Visiting the front counters was a treat for many of the men.

At six o'clock, the store was empty and looked immense. The meat counter was packed with delicious looking cuts of meat and sausages, just as Charles remembered from his first visit.

He inhaled the greasy, aromatic spiciness of the mixture of sausages and aged cheeses. Even though he had eaten a leftover piece of cornbread for breakfast with his coffee, Charles's stomach began to growl.

Mr. Czarnik stopped by a large sausage in a shiny, red casing. He pulled it out and set it on the cutting board.

"This, gentlemen, is baloney!"

There was a low murmuring at the size of this particular sausage. Mr. Czarnik sliced it into ten thick slices and proceeded to cut them into pie-shaped wedges.

He carefully arranged them on an enameled, tin platter emblazoned with Uncle Sam that read, "I Want You!"

The wizened old man wearing a tall, Lincolnesque hat with a shock of white hair and goatee seemed to point his finger at anyone who latched onto his gaze.

As the men passed the tray around the assembled group, Charles caught himself smiling.

Looks like nobody's escapin' ol' Uncle Sam, he thought.

The sounds of men chewing filled the quiet room. Charles savored his piece, chewing it slowly. It was difficult to discern what it reminded him of, but he enjoyed the texture.

Someone finally broke the silence.

"Could I have another piece to check that flavor out, sir?"

Laughter filled the room as one after another, the men asked for seconds. Soon there were more than a few comments on the tastiness of the new meat product.

Mr. Czarnik sat on one of the stools, basking in their interest and enjoyment of the baloney. He took a slice and munched on it himself.

Soon, he cleared his throat. The room became quiet.

"Okay, my friends. Enough of the tasting! We've got to get this big sausage into production!

"I don't know about you boys, but I'm trying to do my part in helping our country. It looks to me like we're at the beginning of a war effort. If I can keep prices down at the table and take care of a hungry family, we all win. This meat is priced at seventeen cents a pound!"

They murmured among themselves. The war. That was a disturbing thought.

Charles's mind, however, was fixed on the baloney production. He wondered how it would be handled, stored, and eaten.

They were still feeling the effects of the Depression, after all. Who would be able to keep this meat when only a few people could afford refrigerators?

Would a thick slice of it be served up with potatoes like a steak, or would they eat it with eggs for breakfast? Both choices demanded a lot of pieces, and the pound of meat would go quickly. Perhaps mixing it with other vegetables would stretch it out?

There were so many questions on his mind, Charles found himself speaking up.

"But, sir, how are they going to keep this meat from going bad? And how will a family be able to stretch it out to keep their budgets low? As good as it tastes, at seventeen cents, one pound may not be enough for a family for more than a couple of days."

Charles's coworkers stared at him. It was one thing to have a question, but quite another to gainsay the boss!

"Uppidy ni--" someone whispered.

Charles felt the hairs on the back of his neck rise. His upbringing and experience commanded that he ignore the comment.

He hadn't seen his question as impudence or his speaking out of place. He simply wanted to know how this meat would help families. It was a good question, to him, especially during the country's financial fallow period.

Buster did all he could to cover his broad smile. When he saw that Todd was equally amused, he poked him. Todd let out a little wheeze that he covered with a cough.

Charles saw none of their humor. He was deep in thought, calculating the costs and reviewing the variables as his father had taught him regarding their crop production.

"I mean, it takes up a lot of space, and many folks I know don't have ice boxes."

It was as though the air had been sucked out of the room. Mr. Czarnik stared at Charles too. But, unlike the others, he wore a wry smile.

"Fancy that! We have a thinker in our company!"

He clapped Charles on the back and laughed. The tension was gone.

"First of all, this meat don't require much refrigeration, son. It's kept like the sausages because it's smoked and cured.

"As for your second question . . . oh, one moment!" Mr. Czarnik held up a finger.

He walked around the counter to the bread bin near the register. At times, a customer asked for a sandwich, which Mr. Czarnik was happy to sell for an additional nickel.

Slicing a couple of pieces of bread, Mr. Czarnik slathered both slices with a lot of mayonnaise. He topped one slice with a new, thinly cut piece of baloney.

Putting the other slice of bread on top, Mr. Czarnik cut the sandwich in two and handed one half to Charles. He nodded for Charles to take a bite.

Charles chewed the sandwich. A big grin spread across his face. Mr. Czarnik had answered both questions with one example. He nodded with new understanding.

"Yes! This would certainly work!"

"You're darn certain about that, Charlie?"

Mr. Czarnik laughed and cut up the rest of the sandwich into small pieces to pass around.

Charles broke his half into to three pieces and passed one each to Buster and Todd. The men's eyes grew large as they appreciatively ate their samples of the sandwich.

"So you see? Families can store this meat easily—along with their eggs in a cool spot. Make bread and baloney sandwiches for the entire family for a week or more with just a pound of meat!"

Mr. Czarnik saw he had everyone's attention. He waved his hands toward the rear of the store.

"And this is the best part! We've already got most of the ingredients! Just need some spices, garlic, and sugar.

"This meat is going to be made from our scraps—the stuff we've been throwing away!"

Buster held up his hand.

"Now, Mr. Czarnik, which scraps are you talkin' about? 'Cause we don't have nary one piece of meat that's thrown away!"

Buster was very proud of his cost-reduction policies. He kept the men who worked on his sausages under sharp scrutiny. He would rove around the tables when he stretched his legs. No one got away with leaving anything on the tables without the meat coming to him for sausages.

"You are very right, Buster!" Mr. Czarnik nodded and grinned as though he had a big secret that he couldn't wait to tell.

"This meat will be made out of everything we've been throwing away—the non-meat products! The tripe, the lips, the stomach of the pig, and we'll mix it with the leftover pieces of pork I'll get from the pens! They're pretty much giving it to me for three-quarters of a penny a pound! And, get this—they're so happy to get rid of it, they'll even bring it to us!"

They all laughed at the irony of this venture. "I'm making money from what no one wants! You see? I'm creating a delicious new meat for almost nothing, which means you men will benefit—when Czarnik's grows, you grow with me!"

The men murmured in excitement. Charles nodded. He knew his instincts were right. He stepped forward.

"Mr. Czarnik, I'd like to learn how to make this baloney!"

Two others stepped forward. One of the men was Carl Westharden, the older man who had been less than eager to have Charles share his job of collecting scraps. The other was a young man, Charles's age, with curly, bright yellow hair.

Carl cut Charles a look that was pure venom. It was as if he meant to chide Charles for taking the initiative for stepping up. Charles knew instantly who had made the evil comment earlier in the meeting.

Charles ignored Carl's bitter expression. Once again, Dr. Carver's words came back to him: *"Fear of something is at the root of hatred for others, and hate within will eventually destroy the hater."*

He figured that whatever Carl was afraid of was his own problem. Instead of Carl, Charles chose to concentrate on Mr. Czarnik.

"Thank you! This is a small experiment to see if we have a good product, so your time and commitment is truly appreciated!"

He looked over the three men and pointed to Carl.

"Carl, I'll make you my lead baloney maker. You know the meat-packing business inside and out. I want you to be the quality control."

Carl looked as though he had been handed the Medal of Honor. He gave everyone a nod, seeking acknowledgment.

Mr. Czarnik turned to Charles and the other young man.

"You two are going to shadow Carl on the making of the baloney, gather the meat that comes in from the stockyard and make sure that the meats that would otherwise be thrown out are retained and put in our baloney bin." Mr. Czarnik glanced at his watch fob.

It was 5:30 a.m. He cleared his throat and motioned at the clock.

"Okay, everyone, no such thing as a free lunch—get to work! You three, come with me!"

Buster rested his hand on Charles's shoulder for the briefest of moments. It was his way of saying "Atta boy!"

With a spring in his step, Charles followed Carl, the other man and Mr. Czarnik into a room that contained floor to ceiling boxes and one big tub.

"I need this room for the baloney—move this other material into the back of the building and clean it up, top to bottom. No dust or hairs anywhere. I want this tub to be clean enough for someone to eat out of it." Chuckling at his joke, Mr. Czarnik left the room.

CHAPTER 21

AUNT THELMA'S HELP

My life changed drastically from that moment on. Mother 'put her foot down' on how my days were to be ordered from the moment of that kitchen conversation. As expected, the workload bellowed.

I had already been taking care of my brothers and sisters while Mother took her orders for the laundry that she did with Big Mama Dee. It was my weekends that changed entirely.

Usually, after breakfast, I had had time for myself. I would either practice with new makeup, try different hairstyles, or mend my clothes. After ironing the clothes for extra money, I could go down to the Branch to read. Sometimes, I have to admit, my reading included Mother's romance magazines.

Now I had all of the responsibilities that Sherrie Lee had and more! Besides the preparation of the weekend breakfasts, I was in charge of cleaning the house for Sunday. I also had to cook our Sunday dinners!

Sundays were busy days for our family. Mother would have the minister over for dinner, so the house had to be in apple-pie order. She created a list of things for me to do, just to make sure I didn't forget a detail.

I had to take all of the linen off the beds and wash and hang them out to dry, clean the cobwebs down from the ceiling, dust furniture, clean and wax the floors, and make sure that the table linens were in good order for the Sunday dinner.

The first weekend was a disaster. Mother found fault with the linens—they weren't bright enough.

"Didcha use my brightener? Lye soap ain't enough all the time."

My floors were too dull.

"Lil' Sister, didn't I learn ya how to mop and wax? Didcha ever watch how I did it, chil', or were you wool gatherin'?"

And the dinner I cooked for the minister was awful. The only salvation from that meal I thought was the chicken that Daddy cooked. My greens were not cooked as thoroughly as Mother's and my mashed potatoes were lumpy.

Before he arrived, Mother rescued the meal by putting the greens back on the stove and whipping the potatoes with more butter and cream, muttering all the while about how I had to get my feet on the ground and my head out of the clouds.

That second Saturday, as I prepared biscuits for breakfast, I was in the dumps. How in the world was I going to accomplish all that Mother had written out for me to her level of perfection?

That's when my prayer was answered. A light knock at the door was followed by my Aunt Thelma's surprise arrival.

"Honey, I heard about what went on. You's got a heap of work ahead of ya! Funny thing that I got an extra bit o' time today," Aunt Thelma leaned on the counter. Her broad, toffee-colored face bore a smile that was infectious.

My aunt was younger than Mother by twelve years. She was my favorite aunt and, it seemed, she took a liking to me. That day in particular, I was very grateful for her visit.

"What do you mean, Aunt Thelma? I thought you worked long hours with Banker Lewis on the weekends."

She chuckled, causing her full figure to bounce in ripples.

"Well, honey, I tol' 'em I got a special project, this af'ta noon. One of my relatives had run into a bit o' trouble and I had to help 'em out."

My eyes flew wide open in excitement.

"You meant me? Oh, Aunt Thelma!"

I gave her a big hug. Tears of gratitude flowed down my cheeks.

"Now, now, chil' It ain't no big thang! Ya gots the basics, I'm just here to show ya how to pull it all together."

She motioned at my salt pork. I had completely forgotten it. The edges were getting too crispy. I had to yank the pan off the fire.

Wiping my hands on my apron, I took an extra tea towel to wipe my eyes. I was overcome with emotion. The Lord was certainly watching over me!

I must have been so downhearted that it showed up in my expression and demeanor. The day after Mother's "sentence," Harriet had become anxious about my new, quiet nature.

"What's wrong, Dee Dee? Why are you so sad?"

I didn't have the heart to tell her about my punishment. As she had been my partner in the venture, it would only make her feel responsible for the situation.

"Just a little tired these days, Harriet. You know, that time of the month." I feigned a smile and patted her on the shoulder.

"But we've got everyone talking in history class! Did you see how big their eyes got when Mr. Wilson pulled out that stack of books?"

Harriet had grinned broadly.

"And it's our secret! I feel like one of God's angels, visiting Peter at night and letting him out of prison!"

She strutted around with her hands tucked under her armpits.

"Aren't we the best? I'm almost bursting at the seams to tell someone!"

"Tell them what?"

We both jumped. Cleophus, Penny Head, had snuck up on us and was peering over our shoulders.

Could it have been only seven years earlier that Aunt Thelma had staged that Tom Thumb Wedding? What led me to believe that the event would be a lark?

Against my best efforts, I felt myself dreading the times he appeared. He wanted to pursue a relationship, hoping what began with our fake wedding would blossom into a real romance.

Did Penny Head really believe that I would someday be his wife? For real?

"Oh, nothing, Cleophus. We're just excited about getting our history books. Can't imagine what information Mr. Wilson is going to present this year now that we have those books. Every day feels like something new . . ."

"But I thought I heard Harriet say she wanted to tell someone something . . ."

I gave him credit for being persistent. Harriet shot a scared look at me. She wasn't good at lying, not that I was any better at it. We just exchanged a worried glance.

"Well . . ." I began.

Somehow, at that very moment, our lack of guile seemed ridiculous. It was so silly to be trying to keep our secret from Penny Head, of all people.

I burst out laughing, which caught Harriet by surprise. Then, she started laughing too.

Penny Head stood there gaping at us with a confused look on his face. His perplexed expression became one of concern.

Bill White appeared and clamped a hand on Penny Head's shoulder.

"So, Cleophus, what did you say to get these young ladies all worked up? Let me in on the joke!"

By this time, Harriet and I had tears pouring down our cheeks. She happened to look up at the hallway clock and gasped.

"We . . . we better get going! We'll be late!"

I smiled at Bill and said, "We'll have to share it with you later!"

We walked as fast as we could to get into our sewing class. Still giggling, it was a miracle that we got there in time.

Yes, Aunt Thelma's offer to help was a huge blessing. I hugged her, believing that my life as a senior would return, once again, and be a happy event.

This reward came after a horrible week of labor, toil, and criticism. I had certainly paid for not being on Mother's good side.

"Now, chil', I gots to go, but when I get back around one, we'll knock this housework out of the park!"

"Will you show me how to make the potatoes like Mother? I have to admit, Aunt Thelma, I didn't watch her very closely when she was cooking."

"Honey, yo, mama don't show nobody what she does in the kitchen! Ya notice she shoos y'all out befo' she starts? She's a peculiar woman, that sistah of mine!"

Thinking back, Mother was very secretive about what she did in her kitchen. She would even have the work area spotlessly clean after she'd finished cooking her delicious meals. This was something that Sherrie Lee and I had always thought magical!

With a new attitude of hope, I got the children squared away for the afternoon. I wanted to focus on whatever Aunt Thelma wanted to share about housecleaning.

Aunt Thelma arrived as planned at 1:00 p.m.

"Bring those chillens in here, Lil' Sistah! They got hands and feet, put 'em to work too! That's how y'all be able to get this work done and get some time fo' yoself afore yo mama gets in here!"

We started as soon as Aunt Thelma hung up her hat and coat. She put her purse on the telephone table and rolled up her sleeves. It was comforting, and even a little exciting, to be in her company.

First, she started with dinner. Aunt Thelma explained that the vegetables could be simmering while the bread cooked. She was quick to add that these things needed constant attention, so we'd have to peek in on them every so often.

The meat was the last thing to cook. Today we had pork chops. Aunt Thelma promised to not only show me how she made her mashed potatoes, she'd also demonstrate how to make her delicious white gravy.

Aunt Thelma smiled when she saw that I had already taken down and washed the lace curtains in the living room and dining room. Laundering them on the galvanized scrub board would have torn them, so Tommy showed Junior and our sisters how to suds and rinse the curtains by hand.

Tommy and I hung them on the nails Mother had pounded into the sides of the house, between the windows, so they could be stretched as they dried. We started at ten, so they were almost ready to take down given the hot afternoon sunlight.

The little ones dusted the cobwebs down from the corners of each room with a rag tied around a broom. They even dusted behind the chiveraux, Mother's favorite chest for linens.

Aunt Thelma gave each brother and sister a cloth and had them dust the baseboards while she prepared the floor for its wipe down. She told me to damp mop the wooden floor while she used a bit of lye soap in hot water for the linoleum in the kitchen.

The floor polish was from a tin of wax that had to be rubbed into the wood with some "elbow grease." We did this together in little circles (it required a lot of energy) until we covered the entire living room and dining room. It took the two of us about thirty minutes.

We tied old cotton sacks on my brothers' and sisters' feet and let them skate along the floor to buff off the extra wax product. After their skating game, the floors glowed with a sheen I sure hadn't been able to achieve!

While they polished the furniture, Aunt Thelma and I set the curtains up for my ironing.

In the kitchen, we checked the Roosevelt clock over the door. It was 3:30 p.m.

"Okay, honey. Got to pop into check on yo' uncle, but you get the poke chops goin' and I'll be back in a half an' hour."

"Thank you so much, Aunt Thelma!"

"We ain't done yet! Yo' mama'll be in at 5:00 p.m. and yo' Daddy is soon to be in afta that! Dinner's got to be on the table by 4:45!"

I started dusting the pork chops with the seasoning we'd made up earlier. They had to rest after cooking, so I planned to get them going at 3:45.

The potatoes were cooking away while I lightly fried the pork chops as I was instructed when Aunt Thelma returned.

"Okay, chil', let's get the gravy started."

By 4:30, I had ironed the tablecloth and was ironing the edges of the last of the lace panels. Tommy and I hung them together. I gave him a big hug of appreciation for all of his hard work.

"Hey, we family! We got to stick together!"

I nodded as I looked around in amazement at how nice the house looked. Aunt Thelma grinned at my expression.

"Now, the best thing is ya bein' here on y'own when y'mama walks in that door! I gots to run. See ya' later, baby!"

Mother was thoroughly surprised when she walked in the door. She stared at the food on the stove, the children dressed and clean and the house, spotless.

Glancing over at the coatrack, she noticed Aunt Thelma's hat. A slow smile spread over her face.

"Best help anyone can find, that sistah of mine!"

Mother patted me on the back. Even though she knew Aunt Thelma had helped, Mother could see that I was trying my best.

"Good job, Dee Dee! Now, let's get the dishes down fo' supper afore ya daddy walks in."

CHAPTER 22

ALL IN A DAY'S WORK

"You heard Mr. Czarnik, get to work!" Carl yelled. With his hands on his hips, he stared angrily at Charles. He motioned to the other man too and gestured for him to join Charles in moving boxes.

Charles laid his apron and hat to one side and started right in. He began by pulling the crates and boxes off the shelves and carrying them out of the storage room to the rear of the building. The other man followed suit.

They continued to make progress. But it was easy to see that Carl felt he did not need to work alongside them.

Periodically, he would bark out orders and scathing remarks at the men, aiming most of his comments at Charles.

"Hey, boy, get your lazy ass over there and get another box. Cain't you pick up two of them boxes at once? Y'all act like you haulin' concrete in your shoes! Slowerin' molasses in December!"

Out of earshot, the other man turned to Charles.

"Hey, I'm Mike."

The two men shook hands.

"I'm Charlie," Charles said, continuing to work.

"Nice meetin' ya!"

They hefted the boxes off of their shoulders and returned to the storage room.

By this time, they had carried most of the loads out of the room. On their way to the baloney room, Mike clapped Charles on the back.

"You're sho-nuff a hard worker, Charlie."

He nodded his head in the direction of the baloney room.

"You'd think he was the boss and Old Man Czarniks' worker, the way he's carrying on over there!"

"Looks to me like he's never had much authority. Let 'em have his fun. I'm just happy to be workin'."

Mike stared at Charles, not sure of what to make of his comment. After a moment, he grinned.

"I've got to bring back some dough to my old lady. We got two hungry mouths at home to feed and one on the way!"

Charles turned to Mike, taking in what he said. The young man looked no older than himself. Charles wondered how he was able to manage on the money they were being paid by Czarnik.

Earlier, Buster told him that the white workers got paid more for doing the same job as the colored men. He said not to let that bother him because he had become a valuable worker and was paid a supervisor's wage.

"Few people know it, Charlie, but I'm paid more than most of the white workers," he confided.

Over the years, Felix Czarnik knew he could place his trust in Buster. During that first week, Buster told Charles that Mr. Czarnik was looking for more good men.

"If you put in more than one hundred percent effort and play your cards right, you'll move up just fine. Old Man Czarnik is fair when it comes to payin' good workers, Charlie."

Charles saw this was the key to getting better pay. He became more determined in his work. From that moment on, Charles decided that he would "find a way or make a way" to increase his pay.

I've got to work harder and maybe Czarnik will give me an extra shift. Make my work a showcase of potential, he thought. While it's a good start, ain't no way I can support a family on this salary.

By noon, the storage room and big tub were clean. Carl brought Mr. Czarnik in.

"Y'see? We got this ready for your baloney makings, boss!" Carl proudly announced.

Mr. Czarnik took a long look around the room. He ran a gloved finger over the inside of the tub. Finally, he nodded in satisfaction.

"Okay! During everyone's lunch, we need to load Buster's meat grinder with the other meat parts. We just had a delivery from the stockyard along with the pieces the men collected from our operation."

He indicated three large wooden boxes that green flies had begun swarming. The bloody canvas bags inside of the boxes were filled to the brim with pork cuttings.

"When this tub is half-way filled with the mash, I'll show you boys how we're going to make it into baloney. But right now, you need to get a tutorial from Buster." Mr. Czarnik motioned for them to pick up the boxes and follow him to the back room.

Unable to escape notice, Carl picked up one of the boxes along with Charles and Mike. Trailing behind Carl, Mike dug an elbow into Charles's side. Charles had to struggle to keep a straight face.

"I'll leave them in your capable hands, Buster," said Mr. Czarnik. He immediately returned to the store.

Buster was in the process of cleaning up the grinder before his lunch break. He handed that job over to Todd and became very businesslike in his presentation.

He proceeded to give a point-by-point lecture on the parts and use of the machine.

"So ya see, turning the toggle this way turns it on, and you turn it off by flipping the switch the other way. And remember, once the filled bin gets down to this level, you gonna have ta turn it off and add more product."

When Buster and Todd left for lunch, Carl put his foot on one of the boxes. He slowly looked around the warehouse.

A couple of the men from the butchering section waved at him to come and join them. Carl glanced up at the clock. It was twelve noon.

"I think Old Man Czarnik forgot we have ta eat lunch at this time too. Tell you what. I'll let you fellers off so we can all get our lunches and start right back afterwards."

Charles and Mike exchanged a glance as Carl walked toward the locker room.

Mike turned to Charles.

"Well? I am getting' hungry, how 'bout you, Charlie?"

Charles watched Carl's retreating back. He took in the time, too. He shook his head.

"Naw, I 'spect I'd better stay, Mike. I think Mr. Czarnik knew exactly what he was doin' when he said to grind this meat now.

"We only got forty-five minutes. Before long, Buster and Todd'll be back in here. Buster's got to clean the head of this meat grinder before he can get back to work, too. In fact, he might even be back in here fifteen minutes earlier."

With that, Charles picked up his box and began shoveling the meat into the grinder. One box's contents fit neatly into the large trough where pig remnants had been earlier.

They powered up the machine and pushed the meat through the grinder, fat and gristle and all. The bloody canvas box received the mash perfectly.

They had begun loading the third box when Carl reappeared. His eyes widened and were fixed on the mash as it poured out of the grinder into the last box.

"You boys did all this on your own?"

Mike and Charles gazed at him, unable to reply to his question. It was obvious that they had continued working throughout their lunchtime.

At that moment, Mr. Czarnik appeared. He spied Charles and Mike in their work aprons, hats, and gloves.

Then he turned and took a long look at Carl, who was frozen in the doorway with a toothpick stuck between his teeth. He rolled it around his mouth nervously.

Mr. Czarnik's jaw was clenched. He controlled his tone, but his voice was extra quiet.

"Carl, I need to see you in my office."

Charles and Mike grappled the last bin filled with pig bits and pieces. As they pushed the scraps through the grinder and into the trough, Mike turned to Charles.

"Hate to be in his shoes! Thanks for not going to lunch, Charlie—I'da been in a tough place, just like Carl, and I can't afford any mistakes!"

Charles nodded his head.

"None of us can, Mike."

Charles said a silent prayer for his father's lessons. He had always taught them to do the right thing, no matter how much it hurt. He was thankful that he and his brothers and sister had listened to Ben's pearls of wisdom.

That evening, over slices of homemade apple pie and cups of hot coffee, Cousin Viola laughed at the predicament Carl found himself in.

"Brought it on hisself, he sure did! Such a sorry lot, some folk are. They don't get that this Depression thing is as for real! It's as real as the nose on our faces! Too many people out there without jobs!"

The homey atmosphere of the kitchen and the good food was relaxing to Charles. But while he felt at home with Cousin Viola, he wondered if this were too soon to ask her about Mama Edna. What was the reason for her mistreatment of Lula?

Cousin Viola observed Charles's tense jaw. She poked Gertrude and nodded her head at the clock.

Giving Gertrude a stern look, she said, "Young lady, time you went to bed. Go on, now. And I don't want to hear no ifs, ands, or buts about it!"

Gertrude reluctantly scooted her chair back. When its wooden legs shrieked against the linoleum floor, she hunched her shoulders at the sound. Stealing a glance at her mother confirmed her suspicions.

Cousin Viola gave Gertrude another look. Gertrude politely stood, picked up the chair and placed it under the table.

Gertrude was rewarded by a big smile and hug from her mother. But, when she turned toward Charles, the young girl hesitated.

Charles stuck out his hand and she shook it. He grinned.

"Nice eating with you, Gertrude. Guess I'll be seeing you in the morning?"

Gertrude nodded shyly and ran out of the room.

Cousin Viola began cleaning up the dishes. Charles tried to help, but Viola shook her head and topped off his coffee.

"You got somethin' on your mind, don'cha, Charlie? Go on and out with it! Y'know, I had to get the young'un out from underfoot before we could have some grown-up talk!"

Charles gripped his blue speckled mug for a beat. After finishing the last of his coffee, he eased his grip.

He wasn't sure if it was too early to strike up a conversation with Cousin Viola about his visit to the home and his mother's condition. There were too many unresolved parts of the story. Too many raw emotions.

He wondered if he would be able to share Aunt Nellie's account or his own memories. And if he did, what would it all accomplish?

Charles's reservations made him decide to keep his own counsel.

"Nothin' that won't keep, Cousin Viola."

Cousin Viola gave him a wistful glance.

"Y'know, Charlie, Bert's goin' to be back tomorrah with my sister. He picked Ida up to bring her back down here to look for that job I mentioned."

Charles nodded. It reminded him that he was to seek a room at Aunt Lonnie's house. In the wake of getting the new job and the new responsibility of baloney making, it had slipped his mind.

"I'll get right on it, Cousin Viola," he began.

"No need. I spoke to mama this afternoon. She's got a room for ya. She's expectin' you tomorrah. If you could have yo' things ready before you go to work, that'll help me out a big deal, Charlie."

"That's fair enough, Cousin Viola. I truly appreciate your lettin' me stay over."

Cousin Viola squeezed Charles's hand and topped his mug off with more coffee.

"My girlfriend and I, well, we was talkin' aboutcha. Your ears musta been burnin'!"

Charles looked up from his coffee in surprise.

"What about?"

"Y'know, we been thinking. A young man in this new city, alone . . ."

She tapped Charles on the shoulder.

"Ain't ya 'bout ready to meet some nice young woman? Well, she got a niece who's as pretty as a movie star. She's not seein' anyone, either."

"Thanks, Cousin Viola." Charles smiled, happy that the conversation had taken another turn.

"To tell you the truth, my new friend Todd wants to go to the juke joint next Saturday. Bound to be some nice

Bessemer girls there. It's the grand reopening!"

Cousin Viola shook her head.

"Boy, ya cain't find no nice girl in a juke joint! Ya got to go to church. And this girl is real cute, her name is—"

Charles put up a hand to stop her.

"Cousin, no offense, but I got to do this on my own."

Cousin Viola immediately gave him a mysterious smile.

"Okay, now. Doncha be comin' back lookin' for my advice on how ta introduce ya to her. Won't stick my nose in this anymore.

"Ya said it, Charlie. It's yo' ball game!"

CHAPTER 23

SOUL CHOICES

I loved going to church ever since I was a little girl. My earliest memories of Sundays actually started on Saturday. That's when I would take a bath and Mother would powder me up with cornstarch.

Our hot summers were sure to make us sweat so much that Mother wanted to make certain we stayed dry and fresh. After the bath, Sherrie Lee and I'd climb into our "cloud" bed and lull ourselves to sleep by softly singing one of the songs we had learned in the children's choir.

On Sunday morning, I'd sit next to Mother wearing one of the beautiful, freshly pressed dresses she had made. All of us were taught, by threat of a pinch or a spanking, to sit still and listen intently to the pastor.

However, as I got older, I found myself leaning forward and into those sermons. And not only because the intense Alabama heat made the back of my outfit stick to the highly-shellacked pew—I sat on the edge of my seat to hear Pastor Marshall's sermon.

In those early days, Pastor Marshall had a lot to say about living a life of peace and purpose. Especially during those tough times. His words calmed my spirit.

Many times, Pastor had said that we should "hunger and thirst" for the words of truth.

Since Sherrie Lee died, I had become wrapped up in the pain of loss. In a way, those words of the pastor had to go through extra tunnels to make it into my heart.

I heard him, but the scriptures didn't seem to be working. They didn't ease my pain.

I decided to bury the pain, to ignore it. I didn't know, in some ways, I was also burying my blessings.

My belief in and love of the Lord was still there. I knew deep in my heart that someday I would be able to deal with the pain, that one day my heart would soften. This knowledge kept me from giving up.

Big Mama Dee taught me about having patience. Although she was the first to admit that patience wasn't her virtue, she always reminded us that no matter what our faults were to keep our eyes on Jesus.

"He's the author and finisher of our faith. I jes' hope you chilluns are listenin' to what Pastor Marshall is sayin' on Sundays! You cain't go wrong with the Word of God!"

Saturday mornings were special to me because I got to spend time with Big Mama Dee. It was just she and I alone at the Branch. It was our together time.

Big Mama Dee would share her faith as well as her great knowledge of herbs and berries that could heal many illnesses. The gurgling of the waters lapping around the mossy stones and robin calls made background music for her teachings.

"Y'see, the good Lawd gave us all of these things to heal our bodies wid," she would say as she offered me a cluster of elderberries.

Munching on them, I would prance around barefoot on the grassy banks of the creek. I loved the beauty of our surroundings and the feeling of the earth under my feet.

I'd hunt for poke greens and dandelion leaves for our dinner under Big Mama Dee's watchful eye. She had me help her collect the rosemary, sage, and mint to replenish her medicinal cabinet.

"God can heal anythin', if'n ya give 'im time. 'Cause time heals all wounds, chil'," Big Mama Dee told me.

Now, in my senior year, I felt her statement was true.

The Sunday after Aunt Thelma helped me with the housework, I felt a great amount of excitement about going to church. I thought it was odd, but there was a change in my heart. I hadn't felt that way for such a long time.

When Mother had wanted me to get the Sunday dinner on the table, this time, I took it as a challenge.

I had planned every dish to perfection. I even stayed up the night before to prepare some of the vegetables.

My challenge was to start out this week with a great attitude and stylish look! I would have dinner ready for the table and be dressed to the hilt. This Sunday would be different from that first, miserable week.

I planned to go to church with my old expectancy and excitement. I was determined to relive the wonder and joy that I had as a child.

I had hope.

I knew it was from Aunt Thelma's visit. She not only gave me hope, she fueled me with extra energy to do my best.

"Young lady, when youse gets hitched, ya gonna havta take care of a household by yaself," she added, "and with some chilluns holdin' onto ya skirt! Ya got ta use this as practice!"

I had never thought of this time of my life as a practice run. But it made a lot of sense.

All this time I had been pining for my prince, and I wasn't even ready for him! I chuckled as I cut up the potatoes.

I'd be a sorry princess if I couldn't uphold my part of the bargain, I thought.

Daddy's routine was to stay home during Bible class to take care of the last few dishes for our Sunday meal. He would fry the chicken that he'd dusted the night before.

I had made a double portion of biscuits for breakfast and would just make up my hot water cornbread after church, if it were needed. That left me with the mashed potatoes and gravy.

Aunt Thelma's recipe and steps were seared in my brain. It was going to be a great dinner for our minister.

After breakfast, I helped get my sisters dress and had just enough time to arrange my hairstyle. I couldn't believe how something as simple as taking a bath the night before and putting on my makeup before breakfast shaved off so much time!

Even Mother was surprised when I walked out of the bedroom, bandbox fresh. I had chosen to wear my blue serge dress with the white collar and cuffs she had made for me the year before.

"Lookin' good, Lil' Sister!"

I turned in surprise. Tommy was nodding appreciatively at my style. Giving him a hug, I noticed that even though he was fourteen, he was as tall as me. I laughed.

"I bet you say that to all of the girls!"

He ducked his head, embarrassed, and ran outside.

Florence brought little Mae out. The girls always wanted to be the first to take her hand and walk her to church.

Usually, any of the girls would suffice. But this time, Mae squirmed and held out a hand for me.

I had to blink back tears. My heart melted. How lovely it would have been to have Sherrie Lee there to see how much her little baby had grown!

"'Seek ye first the Kingdom of God and His righteousness and all these things shall be added unto you!'"

Pastor Marshall stretched out his arms, motioning to the organist. She played a chord that emphasized his words.

"Ya see, church, this here is your foundation, the only promise that you have or need." He chuckled and surveyed the auditorium.

"Now, Jesus says you have to 'hunger and thirst for righteousness.' How is that seen in our lives? By doing the first things first. What was that, church?"

Pastor Marshall looked anxiously around. The fans were going like nobody's business in that hot building.

"Seek the Kingdom!"

Pastor smiled broadly as he dabbed his face. He nodded at the parishoner's proclamation.

"That's right, 'Seek ye first the Kingdom of God.'"

"Now, 'first' don't mean tomorrow, or after you get ya husband, young ladies!"

I felt my face flush. Was he looking straight at me?

Was I really seeking God's kingdom first? What did that mean for me at this time in my life?

It struck me, right then and there, that maybe that was my problem—I hadn't been seeking God's kingdom first! Maybe that was the cure for healing my sadness in losing Sherrie Lee.

Maybe it was time that I did more in my church service. I'd try out for the choir!

Aunt Thelma had been asking me to get involved again. She played every other Sunday and said she missed hearing my soprano voice.

At first, starting high school made me wonder if I'd ever have time. Was this something that I could do now?

I panicked. That couldn't be the answer! I had so many new responsibilities.

The thought had come to me so fast, it had to be what the Lord wanted me to do. Was the Holy Spirit talking to me?

Big Mama Dee said she always listened to God. When we were together at the Branch, she taught me about how she allowed God direct her life.

"It's a 'still small voice,' baby. Yous mighta been doin' somethin' o' thinkin' about somethin' else, then bang!"

She clapped her hands to emphasize this change.

"He comes up on ya and tells ya somethin' diff'rent!"

Big Mama Dee leaned over to me and whispered, "But, baby, ya gots to trust Him. Tha's the first thing."

Straightening up, she pointed at the sky.

"Second thing, ya gots to obey!"

At that time, it seemed that doing God's will took extra effort. But singing wasn't work for me. It was fun.

Just as I was thinking that I should talk with Mother about this, because choir rehearsal was on Saturday evenings, I heard Big Mama Dee's voice in my head again.

"Once the Lawd tells ya somethin', don't go 'round askin' every Tom, Dick, and Harry if ya should do it. Tha's between you and the Lawd, baby! Ya just get yo butt out there and do it!"

That did it for me. I had to just do it. But how, when?

Sunday supper went off without a hitch. Even Pastor Marshall complimented Mother on how tasty her mashed potatoes were.

Matthew and Luke had made it down from Tuskegee and the Methodist Seminary to join us for dinner. They had planned to come on Saturday, but couldn't coordinate their rides.

To me, it was the right day for them to come. I was thankful for their presence because it took some of the attention off of me.

Luke nudged me with his elbow.

"House is lookin' mighty clean, Lil' Sister. You seemed to get it goin' on without our helpin' you!"

I grinned, deciding not to share the secret if Mother hadn't already told them.

"Thank you! God sent His angel . . ."

"That would be Aunt Thelma," Matthew said reaching for the gravy.

"Nobody makes gravy like this 'cept Aunt Thelma!"

I was too far away from him to jab him. His loud voice carried all the way up to Pastor Marshall.

"Thelma made the gravy? Well, it's delicious!"

"DeLois Ann made the gravy, Pastor," Daddy offered. He passed the bowl of cornbread around the table.

"She made the hot water cornbread and nearly everythin' on the table!"

"Now H.P., we don't want Dee Dee to get a big head about her cooking."

"You did a great job raisin' your girl, Clare! Mighty good job!"

"I want to sing in the choir, too, Pastor Marshall!"

Everyone stopped and looked at me. This fueled my fire. I knew I couldn't stop there.

"I used to sing in the children's choir, and I want to start back!"

Pastor Marshall slowly wiped his mouth. He held the napkin as he raised his hands up in prayer for a moment before turning to Mother and Daddy.

Mother's expression said everything. She had just begun to shake a finger at me when Pastor Marshall grabbed both her and Daddy's hands in prayer.

"Lord, thank you for answerin' my prayer! One person left the choir, and you done caught us a ram in the bush! Thank ya, Jesus!"

He turned to Mother and Daddy.

"He knows how to answer prayer! I needed to start buildin' up our choir and didn't know how or where to start." He turned toward me.

"Child, I'd love to have you join our group. Clare and Henry, you have a pearl of great price, here!"

Mother relaxed. She smiled at his compliment.

"Mark my words," he continued, "someday, some lucky fellow's gonna get the prize of his life, too!"

The men chuckled. But Mother's lips formed a straight line.

"Right now, she's gotta focus on her schoolin', Pastor."

"You're right, Clare. These are times when our youngsters have got to make a way for the next generation. You and H.P. doin' wonderfully well, directin' your children toward that goal." Pastor Marshall turned to Luke and Matthew.

"I hear you boys are doin' a wonderful job in your college work. Excellent! 'All things are possible when you believe.'"

Matthew and Luke beamed in his praise. They were proud of their accomplishments. They had set the pace for the rest of the family.

Actually, they were only doing what Daddy and Mother hoped for all of us. It made my heart swell with pride.

Later that week, Miss Trudeau wrote on the board, "To thine own self be true. And it must follow, as the night the day."

"William Shakespeare wrote that. He was saying that there are a lot of choices in life, but you've got to make up your mind what's really right for you. Sometimes you've got to decide between things you want for yourself, and the things others want for you. Have integrity and always be true to yourself!"

At that moment, it dawned on me that my pursuit of that history book for Mr. Wilson's class was the start of following my own dreams. It was really a quest for what was true and good for me—a higher education.

Pastor Marshall always said, "Anything was possible with the Lord." I had read in the Bible that if I truly believed, trusted God, and had faith, I would receive blessings from the Lord! Did that include even removing my pain of loss?

Maybe it included having a great school year and singing in the choir. And, maybe, if I truly believed, it meant that I'd meet the man of my dreams!

CHAPTER 24

A CHANCE ENCOUNTER

It was on Saturday mornings that Aunt Lonnie's boarders were most likely to suffer from the clatter of dropped baking sheets and the slamming of cabinet doors.

Jarred awake, Charles sat up and stretched. Then he remembered one of Aunt Lonnie's boarders had warned him this would happen. It was all in preparation for the weekly bid whist party.

Charles rubbed his eyes. He saw the first rays of sun had begun to brighten his bedroom.

Not at all like hearing the ol' rooster, back home, he thought.

Charles carefully padded to the rickety dresser that his aunt had given him. He noted that the coarse floorboards needed sanding and could use a few coats of shellac.

Charles pulled out his towel and shaving materials and glanced around his room. It had dingy wallpaper and unpainted, rough baseboards.

He made a note to attack the grime-encrusted floors, baseboards, and window seals with at his first free moment. He'd sand and shellac the floors for her and apply a coat of paint or two to cover the bad wallpaper.

Aunt Lonnie had a lot of boarders over the years. But she wasn't one for cleaning up after them or even dealing with the general upkeep of her house.

She wasn't a housekeeper. Even Mama Edna admitted her daughter was slovenly.

"She never could keep house and I sure don't know how she keeps them boarders! Thank the Lord Viola ain't nothin' like that!"

He chuckled as he pulled on his pants, socks, and work shoes. Today, he and Todd would shop for a more suitable pair for fancier occasions. While tonight was the juke joint event, Charles was mentally preparing for Sunday services.

The smell of freshly brewed coffee made his stomach growl. Soon the voices of the other boarders in the hallway grew louder. It quickened his preparation.

By late morning, Charles was walking with Todd along the busy Bessemer streets.

"Ya gonna see quite a selection here, Charlie. Probably mo' shoes than a country boy's seen in all o' his natural born days!"

Staring in various stores' display windows, Todd elbowed Charles. "Am I right or am I right?"

"Yep, I think you hit the nail on the head!" Charles remarked.

Charles marveled at the great number of stores, businesses, and people the city held. The steel industry boom had made a huge difference. What had once been a one-horse town had exploded into a city that found itself right on the heels of Montgomery and Birmingham.

He knew it wasn't fair, but Charles found himself comparing the city to Billingsley. He and his family thought shopping at the Feed Store on Saturdays was the height of their weekend. Except for a few trips to Montgomery, the small country town was the commercial center for the people of the farming community.

But the ravages of the Depression had taken its toll on Bessemer. He figured that many of the unemployed people he'd seen on his first day in town were poor farmers who had lost their land to the banks, only to have them close after refinancing them. There were many people who, like himself, had flocked to the city with the hope of finding a job. The labor market especially for the unskilled workers was simply flooded.

Charles said a silent prayer of thanksgiving for his father's teaching. At an early age, Daddy Ben had taught his children how to survive with little or nothing while working the land. The very hard work that it took to make the farm yield a few extra dollars taught them patience and a strong work ethic.

He believed that it was that same work ethic that allowed Bobby, the sawmill foreman, to put in a good word for him with Mr. Czarnik. Without it, Bobby might have had an entirely different picture of him.

They made it to the shoe store before noon. The colored folk had a section in the store where they were allowed to sit and try on the latest styles.

Charles noted that the chairs were old and worn. Some had springs poking out of the cotton batting that oozed from the torn, leather cushions.

The men chose the most comfortable chairs they could find while Charles tried on his selection. He had decided on a pair of well-made black brogues.

Todd brought over a pair of white and black, two-toned shoes that were the latest style from Britain. He pointed to the poster.

"Hey, Charlie, the picture over there said that the Prince of Wales wears shoes like this!"

But there was something about the dark, well-made shoes with their perforations in the toecap that appealed to Charles. The shoes were functional as well as stylish.

Ben had taught his children in making a purchase one should choose quality over quantity. Charles knew that these solid, well-crafted shoes would last him several years, with less maintenance than the two-toned.

When Todd saw that Charles favored the more conservative shoes, he poked him on the chest.

"Thought you wanted ta be some young woman's prince!"

"Yeah, but what if my dancing partner steps on my foot? I'd have to run to the men's room and touch it up so as not to constantly remind her of the misstep."

Todd laughed and punched Charles on the shoulder.

"But let me tell you, these'll set ya on top, Charlie. There are gonna be a bunch of men at that joint. You want to stand out, right?

"And I think ya havta first get the dancing partner before ya start worrying about her steppin'."

Charlie weighed Todd's comments carefully. He had a point.

After he had made his purchase, Todd regarded Charles closely.

"You might consider getting a closer shave, too, Charlie. You've got to have a smooth, city look if you want to catch the eye of the ladies. C'mon and I'll show you a good shaver."

They turned the corner and were almost run over by a flash of plaid. Todd was able to sidestep the young lady in the plaid dress with white collar and braids.

But Charles ran right into the second woman. He was stunned. She was a knockout.

Charles could tell that she was not at all like the country girls he had gone to school with. She looked like a movie star.

This young lady was dressed in a navy-blue dress with a softly pleated skirt and high heels. Her hair was soft and bouncy, arranged in the latest style.

But it was her face that attracted him. Her wide-set eyes had a dreamy quality and yet held both intelligence and a sense of humor. Below her small nose were softly curved lips painted in the bright red that the movie stars wore.

Charles doffed his hat. "I'm sorry, miss. I should have been more careful."

"My fault, I was in a hurry." She smiled demurely.

Her friend in plaid looked at him and Todd curiously, and tried to hide a smile before taking her friend by the arm.

"Dee Dee, we've got to hurry!"

Charles smiled. He now had her name. Before he could formally introduce himself, the two young ladies rushed off.

"You can pull your eyeballs back in their sockets, Charles," Todd laughed.

Charles turned to look at them again as they disappeared around a corner. The young lady was very attractive and seemed sweet. She didn't toss her head and flirt as he had seen others do in his high school.

He was intrigued. Maybe Bessemer did hold some promise that he would find the right mate.

"You mighty quiet, Charlie. That young lady must've really turned ya head," Todd joked.

"It might have been the best part of our shopping trip, brother," Charles drawled.

Todd directed Charles to the drug store, and Charles walked right inside, not noticing that a white couple was approaching the exit. They looked at him angrily when he didn't step aside to let them exit first.

Todd quickly held the door open for them and stood to one side. He smiled, looked down, and bobbed his head in deference, apologizing for Charles.

"He's from the country, folks."

"Better teach that n— some manners, boy!"

"Ya-suh."

Charles noted the exchange and approached Todd.

"They weren't even near the doorway."

"I know, Charlie. People here are different from Billingsley folk. We know that they ain't right. But they feel they better than us. So, we play along with 'em ta keep everyone safe. And to keep the peace."

Charlie shook his head. Todd pensively gazed at the retreating couple.

"No, it sho ain't right, Charlie.

"Jes the way thangs is here. Don't lose no sleep over it."

Todd clapped Charlie on the back and walked him over to the shaving supplies counter. A young clerk stepped up.

"What can I do for you boys?"

Todd pointed to the set of shavers. The clerk handed him one that was made of a lightweight metal with retractable doors to hold in the shaving blade.

Todd changed his tone to a serious one.

"This will give ya the cleanest shave in three counties, brother."

Charles worked the doors of the shaver open by twisting the bottom ring in the set making up the handle. It was remarkable how the blade snuggly fit into its housing.

"Jes wait until ya get ta the juke joint. Ya gonna have the finest young ladies in the city in a line wantin' ta dance with ya, cheek to cheek."

Charles laughed at his friend's emphatic statement.

"I don't know about that, Todd. I'd be happy just to shave and not nick myself!"

But Charles's mind wandered off and he found himself thinking about the young lady, Dee Dee. It would make his day if he could meet her again.

What would it be like to dance with her? She had a small waistline, perfect for him to hold as they danced the two-step.

"You boys going to a juke joint tonight?"

The clerk's question cut through Charles's reverie. He appeared to be the same age as Charles and Todd. The clerk looked around and leaned forward on the counter, his eyes dancing with excitement.

"Between you an' me, I wish I could join you! I hear that music is somethin' else!

"You boys are goin' to need a shaving cream. I sold this cream to three other fellas like y'all who were fixin' ta go ta the joint tonight. Let me show you the latest lather kit we've got."

Todd and Charles eagerly followed the clerk to the next counter. He showed them the sample set, where he opened a tube and put some of the thick cream in a little cup.

Checking, first, to make sure no one was watching, the young man pushed the cream toward them and whispered, "Feel this, fellas! It'll make you cheek as smooth as a baby's behind, and will ya get a load of that smell!"

Taking a finger full of the thick cream, Charles felt its smooth, velvety texture. Taking a sniff, he was delighted by its minty fragrance.

"Douglas Fairbanks, you know that actor guy?" The clerk smiled broadly.

"Even he uses it! It's only thirty-five or sixty-five cents a tube, depending on the size! You can't beat it, 'cause it only takes a little to give you the closest shave you've ever had!"

Charles reached in his pocket and pulled out his soft, worn wallet.

"Sounds like you made a sale, sir! I'll take the thirty-five cent one. If I like it, and if it works like you say, I'll buy the bigger one next time!"

Todd pulled out a dollar, too.

"Guess I'll best be buyin' some of that, myself! Here you go, sir. Thanks for the demonstration!"

The men left the drug store and parted at the railroad tracks.

"I'll be by in an hour, Charlie!"

Todd walked briskly away, whistling one of the latest tunes.

Charles hurried back to Cousin Viola's. Earlier, she had told him that he could get changed at her place.

Aunt Lonnie's boarding house only had one tub with a shower. Most likely, it would be occupied by the time he got back.

 Charles's step quickened. He'd only have a short while to change into his dance clothes.

He held an eager anticipation for what the evening would hold. Perhaps a certain young lady with dreamy eyes was in his future?

CHAPTER 25

A NEW LEASE ON LIFE

"What challenge do you face today and how are you going to solve it?"

When our English teacher, Mrs. Trudeau, wrote this writing prompt on the board, I sat up in my seat. Bells and whistles went off in my mind. Had I really been true to myself?

My senior year was supposed to be the year. I had begun to grow and change over the last couple of weeks.

I discovered courage meant taking action to do the right thing even when you're scared. My stomach still churned every time I passed Bessemer High School. But we had done something great for our classmates.

I paid an enormous price for that trip with Mother piling all of that housework on me. But the Lord blessed me with Aunt Thelma, and I came out feeling more capable and stronger. All of it happened because I made a decision and carried it through.

And it had given me the courage to sing in the choir. I had chosen to do something that brought me closer to the Lord. I felt I was following God's lead, and, in doing so, it made me feel satisfied.

Aunt Thelma was surprised but tickled about my decision.

"Honey! Let me tell ya, even ya mama is proud of ya! She's practically bustin' at the seams, goin' around tellin' all of the neighbors! And Mama Dee says ya did it 'cause the Lawd tol' ya ta do it! I'm so proud of ya, baby!"

That Mother had changed her mind about me since that Sunday was tremendous! I knew it was because of prayer.

Aunt Thelma gave me a big hug and proceeded to give me other tips to help with my housework.

"Ya gots ta stay on top of it, honey! By doin' a little bit ev'ryday, things won't gang up on ya."

But even after all these successes, the old sadness still lurked around in my mind. I wasn't really aware of them until I read Mrs. Trudeau's question.

The one challenge that loomed largest in my mind kept coming back to me. It had to do with the last direction Sherrie Lee had given me.

What was I doing to with the dream of meeting my true love? Pursuing that dream filled me with my old familiar spunk to get started on a new adventure.

Maybe spunk was another form of courage? That thought filled me with faith. The Lord had blessed me in the other challenges. I believed he would bless me in this one.

Big Mama Dee often quoted a verse, "'Faith is the substance o' things hoped for an' the evidence of things unseen,' chil'! That means ya gots ta carry on like it already be yo's!"

Suddenly, I began to smile. It wasn't a dry essay prompt after all. It was a life changer!

The tension began to ease out of my shoulders. My challenge had always been how I would find true love.

This realization was the start of my new direction. From this assignment, I discovered how to conquer my depression once and for all. I would start my new life by taking charge and acting like I already had it!

Harriet was waiting at the door for me.

"Harriet, I have to level with you. I've been feeling blue for a while, but I've figured out a way to snap out of it."

Harriet brightened up.

"You haven't been the same old Dee Dee. Not since your sister died. I knew, but I didn't want to say anythin'."

I thought my periods of silence hadn't been noticeable. While it hadn't taken a toll on our friendship I could tell, at times, Harriet had wanted to say something to me but held back.

Should I tell her my plan? Perhaps she might even champion it. I could only do it if Harriet was onboard.

"I'm going to go to that juke joint's big reopening."

Harriet's eyes flew open as she stared at me, aghast.

"You said your mother would never allow that! Dee Dee, are you sure? You told me that your Daddy would take down his strap if you did. I can't encourage you in that, DeLois Ann! I just can't!"

I took a deep breath. If I were ever going to show some spunk and gumption, this was the time.

It felt as if several years had passed since we'd had that conversation. Now was the time. I knew it for certain!

"Harriet, I have been dying inside! Sherrie Lee's last words to me were not to give up believing this year was going to be my best year ever—and to keep my spunk!

"I've got to go. Music and dancing help me throw off my grief. It would be great to do something clever and daring on my own, at least just once!"

As I tightly held Harriet's hand, I knew she clearly understood my earnestness.

"I know it will be a release and a lift to my spirits. I see it as the first step to becoming my own person, the woman I need to be—or I'll always feel I'm not courageous enough to choose my own way in life. Do you see what I mean? Will you help me?"

Harriet took a step back.

"W-wait a minute, DeLois Ann. How am I involved in your plan? I'm not sure if I like this . . ."

The bell rang. We rushed inside our history class.

"I'll tell you at lunchtime. You'll see. It's very simple, and neither one of us will get in trouble," I whispered as we took our seats.

Mr. Wilson strolled around the room. He had a big smile on his face that only grew bigger when he looked in our direction.

"Young people," he finally began. "I started this class by stating that history is a science, although a peculiar science when compared with other disciplines. One would think that it is immutable—things either happened or they didn't. We can't dispute that, correct?"

Some of the students looked around. We weren't sure if we should agree or not. Mr. Wilson had a way of flipping our first answers to show us that we missed something. He was tricky!

But I decided to nod my head. It seemed like a pretty good answer.

"I mentioned earlier how we gain information on historical events. Does anyone remember?"

No one felt brave enough to guess. I thought it had something to do with having the people who saw things happen write them down. But I couldn't remember for certain, either.

Mr. Wilson held up the newspaper. Its headline read, US Constitution Submitted to States for Ratification 153 Years Ago!

"Remember, students, we can't just rely on hearsay, secondary, or tertiary sources as we look for evidence that proves any of the theorems we might postulate during the course of this semester.

"Take this headline, for instance. This can be proven and is true.

"How? We have many firsthand accounts, like someone's journal and their day-to-day observations that were chronicled to substantiate this statement as fact."

I should have followed my first thought!

"Others come from secondary sources, then tertiary sources, and on down the line. But they must corroborate or further elaborate a historical event.

"In world history, firsthand sources included people like Josephus, a Jewish historian of biblical times who wrote about the siege at Masada. Or you might include Thucydides, an Athenian general who wrote about the Peloponnesian War in Greece.

"But in our own history, we have many of these firsthand sources and the documentation for these United States is abundant. We can actually see American history through the eyes of the people of the period, through letters, newspapers, court documents, and diaries. They're what we call firsthand accounts."

I sat on the edge of my chair, eager to see where Mr. Wilson was going with this exciting conversation.

"Actually, we're extremely lucky that our country is so young. Many of the written accounts that make up our history have been logged in various places and are still available in libraries and museums like the Smithsonian.

"These original documents are the basis on which great, accurate history books were written."

Our class was silent. I wondered if my classmates felt like me. I was totally immersed in Mr. Wilson's speech!

What I liked about Mr. Wilson's lectures was he spoke to us as adults. He talked as though we understood all of what he was saying.

I had never studied Greek history or even heard of Josephus. It felt as if we were in a college class!

He held up the textbooks that Harriet and I had helped to get. I glanced at Harriet. She was beaming too. Our efforts somehow were part of this talk.

"This history book is a good one. We were able to procure additional copies because of the courage of a few," Mr. Wilson's eyes rested upon us for the slightest moment.

Harriet coughed back a giggle. I dared not turn around. If our eyes were to have met, I'd be in such a state, myself!

"But I want to give you students the benefit of my additional readings. When you read a variety of firsthand accounts on the same topic, you are able to piece together a fuller understanding.

"To this end, we're going to layer on to this book other material that uses firsthand accounts and build a more thorough view of our country's first years as a colony and as a nation. I can promise you that it will be a very rich history.

"Peoples of different nationalities and color figure prominently in our history. All of these groups have been inextricably woven into its creation—its very fabric. We are part of this tapestry, students. The end product makes this nation one of the most unique in the current history of the world!"

My heart was beating rapidly. I realized that my parents and ancestors were a part of this history! It made me consider that some of my courage might have come from those ancestors.

He continued as he walked around the room handing us carefully stapled packets of papers.

"Here are some musings I've typed out and copied for you to begin your first assignment. Due to the shortage of library books on these topics, I've referred to my private collection. That's something I hope that you will pursue, students. Collect your own library. It will serve you well!"

I stared at the mimeographed sheets of paper. Mr. Wilson had given us a synopsis starting in the 1500s, of how our people were involved in the New World and America's history. Some weren't even slaves!

He didn't number the packets to keep track of who had what copy or even ask us to return them. There were ten pages of material he had taken the time to type and copy— all at his personal expense!

A buzz went around the classroom. It wasn't only about the information the papers held. Mr. Wilson had made a personal investment in us.

Our teacher leaned on his desk with arms folded, wearing a huge smile. He gazed about the room, extremely satisfied by our excitement.

I was so engrossed in reading about indentured servitude and slavery in the New World that the bell's ring came as a surprise. My plan! I had completely forgotten about mapping it out!

Even though it was in a rough form, I knew that it would work. Harriet would be involved for a short while and the rest would fall on me.

I'd tell my folks that I was going to visit Harriet on Saturday to go shopping. I had earned a nice amount of money ironing and truly wanted to go to a few shops. Also, Mother knew I wanted to buy a hat for church.

Harriet and I would be honest in our Saturday plans for the outing. The only thing I would not share was going to the juke joint.

My plan would be to dance with Bill White until 7:30 and then go back to Harriet's to have her brothers walk me home.

Mother need never know about the plan. I had the times mapped out and only needed to confirm with Bill that he still wanted to take me.

Walking to lunch, I shared the plan with Harriet. To her credit, Harriet listened quietly. She even smiled at the idea of going hat shopping, something she loved to do.

Finally, when we arrived out at the lawn, she looked wistful. Slowly, she nodded her head.

"Okay. I'll do it. But please don't get in trouble, DeLois Ann. I don't want to see you even more blue if this doesn't work."

That Friday, I arranged to have Bill walk me out to the lunch area. My heart fluttered as I dredged up enough courage to speak. Clearing my throat, I looked up at him through my lashes.

"Bill, thank you for being such a gentleman these past few weeks."

"Why, you are so welcome, Dee Dee."

His white teeth gleamed in the sun.

My heart leaped. He had become someone I looked forward to seeing every day.

Was it possible that this young man could be the person I had my heart set on meeting? I felt an excitement about Saturday that I had not felt before.

"I thought about your offer to go to the juke joint tomorrow and decided that I would."

Bill tried to recover from this surprise by looking down and rubbing his chin.

"You will? That's great, DeLois Ann! I can pick you up at seven o'clock."

I frowned. I had not figured out that part. How could I tell him that I had to be in by eight? The early curfew was a bit embarrassing.

"I have to be home by eight, so we must leave the dance at 7:30, Bill. I know it's on the early side, but I really hoped we could get there by six o'clock?"

Bill thought for what seemed an eternally long time. What could be so hard about coming by an hour early? Did he have errands to run before the dance? Would he be able to rearrange his plans?

I wanted to go so badly, I hadn't thought about Bill's availability that evening. But my fears were allayed when he glanced at my worried expression.

His easy smile returned.

"Look, DeLois Ann, that is a bit early for going to the juke joint, but I'll take you and bring you back in time, if that's what you want to do."

It was my turn to smile. It was going to happen! I was ecstatic, but I held my composure as I replied.

"Great! I'm going to be visiting at Harriet's that afternoon; you can pick me up from her house. Harriet and I have arranged for my return home."

I cleaned that afternoon with more vigor than ever before. Even the silverware we had used for Sunday dinners had a greater shine.

I found the mindless rubbing useful when organizing my thoughts. By the time I finished, I had my day completely worked out.

Mother had already given me consent to go to Harriet's house. I didn't feel as though I was lying when I said that I was going shopping, I just didn't add on the other part.

The only thing that I hadn't worked out was the return time. Daddy and Mother had strict curfews for each of us. When I turned seventeen, I was expected to be in by eight o'clock, from wherever I was. So, eight it would have to be.

Sherrie and I had gone to matinees before she had gotten married. She had often complained about being on "Douglas time" when she had wanted to go out with her friends or beaus.

Matthew and Luke were able to come and go as they liked because they were young men, and they were older than me.

They had gone to the juke joint many times, but mostly after nine. Matthew had told me many times that that's when things really got hoppin'.

As I thought about the night and how much fun it was going to be dancing to those great melodies coming from that new jukebox, my heart started racing!

I had already picked out a skirt that was wide enough to move to the music and my favorite blouse. I was ready!

On Saturday, I would walk to Harriet's house carrying my purse and a small bag that contained my dancing shoes.

But I knew I'd also be carrying a twinge of guilt. I had never kept a secret from my mother—except when I went to Bessemer High. It worried me that I had started a pattern of hiding things from Mother.

But this time was different. I felt that I needed to be on my own in making this decision. I needed to act on my faith. God would help me.

Later on, there would be plenty of time to share with my parents how this evening had come to pass.

For now, I didn't want to make them anxious or, worse yet, have them keep me from going. I wanted an evening of complete freedom.

* *

Dear Readers, You're almost at the end of this story! To get a free, sneak preview of Making Do: Growing Up Colored in the Jim Crow South During the Great Depression's Chapter 1 of Volume II (Faith and Hope), please email me @: josanwrightcallender.com

CHAPTER 26

A MAGICAL NIGHT

My mind was caught up in the excitement of it all! Instead of being "Lil' Sister," I would have an evening of celebration. It would be the first event that I would go to as an adult!

Even the dress I wore lived up to this very important occasion. My navy-blue serge dress had a plain bodice with bugle beads at each shoulder, three-quarter length sleeves, and had a white collar and cuffs. It was my favorite dress for many reasons.

Its wide tail was perfect for dancing and made my waistline look extra tiny. I was happy that Mother allowed Sherrie Lee and I to purchase our girdles from the Sears catalog.

We had giggled over the description because it promised to do what Mother Nature hadn't. That was one of the few ads that kept its promise.

Although my favorite color was anything green, this shade of blue was right for me. My face seemed brighter.

While shopping for a hat for church, I planned to pick up a tube of that new red lipstick I had seen in one of Mother's Life magazines. This was going to be a wonderful adventure.

I thought back to how I'd checked out my look before leaving. I had pranced in front of my mirror, practicing some steps.

All I needed was some dancing shoes. I remembered the pair that Aunt Thelma had given me.

They were stacked neatly in a box in the back of the closet. I laughed as I opened it. They were perfect!

God was blessing me in every way!

"What you laughin' 'bout, Lil' Sistah?"

I spun around and found little Thelma staring up at me. She held a doll Mother had made of old socks and yarn.

I thought how perfect my plan had been, up to that point. I had even packed my makeup and other essentials into my book bag right after breakfast. I had too much at stake to tell her the truth.

Thinking quickly, I knew the wrong answer to Thelma's question would surely get me grounded for the evening, if not the week! I simply had to stick with my original plan.

"I'm going shopping today with my best friend. We always have a great time together."

Thelma frowned and clutched her doll closer.

"Are we gonna have a fairy story, tonight? You promised . . ."

I registered how the families' events had affected my little ones, and in my haste to take care of my own heart, I'd forgotten about Saturday story time. They loved my stories.

Over the past three years, these stories were a part of our routine. It was my way of showing love for them.

I struggled mentally and tried to keep little Thelma from seeing my discomfort. I calculated whether or not there was a way to get back to the house before their early bedtime. It took me a few moments.

Perhaps, if I danced for half an hour, there was a good chance that I'd be back before seven.

The question was whether I could tear myself away. I would just have to do my best.

There was no way that I could explain the significance of my evening plans. I couldn't tell anyone.

"I'll try to get back in time, dear," I said.

I had walked to the kitchen where Mother was preparing breakfast. Daddy had already left with my brothers to help Papa with harvesting the pole bean crop.

Mother looked up at me and took in my outfit. For the briefest second, she looked at me with pride. Then she quickly covered it with criticism. This mixture of emotions seemed to happen more often since my trip to Bessemer High School. It was as if sometimes she saw me as an adult and other times, a child.

"Girl, don't be going out in public with that slip showing. Ya gots to hike it up. 'Specially when ya put on that girdle, makes everything droop that was held up by the rear, afore."

I was surprised. I thought that the slip was the right length. I adjusted my skirt as I ran back into the room to see how much the thing hung out. If I worked quickly, I figured I could switch slips. I had promised to be at Harriet's by 9:30 a.m.

The mirror confirmed my thoughts and Mother's comment. I had to admit Mother's criticism was biting but, as usual, correct.

Mother gave me her last inspection before I went out the door. This time, I passed.

"Ya have to catch up with yo' chores on Sunday, with this shopping trip, Dee Dee. And get back sooner than later."

"Yes, Mother."

I gave Mother a quick kiss, grabbed my jacket off of the coatrack, and shot out of the door. Free.

Harriet and I had gone to downtown Bessemer to shop several times over the past three years, and each time we had a lot of fun window shopping and taking in the new styles.

The makeup counter at the drug store was one of our favorite places to shop. I had my red lipstick selected even before we entered the store, thanks to the fashion magazines I had been reading.

The clerk hurriedly waited on us and seemed to want to shoo us away. She wouldn't let me try on the raspberry red lipstick demonstration stick. I had to purchase it, first.

"That will be fifteen cents, please."

Carefully counting off my coins, I paid the clerk.

Stepping to the side, Harriet held my purse while I applied the lipstick.

"Dee Dee, you look like a million dollars!"

I observed my mouth in the mirror. It usually looked okay, but with this shade of red, even I was surprised.

I couldn't believe the beautiful curve of my cupid's bow and the sassy color didn't make my mouth look overly large, a fear that I had held for a long time.

I laughed and blew a kiss. Harriet giggled with me.

"You girls got to move along, y'hear? We've got customers coming in."
The clerk gestured to the door of the drugstore.

Only one customer was there. A lady pushed a baby carriage to the far side of the store where sodas were served to white customers.

I held my tongue, but my expression said everything I had on my mind. The clerk saw my displeasure but ignored me.
She started wiping off the counter where we had been. Harriet pulled me along with her.

"C'mon, Dee Dee, you've only got a couple of hours before Bill comes over."

I looked at the time and was astonished. It was almost four o'clock! Shopping for the hat and taking in the sights took us longer than I had thought. Time hadn't gotten away from me like that since the last time I was into a good novel!

We flew down the street. I was a few seconds behind Harriet, and when she turned the corner, I picked up speed and almost knocked down a very handsome, well-dressed young man.

He caught me and took my breath away. I wasn't prepared for his easy smile and white teeth.

I quickly collected myself and almost stuttered as I stared at his chiseled features. He doffed his hat, and I felt like I was on the set of a Hollywood movie.

"I'm sorry, miss. I should have been more careful."

I smiled demurely, not knowing what to say or how I'd get the words out. My heart was racing. Whatever I said must have been the right thing.

His voice surprised me. It was clear and didn't appear to have any of the Southern drawl that I'd expected to hear from most young men in my city.

"Dee Dee, we've got to get going!" Harriet pulled my arm. I nodded and followed her swiftly down the street.

That was the type of man I had hoped to meet one day.

Had I met the man of my dreams? If so, I'd met him with no chance of ever meeting him again!

When Bill picked me up at 5:30, I still had the young man on my mind. I knew that it wasn't fair to Bill, but it was one of those chance encounters that I could only pray would not be my last.

"You're looking lovely, Dee Dee." Bill was extra complimentary. It often seemed as though he laid it on a bit thick, as Mother would say.

But he was trying to win my affections, and I had to appreciate his attention and efforts.

He handed me a little package. My first gift from a young man! It was a small handkerchief with embroidered edging.

"Bill, you shouldn't have! This was very thoughtful of you."

Immediately, I gave him a quick hug and placed my gift in my purse where I had my coin purse, compact, and newly purchased lipstick.

I had made arrangements with Harriet's older brother to walk me home. Harriet had shared with him my situation, and he gladly obliged.

I felt badly that I couldn't ask Luke or Matthew to do the same for me, but too much was at stake. Matthew would surely give me away to Mother, if not on purpose, by accident. A sieve could do a better job of containing a secret!

Bill knew my plan and said that dancing with me for thirty minutes would be as great as an entire evening. It made me feel very sought-after.

We arrived at the juke joint at six o'clock. The place was someone's home near the railroad tracks. I'd heard it was located there because of the loud music.

A large group of people milled around the entrance. It was an exciting mixture of both country and city folk.

But what surprised me was the number of people that Mother would have called high-lifers. Women dressed in tight, revealing clothing with lots of makeup and men in bright colored shirts with shoes to match.

They were people ready for a party or had decided to bring the party atmosphere with them.

The place had raw floorboards and dim lighting. But, oh, the music was wonderfully loud and just right for dancing!

Bill wasn't as sure on the dance floor as he was on the football field, but I felt I could dance with anyone that night. The music transported me and lifted me out of my doldrums.

After we danced for a bit, Bill asked, "Would you like to step outside for some air, Dee Dee?"

Bill was so earnest and sweet, I agreed. I didn't really want to stop but knew that I had to be an agreeable date. I knew that Harriet's brother would be picking me up in another ten minutes.

The day had begun to wane, but the setting sun made the night air cool and breathable. I fanned myself with Bill's handkerchief and noticed that he was staring at me with an odd expression.

Before I could ask what was on his mind, he took me in his arms and kissed me very hard! I was flabbergasted.

I tried pushing him away, but he wasn't having any of it.

"Stop, Bill! Please!"

I managed to move my face. But he pushed my hand away and held me tighter.

Then, I felt someone pull Bill off. It was my mystery man!

He struck Bill on the chin and knocked him down. He then stared at Bill threateningly.

"I believe the lady deserves to be treated like a lady."

Bill stared angrily up at him.

"She came with me . . ."

I adjusted my dress and smoothed my hair. I was more than a bit embarrassed. I should have known better. All of my instincts had been trying to warn me about just such a turn of events.

My mystery man looked at me with such an endearing, querulous expression, I had to catch my breath.

He was dressed in a white shirt and dark trousers. The shoes he wore were the two-tone ones Luke showed me once in a magazine. They were the latest fashion. His smile was congenial, and it made his already handsome face quite appealing to me.

I smiled, despite my upbringing. I didn't know this man and had not been properly introduced. Yet I felt at ease in his company.

I sensed that there was something good-natured about him. Something I could trust.

Bill's eyes grew hard. He squinted at the young man angrily.

"You should mind your own business, bud!"

"Bill, he's right. I've had enough air. I would like to dance."

The mystery man offered me his arm.

"I believe this is our dance . . ."

I took his arm. It was quite natural for me to do so, as was smiling. I walked with him onto the dance floor. I could see that Bill was enraged.

But the music and dancing with this kind man took my mind off of everything else.

He was a great dancer! We danced every record that the juke joint put on. I felt as though I was on the silver screen and my heart was gay and joyful.

People backed off the dance floor and began clapping for us as we danced to the lively music.

"Dee Dee! Mother was so worried she sent us looking for you!"

I turned around to find Matthew at my shoulder. He was holding my book bag and Luke was walking across the dance floor toward us. Both wore worried expressions.

"Oh my! What time is it?"

I looked around and saw the clock on the wall advertising Coca Cola and was shocked. It was eight o'clock!

"Oh, dear! I've got to go." I turned to the wonderful gentleman who had rescued me. My expression was one of panic.

"I have to go!"

I was so worried about getting home late that I allowed Matthew and Luke to whisk me away. It was only later that I realized I hadn't even gotten his name!

THE END OF VOLUME 1

GUEST SPEAKER

Josan Wright Callender
josanwrightcallender.com

Author | Educator | Screenwriter | Filmmaker | Producer
Seen on Facebook, YouTube, LinkedIn, Medium, Twitter & Instagram +

Josan Wright Callender, award winning writer-producer and author is the co-founder of Matjo International, an educational media and publishing company located in Carlsbad, California.

Mrs. Callender's interest in educating students through media had a two-fold beginning. Education became her career focus after experiencing top-notch public school teachers. This interest led to Mrs. Callender's 27+ year career in many different educational programs. She has taught in the classroom, mentored and served as a program specialist for a large, urban school district. Mrs. Callender's desire to provide a quality educational experience for all of her students led her to seek and obtain the highly regarded National Board Certificate in 2002 (renewed in 2011). But it was in listening to her mother tell stories that originated from her grandfather, that gave birth to Mrs. Callender's interest in storytelling. From an early age, she became an avid reader of historical fiction novels and a film buff. These interests and many years of hard work eventually paid off in her receiving an invitation to the prestigious Writers Guild of America-West. Her passion for media production led her to co-found Pparallax Films and coproduce ONE DOWN, a 35mm feature (Charleston WorldFest's Silver Award Winner). Over the years, Mrs. Callender's writing accomplishments included Semi-finalist in the Walt Disney Studios Fellowship Program, finalist in Independent Feature Project/west's first Writer's Workshop and winning an Audience Choice Award for a 168 Film Project which she co-wrote and produced.

Mrs. Callender believes the reason for her many successes is due to her faith and reliance upon God in all things.

Topics:
The Story that Faith Wrote: Making Do
Winning a Triple Victory!
Growing Courage in Challenging Times

Book to Speak:
Email: info@josanwrightcallender.com

Event Venues:
Churches
Schools
Book Fairs
Libraries
Seminars
Conferences